A BETTER SENSE *of* BEING

BRENDA SHERIDAN

To my dad, who gave me my love of books,
taught me the value of a well-written sentence,
and believed that I could do anything.

IS A FUNNY THING.
It can show us what we wish could be true,
but also what already is.

CHAPTER 1

There were no red farmhouses in Paris. Iris Macdonald was quite sure of it. The photos of her trip last summer, laid out on the table before her, were further testament to that fact. And yet, each time she tried to paint the facade of a beautiful nineteenth-century townhouse, or the low curve of a bridge over the Seine, the same image came into her mind, insistent and clear: an old red farmhouse with milk jugs on the porch and a little girl in the window.

It wanted to be painted.

Her fingers itched as she began to sketch the curved arches of the French city. It was as if someone was urging her to turn those complicated arches into the simple lines of a gable roof. Her heart burned with a strange longing to bring a different scene to life than the one she had intended, and it was a longing she was helpless to explain. The moody blues and shadowy greys she had laid out before her were useless now. The farmhouse demanded the fiery reds and vibrant greens she hadn't expected to need, and she shuddered at the strength of that demand.

Focusing on the images, she willed herself to create what she wanted—a gift for her best friend's birthday. Ruby had loved Paris, and she was sure Ruby would love this painting, if she could ever get it done. Determined to overcome whatever was forcing the farmhouse into her vision, she reached for her coffee, hoping the aroma would bring to mind cafés and fresh baguettes. It did, but only fleetingly, as the broad white farmhouse porch appeared stamped in her brain.

It was pointless to fight it.

Resigned, she swept the photos up into a pile, scraped the lovely, muted colors off the palate and into the sink, pulled out a pencil, and began to sketch the unfamiliar lines of a house she had never seen, in a place she had never been, and a little girl whose eyes told a story of loss that ripped a hole right through her heart.

It hadn't always been this way. She had always had full control over what she chose to paint. The walls of her small studio were filled with images of the Massachusetts coast she loved to visit and the mountains and valleys of the Berkshires she called home.

She glanced at the pile of canvases in the corner, hidden beneath an old tarp, silent witness to the interruptions, which had begun about a year ago. They came in the form of houses of various styles and sizes, both familiar and completely foreign. Whatever her intended subject had been didn't matter, as her imagination became fixed on whatever cottage or building appeared.

Ignoring them didn't help. Like today, the visions captured her imagination so strongly that they prevented her from getting her usual work done. And that work was what paid the bills, so she reluctantly gave in. If the images wanted to be painted, she would paint them; but there was no way she was showing them to anyone. In the first place, she had no answer to the likely question of what inspired them. More importantly, and yet again for no reason she could discern, they weren't meant to be seen.

The tactic worked. Usually, the images came together pretty quickly, and once they were done, it was as if a page turned in her mind, her imagination once again her own. And for now, nobody had noticed or asked about the pile of paintings in the corner.

She shivered, then reached for her sweater, wrapping it closely around her. Turning back to the red farmhouse, she noticed a fear rising up, seemingly from the house itself. *This is new*, she thought, shivering once again. She often felt emotions as she painted, but something about this time didn't make sense. The image itself was making her uneasy, and it seemed to have a story to tell. She just wasn't sure she wanted to know what that story was.

She needed to keep going, confident the feelings would disperse once the painting was done. She painted furiously, seeming to know exactly where to dip her brush into the paints to get the right color, giving little thought to the image as she went. She felt herself slip into an almost trance-like state, her hands moving seamlessly across the canvas.

Engrossed in her work, she lost all track of time, and the afternoon sped by. Eventually, the light grew dim, and she paused to grab a lamp and move it closer. Looking up from the painting, she had a sudden sense of someone being in the room with her. She was alone, and yet the sense of presence was too strong to ignore. She reached for her coffee, then spit out the liquid that had long since gone cold.

Stop being ridiculous, she said to herself while shrugging off the unease. The painting was nearly done, and there was obviously no one there. With the same determination that had gotten her through worse things than paintings with feelings, she picked up the brush and got back to work. The sense of relief came the moment she was finished. Her hand shook slightly as she set the brush back down, and with a start she thought, *Maybe I should tell Ruby.*

The thought was barely fully formed before a rush of warmth enveloped her, as if she had just been hugged. She wrapped her arms around herself to savor the feeling, hoping to lift the unease the afternoon had brought. She didn't know where it had come from, but the comfort she was feeling was unmistakable. She hadn't felt such love since her mom died. Maybe even since Michael. And that had been nearly twenty years ago.

They had met in college and begun dating soon after they graduated. It had never occurred to her he wouldn't always be there. He had been her best friend in a way Ruby never could be, and it was he she wished so desperately could be there right now. She hugged herself tighter, and the searing pain of his death began to recede. How could it still hurt so much after all this time?

Again, it was as though someone were in the room. Only this time, she sensed Michael—with a certainty that was stunning. She whipped her head around, half expecting to see him standing in the corner. She tensed, listening for the sound of his voice. But, of course, no one was there.

She began to tremble, overwhelmed by emotions that were both chaotic and consoling. The pungent smell of paint burned her nose, and a hunger for fresh air drove her out the door and into the garden, where she peered up at the wispy clouds overhead. She breathed deeply, inhaling the earthy scent of early fall and the sweet smell of a wood fire nearby.

The panic began to fade.

She was definitely not telling Ruby, or anyone else, about that house . . . or any of the rest of them, either. The need to feel grounded was intense, and she sat down on the steps, letting her hands run over the rough stones that formed them. The stones were real. Her little blue cottage and studio were real. That red farmhouse was not. She was wasting time and money, and if all she ever did was hide them, then what was the point?

Be patient—you don't know the point yet, said a gentle voice in her head. She froze, her body still while her mind searched. It wasn't a thought. At least she didn't think it was. It sounded like a thought, but somehow . . . different. She looked around, as if she could see where the words had come from. Once again, there was no one there.

CHAPTER 2

Iris loved the outdoors, particularly when she was rattled. It was one of the reasons she had moved here in the first place. Lakeview was about as different from New York City as you could get. Nestled in the Berkshire hills of western Massachusetts, it provided all the fresh air she could want, including a lake that was perfect for long walks when she needed to clear her head.

Right now, she was rattled. Stepping off the porch, she turned to the left, intending to cross the street and walk around the lake. She lived just on the edge of the village proper, in a little blue house with a wide front porch. It was the porch, and the little shed-turned-studio out back, which had sold the house to her. She never imagined she'd ever feel the need to escape that very studio.

A piercing screech and a flutter of leaves drew her attention skyward. A red-tailed hawk came to rest atop the telephone pole next door, gaze intent on something below. She'd been here for nearly two decades, but some of the wildlife still scared her. The hawk was beautiful, but it was likely on the hunt. Not wanting to witness an attack on some unsuspecting vole, she turned to the right and headed into town.

Shops lined the main street facing the village green, with its large white clapboard church forming the geographic center of town. On the far side of the green, a parallel road filled with shops, restaurants, and a few old houses drew her attention. That was where Ruby lived, and it reminded Iris that they were supposed to have dinner that night. She stopped, staring across the green, thinking about how much she wanted nothing more than to be alone tonight. She was a terrible liar, and knew she'd never be able to keep what happened back in the studio to herself if they got talking, especially if there was wine involved. And there was always wine.

She pulled out her phone and sent a quick text, "Raincheck for tonight?" Almost immediately, her phone began to buzz. She should have known. Ruby would never let a text like that go unanswered. She should have just called.

"Hey, Iris," Ruby said. "Everything okay?"

"Yeah, my stomach is just off," she said, thinking it was partly true, even as her stomach itself growled in outrage at not having been fed all day. Whatever had gone on in the studio had made her a bit nauseous, though. So, it wasn't a total lie. "Want me to call and cancel the reservation?" she added with a touch of regret. She hoped the owners could fill the slot on such short notice.

"Nah, don't bother. I've been dying for a steak all day. I'll grab a book and head over there myself," Ruby said, with a lightness that made clear she was more than happy to eat alone at a nice restaurant. "Listen, I gotta get back to work. My boss needs this report before I head out for the day. Talk to you later!"

Iris tucked the phone back in her bag with a smile. Ruby could never be mad, and she had such a way of making the best out of anything. The thought lifted her spirits a bit, and with a lightness in her step that hadn't been there before, she headed into the café for a fresh coffee and a cookie. She did need to eat something, even if it wasn't steak and pasta.

Leaving the café, she picked up the pace, hoping to avoid running into anyone. She waved quickly at Lucia in the gift shop on the corner, turned at the end of the row of shops, and headed uphill.

On the ridge above town was the small park that gave the town its name. A row of benches faced the lake, offering a priceless view and an unbeatable escape from her day. She set the cookie on the bench as she sat down, stretching her legs so they rested on the railing. The sun was warm on the back of her neck, and she sipped the hot coffee, letting it penetrate the chill that had settled into her bones back in the studio. *It really is a pretty town*, she thought, recalling the day nearly two decades ago when she had found both it and her little blue house.

It was her friend Charlie who had convinced her to move to the Berkshires, asking her to fill in for his accountant who was on leave. She'd been grateful to get away from New York and the painful memories that had made it so hard to move on after Michael's death. Most of their friends had been his medical school colleagues, and with Michael gone, she just didn't feel she fit in anymore.

Iris had meant the move to be temporary, but when the other accountant chose not to return, she was only too happy to come on permanently. She had a nice little apartment over Charlie's garage, and he'd let her take art classes at his gallery as an added incentive to stay. She loved the quiet, and she loved the painting. And nobody but Charlie knew about Michael, meaning she could leave that heartbreak back in Manhattan.

Sitting on this same bench, looking out over the lake and hills, Iris had wondered aloud if she was making the right decision. She and Charlie had just left the house she would eventually buy, and she was having second thoughts.

"What if I'm not good enough?" she'd asked. "At the painting, I mean."

Charlie had laughed at her before laying out his evidence that she was, in fact, a very talented artist, including the fact that she had sold two pieces just that week.

"Besides, I've known for a long time you wouldn't be my accountant forever." She started to object, but he put a hand up. "I'm not saying you're not a good accountant. I'm just saying when you're at your desk, you look like someone playing the role of an accountant in a movie. You have everything all organized, you wear professional clothes, and you get everything done just as it should be. That makes you a very good employee, but I'm not so sure it makes you happy."

She looked up sharply at that. His words had hit something deep inside, and she had to will herself not to cry. "I'm not unhappy, you know. I just feel like there is something else I'm supposed to be doing with my life." The idea had begun to form the day he'd offered her a spot in the gallery. Something was growing in her heart, and she needed to see where it took her. In the end, it had taken her here, to Lakeview, with its scenery and coffee shops and fabulous chocolate chip cookies.

She licked the last crumbs off her fingertips and took another sip of her coffee. A breeze had picked up, and she grabbed the empty paper bag just before it blew off over the village. She tossed the bag and the last of her coffee into the trash, then crossed the park and headed back downhill.

The walk did its job. The real houses lining the streets made the imaginary ones, like that red farmhouse, begin to fade from view. *It was only another vision*, she told herself, a product of her overactive imagination. She was an artist, and artists had visions. Setting aside the fact these were just . . . different, she drew comfort from the fact they faded if she let them. By the time she rounded the turn back to her house, all worries about the paintings were neatly tucked away in the recesses of her mind. She hoped they would stay there.

CHAPTER 3

Twenty years earlier . . .

The visions had started the night Michael died.

She'd woken in the dark of her Manhattan apartment with a sense of being between two worlds—the one where Michael was sitting beside her on the sofa, and the one where he was gone.

She resisted the waking, closing her eyes in order to again see the ugly brown plaid of his hand-me-down sofa, to feel the warmth of the coffee he'd handed her, to hear his voice. The hiss of the radiators and the glow of the light from outside the window beckoned her back to the real world, and she knew she couldn't hold onto him much longer.

She rolled over, wrapped her arms around the pillow beside her, and tried again. *What did you say, Michael? Say it again . . . please?* Her tears continued to fall, soaking the already damp pillowcase, and the hand that lay tucked beneath her cheek. She yanked the comforter up over her head, and in a cocoon of warmth and darkness, drifted back to sleep.

He was dressed for work, his lab coat thrown over the back of the couch. There was no sign of the accident, no evidence of death at all. His face showed no expression, save for the tenderness that shone in his rich brown eyes—the ones that had always made it impossible for him to keep anything from her. He said something—something that made her smile. She asked him to say it again, but this time, it was as if he were behind a glass wall, and his voice couldn't penetrate.

She reached for him, hoping for the hug she was certain he wanted to give. But just as she reached out, she woke. In the next instant, his words evaporated like a drop of water on a hot skillet. Gone. Sunlight streamed through the cracks in the blinds, and the clock by her bed read 7 a.m. There was no going back to sleep now, and there would never again be the hug she so desperately needed.

She crawled out of bed and stumbled to the kitchen for some coffee. The list of people to call was sitting by the phone, the sheer number enough to make her want to crawl back under the covers and hide.

Michael's things were scattered around the apartment. He was always leaving something behind. A spare raincoat hung on the back of a door, and an old sweatshirt was thrown across a chair. He'd kept a small stack of paperbacks in the corner for nights when he needed to decompress from his training.

She picked up a framed photo of the two of them, taken the year before on a trip to Boston. He had asked someone to take their picture. At the last second, he turned to plant a kiss on her cheek, surprising her. She had made him stand still for another, but he had framed this one anyway, saying it resembled her more than the posed shot.

Eventually, she sat down and began to work her way through the list. Calling his parents and her own mom the day before had been awful and something she hoped to never have to do again. These calls proved easier, but not by much. Michael was well-loved and had a lot of friends. As the day went on, the calls got progressively shorter. She offered fewer and fewer details, promising to let them know when arrangements had been made.

Her last call was to Charlie Hatch, Michael's best friend. She'd tried him first but gotten no answer. When the machine picked up, she'd hung up in a panic. There was nothing she could say that wouldn't tip him off something was terribly wrong. She hadn't ever called him before.

"Charlie? It's Iris . . . Iris Macdonald . . . Michael's girlfriend?" she managed to say with at least enough clarity for him to know who it was.

"Hey, Iris . . . " he began, with a hesitation making it clear he knew something was wrong.

"Michael's dead," she blurted out before he had a chance to say anything else.

She hadn't meant to be so blunt, but the silence on the other end of the line told her she had been. "I'm sorry, Charlie . . . " she began, squeezing her eyes shut in a vain attempt to hold back the tears. "There was an accident yesterday. I'm so sorry. Michael . . . died."

"What happened?" he asked, the disbelief raw in his voice. "I just talked to him the other day . . . "

"There was an accident," she repeated. The story came out slowly as she struggled to form the words, each one an effort to speak aloud. She relayed the details of how he had dropped her off at Grand Central and how a delivery truck had blown through a red light and broadsided him, propelling the car into the back of a city bus. In an instant, he was gone; the little grey Escort was almost indistinguishable, his body lost amid the wreckage.

He'd had no time to react. Neither had she.

Her throat tightened, and for a moment, she thought she might suffocate. Willing herself to breathe, she felt the constriction ease.

She heard Charlie put the phone down, followed by a thud, as if a door had been slammed shut. This was followed by a string of curses and a loud, distinct, "God . . . damn you!" The power of that one phrase struck her below her ribs, and she dissolved into tears once again. They sat in silence for several minutes, each lost in their own grief, somehow bonded by the sharing of it.

Finally, Charlie spoke. "We were going to go to our reunion together. He had made all these plans. I was really looking forward to seeing him again."

"I'm so sorry," she repeated. She didn't know what else to say. "I'm sorry I keep apologizing," she added. Charlie let out his breath with a snort.

She shook her head, scrunching her eyes together in disbelief. *Was he laughing?*

"Sorry," he said. "I mean, it's not funny. It's just something he used to say about you—that you'd apologize to the door for bumping into it."

She almost laughed. Michael was always telling her to be more confident and to stop apologizing all the time. She could still feel the soft peck on the cheek he had given her before she got out of the car, before she apologized for making him drive her in the first place. "I will never regret bringing you anywhere you want to go," he'd said. "Just tell me, and I'll be right there."

"He was my best booster," she said, picking up the photo from Boston to study his face. He'd promised to always be there. Could he have known it was a lie?

"I know," Charlie replied. "He talked about you all the time."

She didn't say anything as she sought to hear Michael's voice once again. Recalling her dream, she reached in her brain for the words he spoke, hoping again to hear them. She failed, dissolving helplessly into tears.

"I'll be there tomorrow," Charlie finally said. She nodded, forgetting he couldn't see her. When he asked if she was okay, she nodded again and managed to squeak out a soft "yeah."

"I'm sorry, Charlie," she said one last time.

"So am I," he answered. "So am I."

The tears returned in earnest before she had even hung up the phone. She lay down on the bed, staring at her drawing books and hearing Michael's words in her head. "You can do this," he had said so many times. "Believe in yourself," he had said just this week, as he encouraged her to take that first step of going up to Cold Spring for the artists' retreat.

"I'm sorry, Michael," she said as she pulled the covers over her head to block out the setting sun. "I just can't do this without you."

———

The screech of the buzzer woke her from a sound and dreamless sleep. She reached for the clock as she rolled over in bed. Wondering who the hell was ringing her doorbell at this hour, she crawled out of bed, brushing her hair out of her face. Stumbling to the intercom, still half asleep, she pushed the button and asked, "Who is it?"

"It's Charlie Hatch. I've got coffee. Can I come up?"

The name didn't register at first. Then with a jolt, she remembered. Charlie . . . Michael . . . the accident. A wave of sorrow ran through her so quickly that she reached for the doorframe to steady herself, swallowing a groan. "Yeah. It's the last door on the right."

She pushed the door release button while looking around the apartment. Serviceable, no trash or clothes around, clean enough. She caught sight of herself in the mirror by the door and gasped. Her eyes were swollen and red, her cheeks pale, and streaks of eye makeup were still visible from the day before. She had just managed to wash her face, pull her hair back, and throw on some clothes when she heard the knock on the door.

The deadbolt opened with an embarrassing clunk. The door was heavy, and stuck a bit, but she opened it with a practiced hand. She stepped aside for Charlie to walk by, letting the door swing closed with a bang. He jumped. "Sorry. I forget how loud that is," she said.

"Yup, Michael was right. You even apologize for the door."

She wanted to laugh, but her eyes filled with tears instead. She reached for the tray of coffees he had balanced in one hand and walked quickly to the table with them.

Charlie waited a moment, then handed her a white paper bag smelling strongly of garlic. Her stomach growled audibly. "I figured you probably hadn't eaten much yesterday. Am I right?" She nodded. "Me neither. Michael and I used to get bagels from this place all the time on the way to school." He shrugged. "I hope you don't mind—I always liked the garlic ones."

"Garlic's great," she answered as she pulled the bagels and cream cheese out of the bag, setting them on a plate she grabbed from the cabinet. She motioned for Charlie to grab a seat.

"How did you find me?" Iris asked.

"I stopped by Michael's place first. I still had a spare key from when I stayed at his place a few years ago." His face fell, and he looked away. Iris could sense a deeper sorrow than Charlie was letting on but allowed him to maintain the façade he seemed to have so carefully crafted.

"I figured he'd have your address written down somewhere. Turns out it was pretty easy. He had this on the table ready to mail." Iris reached for the yellow envelope with one hand while setting down the bagel she had in the other, her appetite suddenly gone.

"Is it your birthday?" he asked.

She shook her head no, trying in vain to hold back her tears. She didn't know why he would have written it, but Michael had rarely needed an excuse. She used to joke that he reminded her of her grandmother, who used to keep a file box of cards for every occasion under the sun. And he always mailed them, saying it was part of the magic. A surprise in the mail, left by a stranger, from someone you loved.

Soon, her shoulders began to shake as her tears turned to helpless laughter. She handed Charlie the card. He paused for a moment, then his eyes grew wide, and the corner of his mouth began to twitch. Soon, he was laughing along with her—a deep cleansing laugh that had both of them holding their sides. It was a silly card with a crude joke about working in an office. It wasn't even very funny, but for some reason they both found it hysterical.

When she was able to speak, she explained, "He knew how much I hate my job, but also how hard it is for me to change. We had a long talk the other night about taking chances and trying something new. He kept trying to make me laugh and I wouldn't bite. I guess he hadn't given up."

"Sounds just like him. He was the one who encouraged me to move up to the Berkshires you know. It was after the two of you had started dating, and I was feeling a bit lonely."

"So, he encouraged you to move two states away?" she asked, incredulous.

He hesitated, looking down at his bagel as if deciding whether to take another bite. She waited, not wanting to disturb whatever he was processing in that moment.

"I had a massive crush on Michael in college," he said, his freckled face exploding into blotches of pink. "It wasn't reciprocated," he added quickly.

She didn't respond as she tried to fit this new bit of information into all she knew about both men. She had known Charlie was gay for years. She had just never suspected he thought of Michael as anything more than a friend.

"Michael was great," Charlie continued. "He never let it bother him, but he seemed to know I needed to find my own way, out of his shadow, and away from the two of you. I had been working at a little gallery in SoHo, and one of the artists we worked with told me about another gallery for sale in Lenox. I had the money, and the atmosphere up there seemed like a good place for me. He was right, and we both ended up much happier for it."

She eyed Charlie with a new appreciation for just how devastating this was for him too. All of a sudden, it was all more than she could handle. She picked up the card and walked to the couch, laying down as she held it close to her chest. She began to sob. After a few minutes, Charlie pulled the blanket over her and sat down in the chair beside her.

When she woke, he was gone. A cup of still warm tea sat on the coffee table with a note telling her to call if she needed anything. Looking around, she could see he had tidied up too. *What a sweet guy,* she thought with a pang, realizing she would probably never see him again once the funeral was over.

She glanced at her watch, cringing as she realized it was already early afternoon. She had a million things to do, not least of which was getting some photos together for the funeral. Steeling herself for how painful this would be, she turned on the shower, hoping by the time she had dried her hair and gotten dressed, she would look halfway human.

Going through photos proved to be easier than she thought. Michael loved to have his picture taken, so he was generally grinning or goofing off in every photo she found. But there were a few that made her stop, either because she didn't recognize someone in the image, or because she recalled the occasion so strongly. All she wanted was to be able to talk to Michael about them. She just needed to hear his voice.

With a sigh, she set the pile of photos on the table and picked up Michael's card from the table where she'd left it. Smiling again at its irreverence, she realized she hadn't read the whole message earlier. Below the joke about office jobs, Michael had turned serious: "Be who you are, Iris. Not everyone gets the chance." She broke out in a cold sweat as she realized those were the exact words she had heard in her dream.

And those were the words that had finally driven her to leave the job she hated, and to follow a dream she hadn't known was even there. They had led her here, to Lakeview.

CHAPTER 4

In the beginning, Iris immersed herself in her new home, painting what she saw around her. The hills and lakes were gorgeous in any season, especially in early October. Over time, she took short trips to the coast, and these trips got longer as she became fascinated with painting the ocean waves. Life settled into a pleasant routine, and she was happy. She was being who she was, and she often thought of Michael, grateful for his words that had encouraged her to take the chance when Charlie offered it to her.

Then the houses began to appear. Until the red farmhouse, these visions were silent, seemingly stamped in her brain, but pleasant enough. Fortunately, though she had painted several more houses since then, none of them had filled her with the same emotions it had. And none of them had brought voices with them, and for that, she was grateful.

She shivered, looking carefully around the room to assure herself she was truly alone. She was, and the door was closed. The only sounds were the gentle hum of the heater and the brush of leaves against the window as the wind blew. Still, she couldn't shake the feeling someone was there in the room with her.

She'd intended to do a painting of the huge ocean waves she'd witnessed the weekend before. There'd been a storm off of Cape Ann, and she'd driven out there as soon as it ended, hoping to capture some photos she could use for inspiration. The trip had been a success, but her attempts to get the images on canvas were not.

She closed her eyes, seeing the waves crashing against the rocks, white foam spraying into the air, the waves unstoppable as the tide moved in. She could hear the roar of the surf and the call of seagulls overhead. Even the smell of the salt air was clear to her as she sat, and she sighed, enjoying this part of her process. Then it happened, again.

It wasn't often the houses appeared at least, but there was never a warning. This meant she was virtually always disappointed, as she was today. She'd come back to the waves tomorrow, but still, her heart ached a little for the scene she so desperately wanted to create.

Just paint it and move on, she told herself with a sigh.

It only took a few hours to complete the painting. Most of her work took days to complete, at best. But the houses were always done in one sitting. The urgency and persistence of the images seemed to fuel an ability to create almost without thinking. And the end result, well, that was astounding.

The paintings were all quite good—excellent, if she were being an honest critic. And they were all different, reflecting both the local architecture—clapboards and shingles—and faraway places, with architecture unfamiliar in its beauty.

Iris lifted the corner of the tarp and took in the growing stack of paintings. There were eleven there, so with the newest, that made an even dozen. She knew she should just show them—they were as good as any of her landscapes, maybe even better. But for some reason, some inexplicable yet solid reason, she didn't feel they were ready to be shown to anyone. As she gathered the brushes and put away the paints, she wondered if they ever would be.

A sense of sadness began to wash over her, and as usual, it brought to mind all that had come before. She missed her mom and their long walks through the streets of Manhattan when she lived there. She didn't know what she would think of these paintings, but she longed to tell her about them anyway. Her dad would have called them hogwash. He never seemed to understand why she loved curling up with a book or just daydreaming for hours by the window as the sun streamed in. Michael would have understood. He always understood.

As the last of the paint swirled down the drain, the energy of the painting seemed to go with it. She stared at it drying on the easel. It really was lovely. Thinking that was a good way to end her day, she finished closing up the studio. The days were growing longer, and she was grateful there was still some daylight left to enjoy. She pulled the door closed behind her and turned the key, smiling as the lock turned with a satisfying click.

CHAPTER 5

Outside, she stopped to take in the view of her little cottage and garden. The soft spring air was alive with the sound of the earth waking up from the long winter. A chorus of blue jays called from the bushes, while the chipmunks who had taken up residence under her patio "chip-chipped" in alarm at some unseen threat. The air smelled fresh, and Iris breathed deeply, noticing a familiar stirring in the air, as if someone had gently stroked her face. It wasn't unpleasant, and for a moment, it reminded her of the dreams she still sometimes had of Michael.

She loved this time of the day. The early evening light softened everything, allowing the pink and white of the azaleas to intensify against the deep greens of the ivy and evergreens. Her garden and little cottage, with the sun setting behind it, made her so happy. The stepping stones, newly set into the grass, glowed in the evening light, making the garden feel touched by magic.

Reaching up, she pulled off the elastic keeping her long, brown hair out of her face, vigorously massaging her scalp as she shook the hair loose. She had a sudden memory of her mother telling her she would need to cut it short once it turned grey, and she smiled at both the memory and the knowledge that day had not yet come. A sudden, strong breeze lifted the hair off her neck, and she sighed in contentment before heading across the garden and into her house.

She walked through the back door and kicked off her shoes, feeling the events of the day slip away as she crossed the threshold. The tension in her shoulders eased as she took in the smell of the kitchen and the feel of the cool floor under her bare feet. With a glass of wine in one hand and a cheese board in the other, she stepped out onto the front porch. After the studio, it was her favorite part of the house. The porch was open and low to the ground, making it ideal for visiting with neighbors. Stretching out on the soft chaise lounge, she allowed herself the luxury to sit and enjoy the view.

From her porch, she could see the lake across the way, shimmering in the waning light. The soft hills that flanked the lake were an oscillating palate of burgundies and greens, interrupted every so often by the pink and white of the cherry trees in blossom. A sudden chorus of laughter and shouts foretold the arrival of several young kids rounding the turn on their bikes. She sat back, enjoying their casual, contagious joy.

"Well, now don't you look relaxed!" she heard from somewhere off to her right. She waved as her friend Ruby crossed the street and opened the gate into Iris's front yard. She was wearing a bright yellow raincoat and carrying a purple umbrella under her arm. Her long braids were tucked up under a floppy red hat, and she had a mischievous grin on her face. Ruby posed such a contrast to the clear skies and warm sunlight that Iris chuckled. "Did I miss something in the forecast today?"

Ruby waved a hand dismissively. "Oh, no, I just went shopping, and it was easier to wear this than to carry it! And you know what they say about New England weather—it can change in a minute, so I figured wearing this couldn't hurt!"

Ruby Hendricks had been her best friend almost from the day Iris had arrived in town. She was brash and bold and just young enough to keep Iris from feeling old. She had a soft, deep voice that was calm and soothing, and she could tell the best stories, most often prompted by something that happened at work.

Ruby would go on as if nothing at all interesting could possibly be coming, and then suddenly her brown eyes would twinkle, her dimples would deepen, and she would come out with the punchline of the story. And then she would laugh, her deep voice lightening to a comical squeal, and Iris would be powerless to stop her own giggles.

She handed Ruby a glass of wine and motioned for her to sit down, grateful her friend had turned up when she had. The serenity she had been feeling was fading as she recalled the events of the day. Momentarily lost in thought, she didn't hear Ruby at first. "Sorry, what did you say?" she asked as her friend gave her a concerned look.

"I just asked how your day was. Everything okay?"

"Oh, fine. Fine. I've been working on something from my trip last week," she lied. "The sunrises were just gorgeous, and I really want to get the light right. You know how sunlight sparkles on the ocean?" Ruby nodded. "It's always alive and moving. The waves and ripples make the light reflect differently across the water, and if I don't get it right, it looks artificial."

It wasn't really a lie, she reasoned. The water *had* appeared that way, and she *had* been hoping to capture it before the . . . other . . . happened. Her lips start to twitch as she stifled the nervous giggle that threatened to emerge. She stood and moved to the railing, ostensibly to better see the last rays of the sun as it dipped below the hills.

"Did you get it right, finally?" Ruby asked.

"Not yet, but I did get something lovely done, so it wasn't a wasted day." She reached for a cracker, spreading a layer of cheese carefully as she spoke. She was a terrible liar, but Ruby seemed not to notice this time.

"Iris, do you even know how amazing it is you can imagine something, or see something, and make that something come alive?" Ruby's eyes still held a trace of humor, though her face had turned serious. "I envy you, you know."

"Oh, please—don't envy me!" Iris said. "This is just painting. It's nothing. You can make someone's day just by showing up." Iris waved her hand up and down, indicating the colorful outfit Ruby still wore. "You just walked across town in the full sunshine wearing a raincoat and hat and thinking nothing of it. I know you made more than one person smile on the way here."

Ruby wasn't letting go of it, though. "You don't see it do you—how you light up the room?"

Iris shook her head. She didn't see it at all. When she looked in the mirror, all she saw was a middle-aged woman with pale, sagging skin and lonely eyes. She missed the eager young woman she had been the day she took the job with Charlie. All this time later, she was still trying to figure out who she was, and the strange houses weren't helping her feel any better about herself. She took a slow sip of her wine and then turned to her friend. "Do you ever wonder if you're living the life you were supposed to live?"

"What does that mean?" Ruby asked. "Life is life, isn't it?"

"I don't know. Sometimes I just wonder if I missed out on something along the way, like maybe I was supposed to do—or be—something else." She shrugged helplessly. Wasn't that what becoming an artist was all about? Didn't she do this whole "start a new life" thing once?

Ruby gave her a worried look. "I thought that was why you came here. Are you thinking of moving or something?"

"No, it's not that," Iris said. "I guess I'm just feeling my age. It seems like just the other day I was as young as those kids who went by on their bikes. Remember being so free?"

Ruby nodded, pouring the last of the wine into her glass. "Yeah. I remember laying in the grass at night watching the stars, not caring about mosquitoes, or getting dirty, or making dinner." When Iris didn't immediately reply, she added, "Hey, what's eating at you tonight?"

"Charlie's wedding last month, I think. I hadn't seen some of those people since Michael's funeral. They all seemed so old, especially the guys. I figured I probably looked old to them, too. And ever since then, I've been feeling . . . antsy, or impatient, I guess. I haven't felt this way since I left New York. I kinda thought I had found my calling in my artwork, but all of a sudden, I'm not so sure."

For a moment, she was back in the church in lower Manhattan, sitting with her mom and her sister Alice, the closed casket a silent witness to the violent accident that had claimed Michael's life, just as he was about to finish his residency. His young colleagues and friends, stunned at the randomness of death, filled the rows behind his parents.

His mom, usually a talker, sat eerily quiet, her long blond hair pulled up tightly in a bun, her lips thin and bloodless. His dad reminded her of a stack of books, piled too high, liable to fall over at the slightest touch. He held himself so still and straight she thought he might break. They had been like a second family to her for years, and knowing she was losing them too caused a new flood of tears as she gripped her mother's hand ever tighter.

Charlie sat across the aisle, his face impassive, his eyes dry. He seemed to sense her eyes on him and turned toward her with a flat smile that did not reach his eyes. She wanted to reach out to him, to tell him she understood, but the wide aisle and the rituals of the service kept her firmly in her seat.

They'd gotten drunk together the night before, and she knew some of his flatness was likely a hangover. Her own head throbbed despite the rather large dose of Tylenol she'd taken before leaving home. She fingered the little box of mints in her pocket, hoping her breath didn't give her away. Michael hated the smell of alcohol on her breath, and she apologized to him as she wiped her nose, tucking the tissue into the pocket with the mints.

She took a drink from her glass, surprised to find wine and not Guinness. Embarrassed, she jumped up, reaching for Ruby's empty glass. "Never mind. It's nothing. Just a little jealous of Charlie, I guess. Come on, I'll walk you halfway home."

CHAPTER 6

Every summer, the county held an outdoor arts fair, and ever since the year after she moved to Lakeview, Iris had sold her paintings there. Charlie owned a gallery in Lenox and was one of the organizers of the show. It was a fun event, with people coming from all over New England to browse the various artists and artisans who called the area home.

Usually, she had everything ready long before the weekend rolled around. She knew what people liked and usually had a sense of what she needed to focus on each year. This year, it seemed to sneak up on her. She had plenty of work to showcase, but more than ever, she had found herself relying on a gut feeling she should paint a certain scene. Lists and planning hadn't seemed to matter when her mind had other intentions. She'd given up on the lists six months ago.

And then there were the houses. They were a real distraction, but she didn't know what to do about them. The fact nobody knew they existed only added to her worry about them. So, when Charlie called to ask what she was planning this year, she didn't have an answer.

"I don't know. I'll get something together before then," she said.

"Are you alright, Iris? That doesn't sound like you."

"I'm fine, just distracted for some reason, I guess." Realizing she was being a bit rude, she added, "Sorry. I'm open to suggestions."

"Look. Let me take this off your plate. I'll come by and get everything, take a look, and arrange them in whatever way makes sense. Do you trust me?" She heard the teasing in his voice, sounding so much like Michael for a minute, her own voice caught in her throat.

"Are you sure everything's okay, Iris?"

She took a deep breath. Nothing was really wrong, but she'd dreamt of Michael last night and had spent a good part of the morning running it over and over in her mind. It had seemed so real, yet at the same time, as ethereal as a cloud.

"Do you still think about Michael?" It came out in a rush, as if just the saying of the words would betray what she was feeling inside.

"Sure, sometimes. Why? Have you been thinking about him?"

"Dreaming about him, actually." She paused as the images from the night before flooded her mind. "Can you believe how long it's been since the accident?"

It was Charlie's turn to pause. He was always soft-spoken, but she could barely hear him when he finally responded. "I thought of that recently. There's another reunion coming up. I still half expect him to be there, you know?"

She nodded, as if Charlie could see her, and then softly answered, "Yup."

"What are the dreams about, Iris?" He sounded curious, not just concerned for her feelings. She wondered briefly if he dreamed of his friend. He'd never mentioned it, so maybe not.

"Nothing really distinct. I just see him standing in the background in surprising places. Like last night. I was dreaming about the fair, and all these people were in and out of the tent, but nobody was buying anything. Then there was Michael, standing in the corner. He didn't say or do anything; he just stood there."

"Really? I wonder what that means. Don't dreams tell you something about what's been worrying you?" When she didn't answer right away, he added, "Are you worried about something? The fair maybe?"

She was nervous about the fair, and she didn't know why. "I haven't felt this way since I first moved up here, Charlie."

"Hey, I wouldn't worry about it. Your stuff will sell like it always does. Something strange will happen, or some oddball will offer you a ton of money to paint something risqué—you know—the usual."

She wished she could see his face. Despite being well into his forties, Charlie had the look of someone much younger. His mouth was framed by a mustache and goatee and seemed to be set naturally in a soft, gentle smile. And he had the kindest eyes. They were grey and round yet narrowed into slits when he was teasing her in this way. He would try to hold a serious face, but his eyes gave it away every time. She missed spending time with him. She loved his new husband Andre, too, but it was a change she hadn't expected to make her feel quite so lonely—and unsettled.

She reached for the small key Michael had given her when they were first dating. She kept it on a chain around her neck and often forgot it was there. Right now, the softness of the worn edges and the warmth of the metal felt like a cord that pulled him right into the room with her. "Thanks, Charlie. I know it will be fine. And once it's over, I'm sure I'll be fine, too. If you're sure you don't mind putting it together for me, I'd really appreciate you doing that."

They chatted a bit longer about nothing in particular, each seeming reluctant to end the conversation. When they finally hung up, Iris turned back to her painting with a renewed purpose. She had two good men who believed in her, and she wasn't going to disappoint either of them. "Especially not you, Michael," she said to the wind as she stepped out the back door and headed up to her studio. There was still time to get another painting finished before the sun went down.

CHAPTER 7

*T*sun rose early in June, and therefore, so did Iris. She didn't really mind, counting the extra hours as a gift. With two paintings still needing to be framed, errands to run, and Charlie coming by at four to pick everything up, she had more than enough to fill those extra hours.

By mid-afternoon, she had finished. After grabbing a can of soda from the cooler, she flopped down on the comfortable chair by the door, gazing around at the sheer volume of work she had done. She was momentarily stunned by the beauty of it all. She really was an artist—and a good one, too.

She blushed at the vanity of the thought, even though nobody was around to hear it—even if she had spoken out loud. A slight creak of the floorboards made her spin around to see who had come in, yet there was nobody there. She froze, eyes scanning the room, searching for the source of the presence she was feeling. It was like someone had invaded her personal space, coming in while her back was turned. Yet the door remained closed, her only company the images on the walls.

Great. Now what?

She rubbed her hands vigorously up and down her arms, hoping to dispel the creeping feeling in the process. Then she opened the door, and the window, and let the warm breeze fill the space. It helped. With a determination to will the experience away, she got up and began to sort through the paintings. The stack of canvases in the corner had fallen over, and Iris nearly tripped over them. The edges of the canvases peeked out, and she caught a glimpse of the bright reds and deep blues of the houses she had painted. *Cover them up*, she thought, even as she pulled up a chair and began to sort through them.

They were really good paintings. The little brick schoolhouse was adorable, with its rows of desks and the teacher up front, stern in his suit and tie. Then there was the brownstone, set in a row of similar buildings, but with the single light in the basement window. It wasn't the building that mattered. It had been the little window she had worked to get just right. And then of course there was the red farmhouse. Such love existed within its walls, and such loss, too.

It was those emotions that freaked her out. All of her artwork made her feel something—true artwork always did. But this was different, because the emotions weren't obvious just from the images. They existed within the scenes, much deeper than what was on the surface. And while she painted the exterior of these buildings, it was the interiors that brought the emotions into being. These emotions meant something. What it was, and why, still escaped her.

She was trembling inside, though her hands remained surprisingly still. She put a finger to her wrist, thinking her heart must be racing, but it, too, was calm—pulsing away normally in mockery of the sense she was about to explode. The room was still, and she grasped onto that stillness, willing the feeling of panic to subside.

And yet she wasn't scared. She was absolutely certain. That certainty proved to be the key to getting past what just happened. If she wasn't scared, there was nothing to be afraid of. A blast of a horn from the road out front snapped her fully back to the here and now, and she ran her hands over her face to clear the feeling of cobwebs that remained. The sun had shifted, and she could see it was getting late. She grabbed her keys and phone, scrawled a quick note for Charlie, and headed out without another thought for the pile of canvases lying exposed under the window.

CHAPTER 8

ris had been doing these fairs for five or six years now. She expected a long day, a lot of browsers, and hopefully a few good sales. Someone would grab her a burger or hot dog for lunch, and she'd eat it standing up, gulping a few bottles of water throughout the day. Ruby would be at the welcome tent, Charlie would swing by, and then they'd close it all up and do it again on Sunday.

Her paintings were good, and she had enough confidence to stand firm in the prices she had set. The new business cards she had ordered were tucked in her bag, along with some notecards and small prints she kept on hand for those not interested in or able to afford a full painting. She was ready.

And yet she stood in front of the mirror, agonizing over what to wear. She was on her third outfit, discarding each as looking awful, but without any real reason why. The dress was long, white, and impractical, with a delicate lace around the collar. She felt pretty as she swished the skirt back and forth, and more so when she added the string of amethyst beads and her favorite blue ballet flats.

By the time she had gotten herself together, she needed to rush out the door to pick up Ruby. Fortunately, she had no appetite, so missing breakfast wasn't a big deal. She grabbed a couple of granola bars and stuffed them in her bag for later.

"Excited?" Ruby asked as she tossed her bag in the back seat.

Iris didn't know if excited was the right word. She was nervous, and that wasn't unusual. This was different, though. The best comparison she could make was to the first day of school, when everything was new, and there was an excitement in the air. "Yes," she answered. "I'm really looking forward to it this year."

"Don't you always?" Ruby asked.

"Yeah, but it's like something's gonna happen today. I don't know—I just feel kinda giddy, that's all." She fingered the lace on her neckline with one hand as she turned into the driveway of the fairgrounds. Nothing seemed unusual, just the other artisans heading to their tents before the gates opened to the crowds. Shrugging off the lingering buzz in her gut, she handed Ruby one of the boxes, and the two headed across the field to her tent.

Charlie had done his job the night before, and the paintings were displayed beautifully, grouped by color rather than subject, and the effect was magnificent. Iris turned to the left, drawn in by the serenity of the blues, and the vibrancy of the brighter colors. Ruby turned to the right.

Iris was about to ask Ruby what she thought when she heard a gasp. She swirled around to find Ruby standing with her hand over her mouth, a puzzled look on her face. It was then she noticed the painting on the wall. It was the red farmhouse—one of the paintings she had never wanted shown.

"Where did this one come from?" Ruby asked. "I've never seen it before."

Iris froze, unsure what to even say. Where was Charlie? Why on earth had he hung up this painting?

Ruby appeared startled, eyes wide, almost as if she were in pain. Iris turned from the painting of the old red farmhouse to her friend and back again. She wanted to ask what was wrong but realized Ruby had asked her a question. She repeated it, but with an uncharacteristic edge to her voice. "Didn't you hear me? Where did this come from?"

"It wasn't supposed to be here," was all Iris could think to say. She continued to look at the paintings, avoiding Ruby's confused and shattered stare.

They stood there, each too stunned to speak, the silence growing deeper and darker by the second. Iris desperately wanted to know what was so wrong, but the words stuck in her throat. Just when she thought she couldn't bear it any longer, Charlie stuck his head in the tent and called, "Five minutes 'til they open the gates!" Oblivious to the tension in the air, he turned to Ruby and said, "They need you at your booth."

Ruby grabbed her bag and rushed off without a word. Iris watched her go, wondering what on earth had just happened. Ruby was hurting.

She could see that. But why? She briefly thought of taking all of the house paintings down, but in the end, never had time. Her first customer arrived minutes later, and from then on, she was too busy to do anything about it.

Ruby made her way across the fairgrounds to the welcome tent. It was her job to assist patrons with directions, hand out maps and water, and supervise the crew of teenagers on hand to help with any lugging and toting needing to be done. It was usually a blast.

Right now, though, she was having a hard time seeing how she would even get through the day. Her head was spinning, and her mouth was dry. Grabbing a bottle of water, she drank deeply, wondering how this day would end. Iris could never have known what was in that painting. The house had burned to the ground a thousand miles away from here, when Ruby was only ten. She'd never told her friend anything about it.

How on earth had Iris painted it so perfectly? Why wouldn't she say where it came from? Why had she kept it hidden? Questions whirled inside her head, adding to a sense of being somewhat disconnected from the world around her. She kicked off her flip-flops, needing to feel the grass under her feet. It was cool, soft, and still slightly damp with dew. The sense of disconnection began to lift. She poured a splash of water into her hands and rubbed her face vigorously. *Better.*

Once the fear had begun to ease, a gnawing sense of curiosity crept in. It had to be her grandparents' house, but how? And why? And why did she have a sense something had changed back there in the tent, something as mysterious as the existence of the painting itself? Feeling suddenly lost, and longing for something she couldn't name, she wrapped her arms around herself as she slipped her sandals back on. *Please let everything be okay,* she thought as she tossed the empty water bottle in the recycle bin.

"Are you opening up?"

She jumped.

"Are you opening up? I've been waiting to get one of the maps of the fairgrounds."

She looked up into the face of someone she had never met, but whose concerned look seemed to melt her unease. A well-groomed beard streaked with grey framed a gentle face, and brilliant blue eyes reflected the light of the morning sun. His voice was softly accented, and she thought he might be English.

"Oh, sorry! I didn't see you there." She reached under the table for the maps and handed him one, along with a bottle of water. "On the house," she added with a smile.

"Thank you. Any place I should start?"

"Not really, unless you're looking for something specific." Indicating the map in his hand, she added, "The artists are all listed on the back, with numbers on the map to show you where to find them. They're all mixed in around the grounds, so I really just recommend wandering to see what catches your eye."

"Lovely. Thank you again!" He tucked the water into the bag he had slung over his shoulder, giving Ruby a brief wave as he walked away.

Smiling, she called after him, "Have fun!"

The distraction had done its job. A steady stream of customers kept her busy for the rest of the day, and Ruby scarcely had time to think about the painting, or Iris, or what she was going to say when she saw her again.

CHAPTER 9

Iris took a long drink of her iced coffee as she sat on her stool in the corner. There was finally a bit of a lull, and she was taking advantage of it. A steady stream of shoppers had been through her tent already. A fair number had simply been browsing, enjoying the artwork but not really buying much. She'd had to shoo one man off after she caught him taking a picture of one of the paintings. She'd felt like a jerk when he'd turned red in embarrassment, but she stood her ground.

Charlie had come through not long after, and she'd told him about the mix-up with the paintings. He seemed surprised she had been hiding them, but apologized, nonetheless. The whole situation with Ruby had set her on edge, and the poor guy took the brunt of it. Still, he'd known her for long enough to easily brush it off. When he returned soon after with the iced coffee she was currently enjoying, all had been forgiven.

When her next customer walked into the tent, she sized him up quickly. He was alone, casually dressed, with a brown leather bag over his shoulder. He was not unlike most of the customers she usually saw, but there was something different about him, something she couldn't quite put a finger on. He was friendly, asking questions here and there, and yet he almost seemed to be studying her work. As he stood in front of one of them, he reached a hand out—not to touch it, but almost as if he might. And he seemed to be almost listening—or seeing—something other than what was there.

With a start, she realized she was hoping he would tell *her* about what she had drawn, and not the other way around. The feeling was especially strong when he lingered at one of the houses. Had she been wrong to hide them? They were just houses, after all, and well-done paintings, too. Clearly, they interested people. Although others had considered the houses, with this man, she didn't feel the need to protect them. Quite the opposite.

Gathering a bit of courage, she walked over and asked what he thought as he observed a painting of a little white cottage with a tiled roof.

"It's lovely," he said. "Reminds me of home."

She recognized his soft accent—British. That answered that question. The house had *felt* like it existed far away. But what did that even mean?

"Have you been to Britain? You capture its energy so beautifully!" His hand was extended, hovering over the image as if trying to gauge its temperature.

She shook her head. "I haven't been. I wasn't even sure where that house lived, to be honest." As soon as she spoke the words, her cheeks flushed warm with embarrassment. She sounded ridiculous, even to herself. There was an awkward pause before she spoke again.

"So, what brings you to Lakeview? It's a long way from the UK." She hoped he would accept the pivot. He did.

"I'm in town for work, and I'm a sucker for a good arts fair. I couldn't resist."

Iris laughed. "I know what you mean. I paint all day long, but I rarely walk away from this day without some bit of someone else's work."

A short while later, after selecting a small landscape, the gentleman had gone on his way. Iris thought no more of him until the end of the day as she was cleaning up. As she stood up from behind a table, she spied him standing in the doorway.

"I'm sorry, I didn't mean to startle you," he said. "I was thinking about your work all afternoon and came back to ask if you ever do portraits on commission."

Running over her schedule in her mind, she answered, "I do. Are you in town for a while?

"I am. I would love to get it done while I'm here."

She handed him a business card. "The summer is usually pretty quiet for me. If you are still interested when the fair is over, give me a call."

Iris watched him walk across the field and wondered what it was about him that seemed so different. She really hoped he would call. She was lost in thought when Ruby stuck her head in the door with a gentle,

"Ready to go?" Thoughts of Englishmen and cottages and portraits quickly faded as they tied down the tent flaps together. With barely a word between them, the tension of the morning returned, feeling as tight as the ropes they lashed to the ground.

CHAPTER 10

The ride home was equally quiet. Exhausted, Iris welcomed the silence at first. But neither of them would sleep if they didn't talk about what had happened. As they crossed into town, she glanced over at Ruby. "I'm starved. Want to get dinner before we head home? I really don't want to cook."

Ruby let out a breath. "Me neither. All I had today was coffee and a hot dog." The tension eased a fraction.

"Charlie was just telling me Andre is feeling neglected. You up for some pasta?"

"Sure," was all Ruby said. After making a quick call to the restaurant, she rolled down the window and focused her attention outside. Iris turned on the radio, hoping a little music might lift the mood. She tried not to anticipate what their conversation would be, focusing on trying to soothe the prickling in her spine and the solid lump in her gut. She didn't know what she had done, but she was sure she had caused her friend some pain. Opening her own window, she let the breeze wash over her until they turned into the lot behind the restaurant.

Andre had seemed to know they would want a quieter spot to talk. He greeted them with outstretched arms, drawing first Iris, then Ruby, into a hug. The hug was followed with a kiss on each cheek, and then he led them through the restaurant, packed with customers, to a small table by the fireplace in back. Iris knew this room was generally used for private parties, and she softly thanked Andre for his thoughtfulness.

"You two look exhausted. Beautiful, but exhausted. What can I get you?"

"A couple of salads and whatever you have on special sound okay?" Iris asked, looking to Ruby for confirmation.

"Sounds perfect. Oh, and some wine, please," Ruby answered, her soft tone suggesting she might not be as angry as Iris had suspected.

The wine came quickly, along with warm bread and a large salad to share. They busied themselves with filling their plates, not worrying too much about conversation. Iris really was famished, and it wasn't until she had a bit of food in her stomach that she was ready to talk about the day.

Ruby seemed to have been waiting for the right moment, too. As soon as Iris put down her fork and sat back in her chair to enjoy the wine, Ruby set her own fork down, stared pointedly across the table, and asked once again, "Where did the painting of the red house come from? I've never seen it before."

The directness of the stare was unnerving. She couldn't bring herself to meet it; instead, she focused her attention on the crumbs scattered beside the breadbasket. "I just drew it. It was in my head, so I painted it." It wasn't what Ruby was really asking, but she didn't know how else to answer. "I never showed it to you because I have never shown it to anyone. I'm sorry."

Ruby shook her head, seeming unsatisfied with the answer. "What I mean is, how did that house get into your head? Did you see a picture of it somewhere? Did one of my brothers ask you to paint it?"

Confused for a moment, Iris forgot her shame at causing this whole mess. "What do you mean, a picture of it? It isn't a real house. It's just something I made up, like the mountains and oceans. Those aren't real places either." She didn't add that the house had resembled a photograph in her mind, nor that it had refused to go away until she had painted it. Instead, she asked, "What's so upsetting about it?"

Ruby hesitated, her face clouded in worry—or sadness. Iris couldn't be sure which.

"Iris, that's my grandmother's house. Or at least it looks exactly like it. She always had those milk jugs on the porch and even had a plaque on the front of the house, just like the house in the painting. It's uncanny. How could you have known what it looked like?"

The warm bread congealed in her stomach. She gripped the edge of the table as she grasped for a possible answer. "I guess I must have seen a picture of it at your house somewhere."

Ruby shook her head no. "I don't have any pictures of it," she said quietly, eyes filling with tears as she fiddled with the napkin in her lap.

Iris reached across the table in an instinctive urge to comfort, her focus no longer on her own feelings. "I promise you it was only my imagination. Lots of old farmhouses are red and have milk jugs on the porch. And a lot of the old houses around here have plaques. If I've never seen a picture of it, then it couldn't be your grandparents' house, right?"

Ruby finally lifted her head, the lines of worry around her eyes easing as she did. "Sorry. It just looks so much like it, and I was thinking about her the other day. I guess I let my own imagination get the better of me." She offered a tired but genuine smile.

Iris nodded, breathing a soft sigh of relief. They were alright.

Dinner arrived, and they ate companionably for a few minutes. She hoped they could move onto safer subjects, but before she could bring anything up, Ruby broke the silence.

"Did you sell it? The painting?"

She hadn't, and in fact, she had marked it "Sold" to make sure no one bought it. She shook her head no. "I'll take it down tomorrow. Why? Did you want it?"

"No. You keep it. It's a really nice painting." She didn't sound convincing, and there was a hesitancy that made Iris keep quiet. Ruby took a sip of water, set the glass down, and without looking up, said softly, "You never answered my second question."

She wasn't following Ruby's line of thought. "What do you mean? I told you I didn't sell it. What was the other question?"

"I asked you why I've never seen those paintings before. Were you hiding them?"

They were getting into dangerous territory. She had been hiding them, but telling Ruby would negate the whole argument she had only imagined it. If that was all it was, then there was no reason to hide them. "I don't know. I just didn't feel they were good enough to show anyone," she lied.

She didn't know if Ruby believed her or just wanted to be done with the conversation as much as she did. Either way, that seemed to put the conversation to rest.

Suddenly feeling the full weight of exhaustion from the day, she waved Andre over to get the check.

Before they pulled out of the parking lot, she turned to Ruby. "Hey, are we okay? About today, I mean?"

"Yeah. I just overreacted. We're fine. Let's just forget about it, okay?" Ruby yawned, acting unconcerned. Iris decided to let it go. She wanted to forget about it, too. And for a few days, she did.

CHAPTER 11

Monday morning, Charlie dropped off the paintings that had not sold. Iris was exhausted from the weekend but was determined to get her studio back in order. She had done well. Several of the larger paintings had sold, which would help with expenses until spring when she could begin taking in a little money doing taxes on the side. The steady stream of customers had kept her busy, and their compliments had been encouraging.

She had not sold any of the houses, which both surprised and pleased her. They had garnered some interest for sure, but not enough for someone to buy them. She thought again about the little red farmhouse. That one had attracted attention, of course, but not the kind she wanted. The whole thing made her sad, somehow.

Ruby might have been satisfied with the explanation she gave, but Iris wasn't.

What if it really was her grandmother's house?

"Well, that's impossible," she said out loud, as if somehow it would remove the small ball of ice that had taken up residence in her gut since Saturday morning. With determination, she set about getting her studio back in order, firmly putting thoughts of houses and grandmothers aside.

One of the best things to come out of the fair were a couple of commissions. She heard in her head the soft accent of the gentle man from Britain. *Maybe the weekend hadn't been all bad*, she thought. Recalling his interest in the houses, she shivered slightly. But something about him reassured her somehow, and she realized she was really hoping he would call.

As if in answer to her wish, the phone rang. "Hello. My name is Jeremy . . . Allen. From the fair? I spoke to you about a possible commission?" He sounded surprisingly uncertain, nervous in a way, and Iris hurried to reassure him.

"Of course! I remember. I'm so glad you called." She smiled to herself as she sat down at the table. "Are you still interested?"

"Yes," he said, with a sense of finality Iris found puzzling.

"What exactly are you looking for?" she asked.

Jeremy told her he was looking for a simple portrait of himself to hang on the wall in his home. "I have needed to do this for some time but never seemed to be able to find the right artist. I knew when I walked into your tent, I finally had."

"Well, don't put too much pressure on me now!" she joked, although he was making her nervous for some reason.

"I won't. But I do recognize a talented artist when I see one."

He sounds awfully nice, she thought. Maybe it was just that she was still on edge about the situation with Ruby. And she really could use the extra income a commission would bring. She let out the breath she'd been holding. "Thank you. When you come by, I'll make a few sketches and then take some photos so I can work from those without making you sit still for hours. Does that sound alright to you?"

"It does. When would you like me to come by?"

Looking up at the calendar on her wall, she answered, "How about Wednesday at ten?"

"Sounds perfect. I'm looking forward to it. Thank you again."

As she hung up the phone, an idea came into her head. The man's voice and accent had reminded her of British TV shows and old novels. She was always painting local scenes. Maybe today she'd try something different. Recalling the cottage Jeremy had told her reminded him of home, she decided to paint something that reminded her of one of the little villages she was always seeing on television.

She sketched a country lane with a couple of stone walls lining each side. She began to hum as she added in some sheep and a few trees, fully immersing herself in the scene.

And then it happened again.

The vision of the country lane disappeared from her mind as surely as if she had changed channels. In its place stood a large stone building, three stories high, with large crimson doors on each floor. It was a barn, and an old one at that. She shook her head to clear the image, but it only intensified. It drew her inside, into a space lit by several lamps along the wall.

She stopped humming, her mouth gone suddenly dry. She breathed slowly, willing the scene to come back to her, to no avail. She smelled grass, and manure, and blood. Suddenly, she heard a long, low moan, and the back of her neck prickled. She closed her eyes, searching in her mind for the source of the sound, because it most definitely had been in her head.

The source of the disturbance began to reveal itself. In the back of the barn, she could see a cow, and a man standing beside it, speaking.

"Don't worry," he said. Her breath caught in her throat as she realized this time the house was not just a silent image; this time, it had something to say. Reflexively, she covered her ears, hoping to silence the scene—only the sound was in her head, and with some irony, covering her ears only served to make it easier to hear.

She listened. And as she listened, she began to relax. There was humming, only this time it wasn't coming from her. It was as though she were right there in the barn, feeling the warmth from the animals, seeing the gentleness in the way the man stroked the heifer's side, whispering to her, "It's alright. You're doing fine. Don't worry." He repeated the words, seemingly consoling her right along with the animal.

Her own fear began to lessen, and as it did, she recognized the feelings that seemed to be coming from the barn and those inside of it. There was expectation, and joy, and hope. Beautiful hope.

The man was talking again, the words soothing even if mostly indistinct. This time, she heard something else, struck by its incongruence to the situation. "Be who you are."

A warmth rose within her, spreading out to the tips of her fingers and toes, seeming to exit through the top of her head. She could feel the presence of the man and beast and knew without a doubt she was not alone. She breathed deeply—oddly comforted by the experience.

And then, as suddenly as it came, the image disappeared. The warmth was replaced by a chill that led her to reach for the blanket she kept nearby, wrapping it around her shoulders. Her cup of tea was thankfully still warm, and she let the warmth sink into her fingers as she wrapped her hands around the smooth ceramic mug.

What the hell?

CHAPTER 12

Ruby worked as a project manager for the town of Lakeview, and her office was right next door to the post office. If Iris timed her trip to pick up her mail right, she could sometimes catch Ruby on her lunch hour, and they would grab something to eat together. The line hadn't been too long today, so she got to the town hall a bit before noon. She texted to say she was downstairs, then grabbed a seat in the lobby.

For privacy's sake, she kept a post office box for business related mail. So, she didn't expect much beyond a few payments from clients or bills from suppliers. One piece stood out from the rest. It was an advertisement from a local cultural center she supported. They sometimes hosted events for authors or artists, and this seemed to be one of those. The flyer had an image of a lighthouse at night, its beams spreading out like a starburst over the water. The image drew her in, making her long to be present within it, like the keeper of the lighthouse.

"What's that?"

She hadn't heard Ruby approach and jumped, nearly dropping the pile of mail. "It's something at the cultural center next weekend. Wanna go?" she asked, handing her the flyer.

"Beacons," Ruby read. "Some kind of art show, do you think?"

She reached for it back, looking more closely at the description. "It says it's an evening of inspiration, whatever that means. It's cut off at the bottom, but my guess is it's either a talk or a show. What do you think?"

"Why not? I could use a little inspiration in my life. Come on—they've got potato soup at the diner today, and I'm starving!"

CHAPTER 13

Wednesday morning, Iris peered out the window and noted the storm clouds forming off to the west. Hoping the rain would hold off until she could get a few photos outside, she pulled out her studio light and set it up in the corner. Inside the studio, as small as it was, she had set up a place to sit where she could meet with clients, and where the natural light was brightest. Ideally, she could get everything she needed from this man today. Worst case, she'd have him back again on a sunnier day.

Jeremy arrived on time, dressed in tan khakis, a collared shirt and a navy blue sweater. He appeared casual, comfortable, and smart, and she was pleased that was the impression he wished to give with this portrait. He greeted her warmly, almost as if they were old friends, complimenting her on both the studio and the garden.

As she began to explain about how they would proceed, it soon became clear that unlike at the fair, when he had been confident and at ease, he was feeling a bit out of his element. When he wasn't brushing nonexistent dust off his sweater, he was clearing his throat and adjusting his collar. He looked like a young man at his first job interview.

"Come on, let's go out to the garden before we lose the sun." If she wanted to get good images today, she was going to need to get him to relax.

It was the right decision. His posture changed the minute they were out among the flowers. His face brightened, too, and he seemed genuinely interested in her plantings, pointing out things less common back home. His own garden—or his wife's garden, as he called it—was a true passion. Before long, he was again the confident man she had met at the fair.

"So, where in England are you from?" she asked, hoping to get a better sense of who he was, and then convey that in his portrait. She motioned to one of the patio chairs, encouraging him to sit while they talked.

"Our home is in the south of England, in Somerset. You'll have heard of Glastonbury, perhaps? Home of King Arthur and all that?"

She didn't know England much at all, but she had heard of Glastonbury. "Isn't there a big music festival there?"

He hesitated just a bit before answering, his eyes focused on something beyond her shoulder. He spoke softly. "Yes, there is a big festival there. There is also an ancient abbey and a beautiful little town. Very New Age, you might say. And you've heard of Stonehenge, I'm sure." She nodded. "I live not far from there. It's ancient land with lots of old legends and tales, as well as some beautiful old cathedrals and castles, too."

As he spoke, both his face and mood lightened, and she realized there was a sadness about him, which became obvious only when replaced by that shimmer of joy. She began to snap some photos as he spoke, wondering about his sadness. Perhaps he wasn't so happy being here in the States.

"So, you said the other day you were here for work. Can I ask what you do?"

He reached down to pick up a few of the rose petals that had fallen from the bush beside him. He brought them up to his nose, sniffed, and then scattered them back into the garden. "I'm teaching classes up at the Sanctuary for the summer."

Her only knowledge of the Sanctuary came from the ads that arrived in the mail every once in a while. It had never interested her, and she generally tossed them right in the recycling bin. "You mean the yoga place?"

"Yes, although they have more than just yoga there. They teach classes on meditation and spirituality, and self-discovery stuff, too. You might take a drive up sometime. It's really lovely."

"I'll keep that in mind—thank you!"

Satisfied with the outdoor shots, she stood and directed Jeremy back to the studio. In addition to the photos, she wanted to get some sketches done. "Just relax and try not to worry," she said when he asked what he should do. "Pretend I'm not even here, if you can."

Jeremy took his seat, adjusted his collar, and plastered an awkward smile on his face.

She laughed. "I said relax. You look about as relaxed as someone waiting to meet the new dentist."

"I am relaxed," he said through clenched teeth. She laughed again, and then so did he, and his tension seemed to subside for the moment. She kept drawing, concentrating on her work, trying not to make him any more nervous. He was trying so hard to look natural while achieving exactly the opposite effect. She wondered at this. He had been so relaxed as they spoke, both at the fair and during their conversation. She needed to get him talking again.

"So, tell me about your wife. How did the two of you meet?"

The awkward smile disappeared but was quickly replaced with a genuine one. He reached into his pocket, pulled out a worn leather wallet, and from inside, a well-handled photo of a young woman. She had long brown hair, a bright green sweater, and freckles. "Her name's Clara. That was in Glastonbury when we first met."

She continued sketching, loving the sweet expression on his face. She didn't want to interrupt; she merely nodded to encourage him to keep going.

"I was there with some friends from university. We'd all come down on the train for the festival, and they were much more serious about it all than I was. It was blistering hot, and I realized I'm not one for crowds, so I left them and made my way into the town. I ended up at this little shop called the Mystic's Workshop, where I met Clara.

"She was working behind the counter and dressed for the tourists. She was wearing this long green dress; her eyes were ringed with purple eyeliner, and she had this sparkly makeup all over her face. She had flowers in her hair, and that was what got my attention. The rest seemed a bit harsh, but the flowers were pretty. They made me wonder what she looked like underneath all it all."

Iris laughed, and he stopped speaking, a blank look on his face. Then he realized what he had said, turning as red as the rose petals he had left in the garden. She apologized, but the grin didn't leave her face until he continued.

He cleared his throat. "As I was saying, I was smitten. But I didn't know what to do, so I just started looking around, picking up random things off the shelves. One of those was a book called *Are You Psychic?*, or something of the sort. And she comes up behind me and says, 'You are, you know.'

"I was terribly insulted and told her so. Er . . . politely though. I didn't want to alienate the first woman I'd spoken with all day." He winked, and Iris laughed. If he was half as charming then as he was now; she had no doubt he hadn't had to work too hard to win her over.

"Well, my wife has never had a problem with confidence, or with her intuition. Next thing I knew, she'd invited me to a gathering at her church, so she could prove to me I was not only psychic, but a medium to boot." He paused; one eyebrow raised in question. "Do you know what that is?" he asked Iris.

She nodded, not wanting to interrupt his story. She'd heard of mediums, of course, but would have been hard-pressed to explain what one was—or did.

"Well, to cut a long story short, I found myself in an old church hall with a bunch of middle-aged women, eating biscuits and talking about spirits. By the end of the evening, I'd been taught to meditate. Then I'd been paired up with a woman whose name I can't recall, who handed me her antique watch so I could give her a reading on where it came from. I thought I was making up some story about a red-haired soldier who'd brought the bracelet home to her from the mountains.

"Turns out, it was true. And as I sat there gobsmacked, I'd looked up to see Clara standing with her arms crossed, a proud look on her face, as if she'd just won the Olympics or something. 'I told you so,' she'd mouthed to me from across the room. And from then on, we were inseparable. I finished school, moved to Glastonbury, and we were married a year later."

He sat back, the little photo of his wife in his hands. He was still smiling, but with a far-away look to him. Iris scribbled furiously, hoping to capture his expression before it faded. Finally, she set her pencil down. "You can relax—I've got enough. I just need to make a few notes and then we can chat."

Jeremy let out a huge sigh, seemingly relieved to be able to breathe freely once again. He stood and stretched, then motioned at the paintings around the room, one eyebrow raised, asking permission to look around. "Oh, go ahead!" she said, turning back to her notebook.

She was curious about his reaction, recalling how he had been so interested that day at the fair. Surreptitiously, she watched him as he made his way around the room. He was so different from anyone else she knew. He wasn't just looking at the pictures. He moved slowly, cocking his head as if listening. This made her do the same, and she noticed the birds outside and the soft whoosh of the cars out on the road.

He turned toward her, and she averted her gaze quickly, hoping he hadn't noticed she'd been watching him. "You've a lovely studio," he said. "It's very peaceful. You must love working out here."

She was pleased he liked it. Peaceful is exactly how she would describe it, and she breathed deeply, inhaling the smell of charcoal and paint, enjoying the serenity she associated with those scents. "I do. It's my favorite place to be, if I'm being honest."

He moved to examine the unfinished painting on the easel in the corner. She watched him, fascinated again by the way he seemed to be studying it, not just examining the artistry. She herself felt the urge to hold her hand up to it and half expected him to do the same. As had happened that day at the fair, she realized she wanted him to tell her about her own painting. "Does it look finished to you?" she asked. "I'm not sure myself."

He examined the painting more closely. "It has all the parts one would expect in a mountain scene: clouds, trees, mountains. It could be done, yes." He hesitated. "But I don't believe it is."

She set down her pencils and walked over to join him at the painting. "I'm stuck on it," she said. "I thought it was done days ago, but it's missing something, I think. I was ready to just sign it and call it done, but I won't, since you agree. I'll just have to wait until the inspiration for the missing piece comes to me."

He pointed to the area in the middle of the image, where the mountain met the valley, and she had filled the spot with wildflowers. It was the same spot that was bothering her. "What's going on here?" he asked.

"I think there's somebody on that mountain," she said. "I'm just not sure where."

He glanced sharply at her, then smiled, almost to himself. "I think you're right, but I think you haven't found it yet—their place, I mean."

She picked up the small brush lying on the tray below the painting. She dipped it into the cup of water she'd left there, then dragged the tip across the center of the scene, broadening the line as it moved out from the middle.

"There. That's the path he—or she—is on. It leads to someplace they've always wanted to go," she said, looking to him for confirmation. His eyes widened in understanding, and she blushed, strangely pleased at his response. "Thank you for helping spark my imagination," she said. "I couldn't see it until now."

He turned, pointing to the other paintings she had hung around her studio. "Is it always this way, seeing a story in your paintings?"

She thought about it for a minute, then shook her head no. "Not always; it's a more recent thing, I think. I don't remember when it started. I just realized over time it was what I was doing." She put the brush down and walked back to her sketches, suddenly feeling self-conscious. "I think this will be enough to start with. I will be in touch as soon as I have something more, to make sure I'm on the right track for you."

"I'll wait to hear from you then," he said, as he picked up his jacket to leave.

"Sorry," she said, realizing she'd been terribly abrupt. "I didn't mean to rush you out of here. Sometimes when a painting starts to tell its story to me, I forget everything else. I really appreciate your help with this, and I think the sketches will be great."

"You're not rushing me. I recognize an artist at work when I see one." He handed her his business card so she could get in touch with him. "Thank you for your time with this. I know I'm in good hands here."

"My pleasure." She opened the door for him, allowing him two hands to get his umbrella opened. Seeming to remember something, she called after him as he walked away, "By the way, I lied earlier. I don't know what a medium is. Will you tell me next time?"

"Of course!" he answered with a laugh, neatly dodging a large puddle, raising one hand in a last wave goodbye."

CHAPTER 14

After Jeremy left, Iris turned back to the mountain scene and began to paint in earnest. With the scene now clear in her mind, she had it finished by the end of the day. Pleased to be done with it, she cleaned up her paints and turned to the sketches she had done of Jeremy. There was something about him she couldn't quite place, and she had greatly enjoyed the morning.

She realized that what she had first thought was physical attraction was something else, but again, she just couldn't figure out what it was. His questions about how she painted weren't much different from the questions Ruby was always asking, but for some reason, his questions had disturbed her. She shook her head to clear the feeling away.

Realizing she wasn't going to be able to focus, she pulled on her sneakers and headed out for a walk. The rain had stopped, and the air smelled fresh, especially after a day spent inside with the smell of acrylic and charcoal. She started toward the lake, but the sight of the flowers on the town green drew her there instead.

In the center of the green stood a tall white church, surrounded by walking paths and a small colonial cemetery in the back. The early summer flowers were in full bloom, and the scent of roses and lilacs drew her closer. As she walked under the tall open windows, the strains of "Amazing Grace" drifted out into the evening air.

She sat down on a nearby bench, feeling her tiredness seep away and the unease begin to lift. She remembered singing this hymn regularly in church growing up and began to recall those days before her father died, when her mother would softly sing songs like this as she worked.

A sudden pang of longing for her mother hit her like a gust of wind off the mountains. It had been a few years since her mother had died, but sometimes the loss was still achingly fresh. As she recalled her mother's touch, a beautiful calm settled in, as if being wrapped in a warm blanket. She remained still, afraid to move, lest the feeling of her mother's presence slip away.

CHAPTER 15

The Cultural Center was located across the lake, on a rise overlooking the town. They arrived early enough to sit outside for a while and enjoy the view. There were benches donated by various people, most in remembrance of someone who had passed and had often loved to sit here and enjoy the view. They sat down on "Bitsy's Bench" and spent a few minutes speculating on what might have prompted someone to be given such a nickname.

"There was this tiny little woman who always came by the town hall to vote early. I'll bet it was her," Ruby guessed.

"No, I'll bet she or one of her siblings had a lisp or something. Maybe her name was really Betsy," Iris said hopefully. She'd never had a nickname growing up but always thought it would be fun. She had asked once if she could have one, but when Alice had suggested "Sissy," she had quickly backed off. There were worse things than having to go by your own name all your life. Like being called Bitsy.

Ruby seemed to agree. "Either way, I'll bet she's up there cursing her family for immortalizing that name on this bench." Looking up to the sky, she called out, "Hey Bitsy—if you give me a sign, I'll spill coffee on them or something; just let me know!" Then she dissolved into giggles.

Iris playfully slapped Ruby's shoulder. "Hey, be nice. Maybe she liked the name." She glanced around nervously, hoping nobody had heard. What if Bitsy's family had been nearby? "Come on, let's head inside. Maybe we can get a good seat."

They came around the front of the building and joined the small line to get in. While they waited, Iris walked over to read the sandwich board standing outside the door. It was a larger version of the flyer she had read, but this time, nothing was cut off at the bottom. She drew in her breath sharply with a soft, "Oh!" then covered her mouth with her hand.

"What is it?" Ruby asked.

She pointed to the bottom of the sign. After "An evening of inspiration," it said, "with mediums Jeremy Allen and Amanda Bennis."

"Ruby, I think this isn't an art show." She let out a single nervous laugh. "This guy, Jeremy, he's a medium. He was at my house the other day. I met him at the fair, and he asked me to paint his portrait. He told me what he did, but I never got to ask him what that meant. Do you have any idea?"

Ruby's mouth had formed into an "O," and her eyes were wide and bright. She grinned like a kid who just found out she was getting a new bike. "A medium! Awesome! Have you ever seen that one on TV? She's amazing."

She shook her head no. "I've heard of her but never seen her. What does she do?"

"Talk to dead people," Ruby answered with a shrug. She was trying to look nonchalant, but Iris could see right through her. Ruby was beginning to bounce on the balls of her feet. As soon as they were through the door, she pulled Iris along, making a beeline for one of the seats up front. "I can't believe you know one!" she said, giving Iris's arm an excited squeeze.

She wished she had been able to ask Jeremy more the other day. The urge to turn around and leave was strong, but Ruby's excitement was contagious, and eventually, she gave in to it as well. When Ruby turned to her and wondered with a smirk if Bitsy might show up, Iris shushed her as if Bitsy herself were listening, though she couldn't fully hold back a little grin of her own.

Three people walked onstage and stood in front of their chairs, singing along to the music. Soon the audience joined in. It reminded Iris of a high school assembly, and she laughed. As they sang, she focused her attention on the two mediums. Jeremy appeared calm and self-assured, dressed in a collared shirt and jacket. She resisted the impulse to wave, not wanting to draw attention to herself. As she recalled his insight about her painting, a warmth began to spread up through her chest. She felt a deep sense of calm and a burning curiosity.

She turned her attention to the woman, who had her hands grasped in front of her, looking as if she might bolt if given the chance. With a start, Iris realized the woman was looking right at them. Puzzled, she raised her eyebrows in question, then turned to Ruby. When she looked back, the woman had turned away, her lips tight and her hands still tightly clasped.

Iris swallowed the renewed sense of unease that had risen and turned her attention to the host who had stepped to the microphone. He spoke for a few minutes, explaining a bit about mediumship, which served to once again calm her nerves.

"You okay?" Ruby whispered, as Iris wiped her hands on her jeans.

"Yeah. I'm good," she answered, feigning nonchalance. "You?"

"Just nervous," Ruby whispered back. "That guy Jeremy looks familiar. I think I might have seen him at the fair too. It's like we were meant to be here, you know?"

Iris wasn't so sure. Coincidences were just that, she'd always said. Besides, he was new in town, which would explain suddenly seeing him in different places. She was just about to argue the point when Ruby turned to greet the woman who had sat down beside her.

Lucia Alvarez owned a little gift shop in town that Iris visited from time to time. Iris waved a hello while Ruby turned her attention to the newcomer. Lucia seemed to agree about the whole "meant to be" argument, and they nattered away softly until Iris had to shush them. Jeremy had stepped to the microphone.

He smiled warmly, eyes moving around the room, stopping here and there to look someone in the eyes. Iris could see the audience warming to him, and she realized he must do this often.

"Thank you for the lovely introduction," he began, "and thank you to all of you for welcoming me this evening. Before I get started, I want to tell you a little bit about how I work. How many of you have never been to a mediumship demonstration before?" A scattering of hands went up, and Iris immediately felt better for it. She and Ruby weren't the only novices there that night.

"Wonderful," he continued. "I hope you enjoy the evening. It's a full house here tonight, and I'm not just referring to all of you. We are joined here by your loved ones in the spirit world, those who have passed from this life and now exist in the world of spirit, the world where life continues on."

Images of her parents, and Michael, sprung into Iris's mind. She turned to look at Ruby, wondering who might be springing to her mind. Reaching over, she grasped Ruby's hand in a comforting squeeze.

"You see, it is only our bodies that die in the end," he continued. "Our spirits, the essence of who we are, live on. Tonight, those loved ones of yours have an opportunity to communicate with you. Not all of you will be able to receive a contact, but several of you should receive enough evidence from either Amanda or me to recognize your loved ones and know they live on. That is the reason we do what we do here: to provide you with hope and the comfort of knowing your loved ones remain by your side long after they have physically left this world."

The room had fallen silent, and the silence was palpable. There was something else, Iris noted, as she listened to Jeremy speak. There was an energy in the room—an electricity—and the hairs on her neck stood tall in evidence.

"Because it is so important for you to trust the evidence presented here tonight is real, I will ask you to do a few things. First, be open-minded. You may be hoping to hear from a specific person for a specific reason. Trust there is incredible intelligence in the spirit world, and they know the best way to reach out to you. That may mean someone other than who you hoped for makes contact. Try to not be too focused on one person—it could be someone else here for you tonight.

"The second request is to not feed the medium. What I mean is, don't offer us any information. Let us give it to you. Please just answer "yes," "no," or "I'm not certain" if we ask if you recognize a piece of information.

"Lastly, raise your hand if any of the information makes sense. Then, if we come to you, please answer loudly and clearly so all can hear. It really helps to build the energy in the room, and it also helps to make sure everyone here can follow what is happening."

Iris already felt as if she might explode from the energy she was feeling. She glanced around nervously, half expecting people to be starting at her. The thought of even more energy being present in that room was a little daunting. Taking a deep breath, she willed herself to relax. As she exhaled, her body relaxed a bit, and her mind soon followed.

"Now remember, even if you don't get a connection tonight, your loved ones are still here. If you leave here tonight more convinced spirits are still living and able to make contact, then the evening will have been a success."

He turned, took his jacket off, and laid it across his chair before returning to the front of the stage. He looked out over the audience, his eyes focused, but not on any one of them.

"I sense an older gentleman. He has a beard and white hair, but he tells me it was red when he was younger. He has a large family, and when he laughs, his entire body shakes. He also strikes me as generous, hardworking, and kind."

"Sounds like Santa Claus," Ruby whispered, and Iris gave her a soft elbow, telling her to shush.

When Jeremy said this man also had a tragic side to his life, two hands shot up from across the room.

"Can you take all the evidence I've given up to now?" he asked. "Does it make sense for someone you know in the spirit world?"

"Yes," they answered together.

"Both of you?"

They turned to look at each other and said, "Yes, we're cousins."

Jeremy acknowledged that and continued. After a bit more back and forth, the story of this gentleman came out. He was their grandfather. He had tragically died while crossing the street to get home after church.

"He tells me one of you is worried about something. Am I right?" Jeremy asked.

One of the women said yes, so he continued. "He is showing me a police car. Does that mean anything?"

"Yes!" the young woman nearly shouted.

"He is also showing me a school, and I get the sense someone is thinking of going there—to school for something." They again both nodded yes. "It isn't one of you, is it?"

They both answered, "No."

"Okay, he seems to be putting the police car and the school together. Someone is thinking of entering the police academy, aren't they." He didn't say this as a question but rather as a statement of fact. Not waiting for a response, he continued. "He is asking me to tell you not to worry. He knows that can be a scary thing to do, but he wants you to trust this person will be well trained, and it will help to keep them safe."

"My fiancé is planning to apply, and I have been worried." The woman spoke softly, lifting her shoulders in a gesture of helplessness.

"Well, your grandfather is showing me he was either a police officer or a firefighter, too—is that right?" Jeremy offered with an air of confidence.

"Yes."

"He is pointing out again how he died. I think he is trying to show you just crossing the street can be dangerous enough. It might be a strange way of getting the message across, but I think that is his way of saying, 'Don't worry.'" He reached for his glass of water, and this seemed to be an indication he was finished. They thanked him for the message, and he thanked their grandfather for coming to deliver it. The audience applauded.

Ruby nudged Iris. "Wow—that was great!" Iris agreed. So far, she was impressed at how it all worked, but still a bit skeptical. Could he have known the two women and planned it all?

Jeremy quickly moved on to his next contact. This one didn't go as smoothly. He talked about another man, someone's husband, he thought. "He's at a ball game or a ballpark." No hands went up.

"Someone has a photo of this man on her nightstand." Nothing.

"Alright, now he is showing me an orange bird. Does a bird, an orange bird, mean anything to any of you?" Again, no hands went up.

Jeremy seemed quite puzzled such specific evidence was not being recognized by anyone. He started to go back through it slowly. As he was doing this, Iris noticed the woman sitting next her. She was staring at Jeremy, had pulled her shirt up over her mouth, and was chewing on the collar. Iris asked, "Are you okay?"

The woman shrugged in response. "My husband was a huge baseball fan. He was trying to visit every ballpark in the country. He didn't make it. The picture I have on my dresser is of him at Camden Yards where the Orioles play. Do you think that's him?"

Iris stifled a grin as she realized this must indeed be the woman's husband. Instead, she gently replied, "It sounds like it might be. Why don't you raise your hand?"

Still looking very nervous, the woman put her hand up, and Jeremy nodded. He continued to build the evidence culminating in the delivery of the message that the man knew his wife was lonely, and he didn't mind if she started dating. The woman seemed pleased and said she had been wondering about it. The audience applauded warmly. Iris didn't need convincing anymore. She poked Ruby in the side and said, "Holy cow—this is real!" Ruby laughed and agreed.

The second medium was introduced as Amanda Bennis, an American medium who lived nearby. "I'm honored to be sharing this platform with Jeremy tonight. He was my first mentor when I began studying mediumship ten years ago. He has been an inspiration to me and a true model of integrity in mediumship. Thank you, Jeremy for those wonderful contacts. I think everyone will agree they were very moving." The audience applauded briefly.

"All of the same rules apply for me in terms of yes and no answers and being open-minded. One difference though is I tend to get a sense of who the message might be for, so I may approach you directly. Please don't feel pressured to accept what I present to you, but if it makes sense, please let me know, okay?"

Iris was fascinated by this second medium. She seemed to somehow know just who she was getting a contact for, but Iris couldn't tell how she knew it. In fact, her curiosity was growing over exactly how any of it worked. Amanda said things like, "He is showing me . . ." or "I keep hearing . . ." *Was this out loud? Did she see someone standing there?*

She had so many questions bubbling up inside of her that she realized she had been barely paying attention to what was being said. And now, for some reason, everyone was looking right at her. She turned to Ruby and quickly realized she was the one they were looking at. She was sitting bolt upright, with the same look on her face Iris remembered from that day at the fair. She was so still; it wasn't clear she was even breathing.

Iris didn't know what to do. She looked from Ruby to the medium, and then to Jeremy, hoping he might somehow tell her what was going on. But his eyes were on Ruby as well, and so he didn't see Iris's silent plea for understanding. Iris turned back to her friend, placing a hand gently on her forearm. It was rock hard, and she was trembling.

The audience turned back to Amanda as she broke the silence. She said she would repeat the evidence and asked Ruby to let her know if it made sense. Iris listened intently this time.

"I have a woman here who tells me she knew you well when you were young, and you were very close. She says she passed before you were grown, and you had been less close in the period before she died. I keep hearing the word 'Hope,' and I get the sense it has something to do with you and a big change that happened in your life. I'm also hearing 'Grace.' Does that mean anything to you?" she asked.

Ruby continued to look stunned but answered softly, "Yes."

"Could this be a grandmother?"

"Yes—that's Grace. That's her name." She reached for Iris and held her hand, tight.

"Your grandmother is showing me the color red. It seems to be both a good and a bad memory. She wants to talk about both, but just for a minute. I think it's a sore memory because she is saying to me, 'Don't push it.'"

Ruby grinned. "She said it to me a lot: 'Don't push it.'" That got a chuckle out of the audience, and the energy in the room lightened.

"Now I see the color red again. She is showing me a house—a red house with a front porch. I see laundry on the clothesline and milk jugs on the porch. It seems like a farmhouse—an old one. Does that make sense?"

Ruby nodded. "Yes, that's her house."

Iris began to tremble now, the hairs standing up on the back of her neck.

"She is showing me red again, but this time it feels different— something frightening, I think. There is also a little girl I see. She is in a nightgown. Was there a fire? I feel like this little girl isn't in danger from it, but she is seeing it somehow."

"Yes. There was a fire."

Iris was sweating. She desperately wanted to pull her hand back, to wrap her own arms around her body. At the same time, she desperately wanted to comfort Ruby.

"There is something painful about the memory, so she just wants me to tell you that it wasn't your fault. None of it was your fault." Ruby emitted a strange sound, something between a gasp and cry. Her free hand covered her mouth as she obviously fought to maintain her composure.

"Your grandmother said she knows you left because you thought it was your fault, and it wasn't. She says she wished she could have told you then so you wouldn't have carried that guilt along with you to . . . Hope? She said it just like that: You carried the guilt along with you to Hope?" She stopped for a moment, a puzzled look on her face. Does this make any sense to you?" Ruby nodded, and she was smiling now— just enough for Iris to know she was okay.

Amanda continued. "Your grandmother says she knows why you went looking for it and when you found it, she was sure you would be okay. She really wants you to know she always loved you and always will, and she is so glad she finally got the chance to tell you. She is so proud of you. She sends you a hug and a kiss and says thank you for everything, and especially for coming tonight."

Iris joined in the applause, realizing as she did so that her hands were numb. In fact, her whole body felt numb, except for her heart. It was pounding away as if she had just run several miles. *How on earth?*

She turned to Ruby, who was blowing her nose but smiling, too. What in the world had just happened? It seemed as if the whole room must know the medium had just described that stupid painting she had hidden for so long. And yet they were already turning away, focusing their attention on Amanda as she moved on to her next recipient. Even Ruby seemed less bothered than Iris.

"Wow," Ruby said. "Oh, wow." She sniffed, wiping her eyes with the back of her sleeve. She was trying to smile, which was both confusing and reassuring. At least she wasn't angry. Iris gave her friend a warm hug, but for the rest of the evening, heard nothing. All she heard was her own voice inside her head wondering what the hell just happened.

By the time it was over, Iris was spent. Her mind hadn't stopped racing through the evidence Ruby had received and her memory of the painting and Ruby's reaction to it. She was paying no attention to anything else around her until she heard a soft, "So, what did you think?" It was Lucia, who had glided up alongside of her as they walked down the center aisle to leave.

"It's my first time at one of these," she replied. "I don't know how it's supposed to go, but it seemed pretty good to me." It was a lame response, but better than the truth, which was that she was excited by it, worried about Ruby, and terrified of what it all meant.

"They were really good tonight," Lucia answered. I've seen quite a few mediums work, and these two did a great job." She turned around to Ruby, who was lagging behind them a bit.

"How are you doing? That was quite a reading to get for your first time at one of these things."

"I'm good," Ruby answered, speaking softly, and without her usual brashness. Her expression made it clear her mind was elsewhere, and Lucia seemed to see this and didn't push for more conversation.

"Let it sit with you," she said. "She sent it with love, you know."

Ruby nodded, her eyes soft and bright. "Thank you."

CHAPTER 16

They drove for a bit in silence, each mulling their own thoughts. Iris was afraid to say anything, lest Ruby ask her about the painting. But perhaps listening to her friend would stop her own internal monologue, the one asking how in the world she knew about that house.

"What did you think?" she finally asked as they merged onto the highway. There was a surprising amount of traffic for this time of night, and she instantly regretted asking the question when she couldn't look Ruby in the face. She risked a quick glance and was relieved to not see tears, at least.

"That was something else. To be honest, I'm not sure what to think about it," Ruby said. She shuffled a bit in her seat, rubbing her hands across the front of her jeans. "Do you think it really was my grandmother?"

"I don't know. It was all so convincing, but I don't think I can answer that for you. What makes you believe it was real?"

"She couldn't possibly have known those things. I mean, there's just no way . . . "

"Did you ever tell anyone in town about it? She did say she is from around here. Could she have heard the story somewhere?" Iris asked, immediately regretting the question. Just the thought of someone doing something so cruel as to make this all up made her chest hurt.

"No, so she really couldn't have known anything about it," Ruby replied. Then with an almost childlike plea, added, "It has to have been real."

They drove for a couple of minutes in silence again. Iris could sense an earnestness in her friend that was unfamiliar. She was usually so confident and unconcerned, but tonight, there was a striking vulnerability. Wanting to comfort, yet still grappling with her own unsettling emotions, she chose her words carefully. "I'm sorry this brought up such a sad memory for you. Are you okay?"

"Thanks. It's a lot to think about, but I'm okay," Ruby answered. Then, as if she, too, needed to lighten the atmosphere, added, "What a wild night, huh?"

Iris accepted the pivot. "How about that woman next to me? I think she would have let the whole thing slip by her if I hadn't said something."

"And it was her husband!" Ruby laughed. "I hope she finds someone new. She was awfully young to be a widow."

"I'll bet she will. I'll bet she's already found someone and that's why he was there—he probably knows all about it." She paused, thinking for a few seconds before continuing. "I wonder what that's like, being dead and watching your spouse move on. Makes me kind of sad for him in a way."

"Well, maybe you don't feel sad after you die," Ruby said, although she sounded doubtful. "Do you think my grandmother sounded sad?"

"Not at all, actually. She sounded kinda happy to talk to you, I think." The conversation was veering back into dangerous territory. And Iris realized she was believing in the evening more than she ever would have expected to. She wished she could know what Ruby was thinking.

They had arrived back in town, and she pulled over in front of Ruby's building. "You sure you're alright?" she asked as Ruby undid her seatbelt.

"I'm sure," Ruby answered, with a modest but genuine smile. "Go on, get outta here. I'll see you tomorrow."

She waited until Ruby was safely inside the front door, then let out a massive sigh, relieved she hadn't mentioned the painting. Her head was spinning with everything she had seen, and she wanted nothing more than to get to bed and shut it all off. Her last thought as her head hit the pillow was of Jeremy. *I've got an awful lot of questions for that man.*

––––––––––––––––––

Ruby pulled the door closed behind her, turning the lock with trembling hands. She seemed to have convinced Iris she was okay, but it wasn't really true. Thank goodness they had just headed home. It had been comforting to hear from her grandmother, if that's really what had happened. But she hadn't ever talked about the fire for a reason. And she wasn't ready to do it tonight.

The events of the evening kept running through her head, like a reel that wouldn't stop. Her emotions swung from relief it hadn't been her fault, to fear it had been, and that the evening was all some sort of a scam. The latter thought took over, and she dropped onto the couch in despair. *Please don't let it be a scam*, she prayed.

After a few minutes, a calm seemed to settle in. Feeling comforted, she headed to bed. The evening was again running through her head, but more like a story being told by someone she loved. Just as she was nearly asleep, it hit her. It wasn't only the medium who had seen her grandparents' house—the one they had lived in until it burned to the ground. If the demonstration was a scam, then how had Iris seen it too?

CHAPTER 17

It had been a week since the demonstration, and Iris was still rattled. She had spent the day moving from her studio to the front porch, to the kitchen, and back. She couldn't figure out what to do, and everything she tried seemed wrong. Unable to sit still long enough to paint and too distracted to read, she had resorted to cleaning every room in the house. Recalling the day she had sat outside the little church on the green and listened to the organ playing, she slipped on her shoes and headed into town.

If the church were closed, she had planned to sit on the bench in the shade. Fortunately, it was open, and Iris went quietly inside. She wasn't much for church services but did love the way churches felt inside. The sun was streaming through the large windows, and she slipped into one of the benches, sighing as the warmth of the wood seeped into her body.

She still hadn't spoken with Ruby about the painting, and this was bothering her. The fact neither one of them had brought it up should have meant they were letting it go, but the opposite was clearly true. They were avoiding each other, and if they didn't deal with it soon, she was worried their friendship might collapse.

Usually, when she was feeling off, sketching or painting was all she needed to do to again feel right with the world. But her attempts at sketching were proving to be even more unsettling, and if she couldn't get the sketches done, she couldn't start on the portrait she had been hired to do.

Her mind logically moved onto Jeremy, and this brought a surprising feeling with it. She wasn't attracted to him in the normal sense of the word, but she did feel a strange longing to be around him. She wondered if he would be able to help her with the situation with Ruby, but that would mean telling him about the painting, and that might lead to the other houses, and . . . *Stop.* She rubbed her hands vigorously over her face and said it again. *Stop.* She was letting her worries get the better of her.

69

Telling herself to breathe slowly, she turned her attention inward. With each exhale, her muscles relaxed a bit, which helped at first but soon left her feeling unmoored and adrift in the sacred space. She shifted her attention, looking around the church for something to center her. Taking the focus off herself seemed to help. As she scanned the room, she placed her palms on the wooden bench, noting the smoothness of the well-worn surface. A faint smell of beeswax filled the air, and she inhaled deeply. *Much better*, she thought, as she began to feel settled for the first time all day.

Following the shafts of sunlight streaming in, she noticed several small plaques on the wall. One in particular stood out from the rest. As she approached the plaque, the words came into focus, filling her with a warmth that seemed greater than what the sun was bringing. It read:

> *Organ donated in honor of*
> *John Newton (1725–1807)*
> *whose hymn, "Amazing Grace,"*
> *continues to inspire all who hear it.*

There was something about that song. Walking around the perimeter of the church, she admired the other plaques and the view out the windows before returning to the seat in the sun. With a determined effort to maintain the serenity she was feeling, yet feeling surprisingly safe, she let her thoughts return to the demonstration. She ran through the evidence the woman had presented to Ruby and compared it in her mind to the house she had drawn.

As she thought about what had happened, something in the back of her mind began to surface. *If that woman saw a red house with milk jugs, and she's a medium, does that make me a medium because I saw it too?*

She couldn't be a medium. She still didn't even understand what one was. She was nothing like Jeremy or the other medium. She wasn't even sure she believed in heaven. Swallowing, she grimaced at how dry her throat had become.

She reached in her bag for a mint, noticing the program she had grabbed at the demonstration the other night. She pulled it out, suddenly curious to read about the two mediums. Amanda lived locally and had been working as a medium for a few years after spending several years developing her abilities. Iris wondered what it meant to develop one's abilities. Weren't mediums born that way? Her throat tightened a bit more, and she swallowed deliberately to clear the feeling. She began to notice her heartbeat, throbbing loudly in her chest. She kept reading.

Under Jeremy's photo was a quote that read, "A medium is one who communicates in a meaningful way with those who reside in the world of spirit." She read the quote again slowly, focusing on each word to be sure she understood it correctly.

Ruby had certainly believed something was communicated that night. But was Iris herself communicating something through the paintings? She wasn't willing to say she had done anything meaningful, but neither was she willing to dismiss this out of hand any longer. Could she really be a medium too?

Her hands began to shake. She reached up, running her fingers through her hair. Her scalp was tingling, and she felt like she was going to explode. "And explosions are never a good thing," she said out loud, letting her voice reverberate in the open space.

Unless they are fireworks. The words came into her mind like a thought, only she was sure they weren't her own. She whipped her head around to see if someone else was there. She was still very much alone. She stood, wanting nothing more than to get out of there. As she walked down the aisle, the feeling of an explosion kept coming back, along with an image of fireworks.

The feeling she was no longer alone became overwhelming. She nearly ran the last few steps to the door, slamming it open and racing out onto the green. "You are *not* a medium. You are *not* a medium" she repeated in time with her steps. When she arrived home, she looked back uneasily over her shoulder as she slipped inside, locking the door behind her.

She stood there in the living room, looking around at everything solid and real. She kicked off her shoes, enjoying the feel of the smooth wood floors under her feet. It only took a few minutes to brew a hot cup of tea, adding a spoonful of honey and a splash of milk. The need for comfort was strong, and the drink reminded her of the days when her mom would come visit, and they would sit, drink tea, and talk. *Well Mom*, she thought, *what do I do now?*

There was a notebook on the coffee table, and Iris grabbed it as she sat down on the couch. She'd handle this like she handled anything that troubled her—with logic and reason. At the top of the page, she copied the quote about mediumship from the brochure she still had in her pocket. Below that she wrote, "Communication" and wrote down a definition she found in the dictionary: "An exchange of information; a means of sending or receiving information."

Then she made three columns on the page, one each for Jeremy and Amanda, and with a shaky hand, put her own name atop the third one. On the left, she listed the ways the mediums had said they were receiving the evidence, which Iris presumed was the communication from the spirit world.

Recalling what they had said, Iris first thought about Jeremy. He had told them about seeing the man with the orange bird and the other man who reminded her of Santa Claus. She put a check mark under Jeremy in the row labeled "Seeing." Amanda had also told Ruby she could see the color red, the house, and the little girl in pajamas, so a check mark went into Amanda's column as well. Looking at the last column, Iris very firmly said, "Not yet," and turned back to the demonstration.

Hearing was the next category. Both mediums had said the spirits wanted them to know something and had given a message. Tears came to her eyes as she recalled Ruby's response to being told she had done nothing wrong. Yup, hearing was a big one, and they both had done it.

The last category was feeling. She added this because she recalled distinctly how Amanda had described what she was feeling to Ruby. She had said that the memories felt painful and that the color red felt different when it referred to the fire. She put a check mark under manda's column but left Jeremy's blank. She couldn't recall if he had spoken about feelings at all, and she was trying to be as precise as she could.

So that left the last column, Iris's own. She thought back to when she had painted the red house. She had most definitely seen it, so she added a check mark to the row. She wanted to leave the hearing row blank, but a shudder ran through her as she recalled the comment about fireworks and the voice in the barn when she had painted that image. With a trembling hand, she added a check box under her name and moved along. She couldn't recall feeling anything about the red house as she drew it, so she left the column blank. And then she remembered the other houses. *No,* she thought, *I definitely feel something.* She added the third check in her column.

Iris sat there, staring at the paper, trying to sort out what she had found. If the table she had made was to be believed, she was a medium. She picked up the pencil again and at the bottom of the page began to write down everything she could think of to back up that possibility, followed by all the reasons it couldn't be true.

The list of supporting evidence soon grew to be twice as long as the one against it. As she sat looking at the exercise she had completed, the feeling of an explosion returned. But this time, she thought of the fireworks and realized fear and excitement feel very much the same. She was most definitely excited now, but also still a bit afraid.

The best way to overcome fear was to learn about what was scaring you. This was something her dad had taught her when she was a young girl, and it was a mantra she had always followed. She'd need to talk to Jeremy, but in the meantime, she would begin researching this mediumship stuff, hoping that would help.

But first, she needed to paint. The feeling of urgency was strong, and Iris hurried out to her studio. She began to sketch in the outline of a building, with a set of double doors, some steps leading up to them, and a glow coming from inside. Picking up the paintbrush, she added in yellow and orange trees, a few pumpkins out front, and a steeple up on top, glowing with the light from within. A warmth spread through her as she painted, as if being embraced by an old friend. It was love she felt, and love could only be expressed through light.

As the image took shape, Iris began to forget all that had been troubling her. It was as if the worries of the day had vanished into that light. By the time she had finished, the little white church radiated a palpable sense of home. She titled it *Amazing Grace* and left it to dry on the easel in the center of the room. As she left it, she knew without a doubt she had painted it for a reason, and it was hers. She rarely kept paintings, always feeling she painted for others, but this one belonged to her. She closed up the studio and tucked her key away in her pocket, feeling inexplicably held, comforted, and safe.

The next day, Iris had the photos of Jeremy laid out in front of her. She was pleased with them. They captured his likeness well, but for some reason, she was having trouble getting that likeness onto the paper. Something was distracting her as she examined the photos. The images kept changing—enough that she wondered if she should get her eyes checked.

In one picture, Jeremy resembled an old woman. In another, Iris could almost see a dog beside him, though no dog had been present when she took it. Frustrated by the distraction, and cursing her overactive imagination, Iris returned to the method she had used to deal with the houses. She sketched the persistent images on a separate page and set them aside.

Well, that was oddly satisfying, she thought. In fact, it had filled her with the sense she had completed something important. And as with the houses, somehow the characters she had drawn were happy she had done so.

"Now that is nonsense," she said out loud, rubbing her face to dispel the strange feelings. "Stop your musing, Iris and get this done. Photos don't have feelings, and you are letting your imagination get the better of you."

CHAPTER 18

The smell of lavender and sage greeted Ruby as she walked through the door of Lucia's Landing, hoping Lucia would know where she could find Jeremy. She wanted desperately to speak with him but didn't want to ask Iris. It would have opened up the conversation again, and she just couldn't bring herself to do that. Not yet, anyway.

As she walked in the door, she had the sensation she had actually gone outside instead of in. The air in the store was fresh and earthy, and surprisingly, she could hear birds. As she approached the counter, a sound machine on display revealed the source of the birdsong but did nothing to diminish its effect. A calmness settled into her very being, and the fear she had held onto since the other night suddenly lifted.

Lucia was with another customer, so she had time to look around. It was early in the evening, and the sun was low in the sky, resulting in beautiful beams of light spreading across the store. To Ruby's delight, someone seemed to have recognized the usefulness of this light and positioned certain items to take advantage of it. On top of one pillar was a large, faceted crystal sphere that dispersed the light into dozens of little rainbows around the room. The jewelry case was equally well lit, and the various stones inside sparkled in the sunlight.

Her eyes wandered along the wall to the collection of books on display. Thoughtfully, there were a couple of soft and inviting chairs set next to the bookcases, with additional books stacked on a small table between the chairs. Realizing she might have to wait a few minutes, Ruby headed over to take a seat. On the table was a stack of books, and she reached for the one on top. It was titled, simply, *Believe*. She snorted softly, wondering if it was some sort of sign—if she believed in signs, that is.

When Lucia finished, she walked over and sat down in the other chair, her eyes twinkling in curiosity. "I was wondering if I would see you after the other night," she asked. "Did you have fun?"

Ruby brushed aside the question. She wouldn't have called it fun, exactly. The experience still seemed unreal, as if it all had happened to someone else, and she was the bystander. Better to cut to the chase.

"I was hoping to find Jeremy—the British guy. It sounded like maybe you knew him?" She paused, hesitant to presume too much about Lucia. She gestured toward the books and crystals surrounding them. "This seems like the kind of store a medium might like."

"*¡Si!* I know Jeremy! He's come by here a couple of times, and I took one of his classes up at the Sanctuary last summer." Lucia leaned forward, hands clasped in front of her, adding, "Were you hoping to get a reading from him?"

She shook her head sharply, putting a hand up in protest. "Oh no, not at all—I don't even really know what that means." She laughed, nervously. "I just . . . want to ask him some questions. Do you think he'd want to talk to me?"

"Is everything alright?" Lucia asked.

She didn't know how to answer. She wasn't used to feeling this way. She was nervous, wanting to hide her face in a way that felt wholly unnatural. Seeming to sense this, Lucia added, "Is there anything I can help you with?"

"No, not really," she answered. "I just wanted to talk to him about the other night and the message I received. I thought he might be willing to talk to me." She was beginning to think this was a bad idea, looking around as if something in the store would get her out of this conversation.

Lucia reached for a pad of paper and began scribbling some contact information. "I know he'd be happy to talk to you. I told you he teaches this stuff, so he's used to questions. I know he is in town for a while. Just send him a text or an email. He'll get back to you pronto. He's good about stuff like that."

Ruby let out the breath she had been holding as she accepted the slip of paper. Good, now she'd just need to get up the guts to call him. As she stood to leave, the book she had picked up slid to the floor. She reached for it, but before she could put it back on the table, Lucia asked her if she wanted it.

"Oh, I don't know. I just picked it up while I was sitting here." Then, as an afterthought, she asked, "Do you think it could be some sort of a sign?"

Lucia grinned broadly. "*¡Ay bendito!* The best signs are the unexpected ones. That book is always getting picked up and put down somewhere, so I think it ended up on top of that stack for a reason. You're not sure about the other night, so maybe this was meant to help you. You never know with the spirits, Ruby."

She left the shop with the book, the contact information, and a little crystal sphere to bring a bit of magic into her own home. Walking down the street, her worries began to lift, just a bit, replaced by an unmistakable sense of hope.

Life being life, it was over a week before Ruby was able to meet with Jeremy. He had responded quickly, just as Lucia had said he would, but between his classes and her work schedule, they hadn't been able to find a time. He seemed to like the outdoors as much as she did, so he had agreed to meet her at the park across the lake from town.

She arrived early but was too nervous to sit still and wait. The lake was nestled in a valley, and a ridge sloped up just behind the park. There was a path that led uphill through the trees, and Ruby took off running, hoping to make it up and back before he arrived.

The run did her some good, expelling her nervous energy as she climbed. On the way back down, she realized she was going to be a sweaty mess when she met the poor man and slowed down to allow her breathing to slow to a normal rate. When she finally arrived back at the lakefront, Jeremy was waiting.

He was sitting at a picnic table, his back to her as she came out of the trees. She was about to call out to him, to alert him to her approach, when he turned, as if fully expecting her to be right where she was. She waved, and he waved back, his face telegraphing his utter confidence she would be right where she was, even though she was still too far off for him to have heard her approach. Iris was like that too, always seeming to know when she was coming. Strange.

They spent the first few minutes admiring the view, talking about where they were from, and generally sidestepping the reason she had asked to meet him there. He was exceedingly patient, accepting each diversionary topic. Finally, with the deftness of someone used to dealing with reticent students, he simply stopped answering her cocktail party questions and asked one of his own.

"Am I the first medium you've ever met?"

It wasn't the question she had expected. She started to say yes, then thought of Lucia, who seemed to know about more than just selling books and crystals and answered honestly. "I don't know."

That made him smile. "Good answer. You're probably right. Most of us don't walk around with signs all over us advertising what we do." She blushed.

"Don't worry," he said. Lots of people think mediums are a bit strange, and television and movies give the impression we spend our lives pointing out dead loved ones to unsuspecting neighbors." He laughed as she ducked her head down to hide the flush she could now feel in her face. "I'm not one of those people, Ruby. And I'm not judging you. I promise."

Gosh he was a gentle soul. She took a deep breath, with a silent prayer to whomever might be listening, to help him know the answers to her questions.

"Was that all real the other night?" she asked, hoping the question wasn't insulting.

He didn't seem bothered at all but rather seemed to expect or at least not be surprised by it. His eyes were soft, and kind, but directly focused on hers. "Did it feel real to you?" he asked, once again turning the question to her rather than answering it himself.

"Well, yes . . . and no. Actually, it felt very real as it was happening, and then after I got home, I thought about it and thought it couldn't have been. I wondered how you did it, and I sort of wondered if it was all faked in some way." Afraid to look him in the eye, she focused instead on a small ant, lazily making its way across the table.

To her surprise, he laughed. That made her look up, and the twinkle in his eye assured her he wasn't mocking her either. "Don't worry," he said. "Most people are suspicious the first time, and to be perfectly honest, not all those who call themselves mediums are to be trusted."

She was confused. "So, how can I know it's real then? I mean, I don't *think* you're faking it, and you seem nice enough, so how can you tell what's true and what isn't?" She stood up, the intensity of the conversation causing her to want to flee. Only his kindness kept her from doing so. Instead, she moved closer to the lake, leaning against the fence running along the shore, her arms crossed in front of her.

Jeremy didn't follow right away, and she was grateful. It was a warm day, and even with a soft breeze, she quickly grew too hot to maintain the defensive pose. As she relaxed, he turned and followed, stopping just close enough to be heard.

"Ruby, there's nothing to be afraid of. When I said there are those who are not honest, I wasn't trying to frighten you. I promise." She nodded for him to continue.

"Look, I want you to think about the first thing you told me. You said it felt real as it was happening. That was your instinctive response, and your most reliable reaction. Later, you began to worry about it, and you convinced yourself it must not be real because that is what makes the most sense to a fearful mind."

He was right. She recalled how certain she was as she sat there in the hall, that it was her grandmother. "It was comforting when she told me those things. Is that what you mean?" He nodded, and in that moment, the urge to flee vanished as suddenly as it had come.

"Ruby, any time a medium is demonstrating, they should have one goal in mind, which is to provide you with the evidence that what they are bringing to you is accurate and truly from someone you love in the spirit world. What was it Amanda told you that made you think this was your grandmother?"

Ruby took a deep breath. "She told me it was my grandmother, and her name was Grace. She said the name of the school I went to—the Hope School—and she described the house she lived in. She also knew how I felt about my grandmother and her house. I can't explain it, but it just seemed like she really was talking to my grandmother. It all just made sense . . . you know?"

"It sounds like pretty clear evidence this *was* your grandmother. Now tell me, what is your evidence it was all fake?"

She thought about it for a minute. She couldn't actually come up with any evidence, as he had asked. "It's just that it doesn't make sense she would know all those things about me. I have never told anyone around here, not even my best friend. The things about the fire I have never told anyone at all." She stopped and thought about what she had just said. "I guess I don't have any evidence—just a feeling."

"I think these events in your life have lived inside of you for a very long time, Ruby. I think having them come up to the surface like that must have been pretty frightening for you, am I right?" She nodded, willing herself to relax.

"I think once you got home, you likely began to go over those events in your head, and you became scared. Once fear gets into a situation, it can really cloud a person's perceptions. That is why I said it is best to trust what you felt at the beginning. Those feelings are the most accurate response to a situation. Your instinct told you this was true. Fear is the only thing telling you it wasn't."

With a conscious effort, she recalled again the way it had felt to receive that message. She imagined her grandparents sitting on the front porch, smiling at the memory. "They were wonderful, you know—my grandparents. They used to take in my brothers and me for a couple of weeks each summer. We'd camp in the field behind their house, and my grandmother would take us walking in the woods. She knew every plant, every bird, and every inch of those woods. I think that's where I get my love of hiking from."

Her mood began to lighten, and she was glad they had met. Jeremy didn't push her to say more, and she accepted the silence gratefully. As they headed back along the path to town, she pointed out the various birds she recognized and suggested some pretty hikes he might want to take while he was in the area.

As they reached the parking lot, she had one last question. She told him about the book she had picked up the other day. "Lucia thought it was a sign. What do you think?" she asked.

His reaction was the same as Lucia's had been. He grinned, and said with a laugh, "That's about as direct as it gets!"

"But where would this sign come from?" she asked. "Who put the book there?"

"Well, signs aren't usually a matter of putting something somewhere but rather of drawing your attention to something that already exists. The book was already there, but your attention was drawn to it. What's more, it had some meaning for you. On another day, it might have just been a book with an interesting title, or you might not have noticed it at all. But on that day, in that moment, it did make sense and had a powerful meaning for you. This is what makes it a sign. And signs from the spirit world are always given to you out of love, to help you feel better, or understand, or see something you need to see."

He smiled broadly, waving his arm in a circle that encompassed not only the lake and town but the sky and clouds as well. "A world has opened up for you, Ruby, but it is a world that was always there, existing right alongside of you. I can promise you the spirit world is so happy they were able to connect with you. I am sure they are so proud of you, too, for being open and willing to receive the gifts they sent. Trust the love you are feeling in all of this, and know even should you never hear from them again, they will still be there, walking beside you and supporting you in all you do."

CHAPTER 19

They reached the end of the marked trail, and Iris stopped to admire the view. She had never been to this place. In fact, she hadn't known such wilderness existed so close to the town. Ruby looked back at her with a mischievous grin, then parted the branches before her, beckoning her to follow.

The branches brushed at her sleeve as she passed. The sounds of the town softened as they got further into the brush. They began to climb, and the steepness of the incline required her to hold on in spots. The rocks were rough, but by following Ruby's lead, she easily found handholds to pull herself up the last few feet. Stepping out onto a ledge, she could see the lake below them. The air smelled fresher up here, despite the acrid smell coming from the pasture on the other side of the rise.

Ruby's demeanor had changed as they climbed, the set of her shoulders relaxing the moment she stepped out on that ledge. It was as if she became lighter as she climbed, almost able to float on air. She'd never told her about this place, and now Iris could understand why. It was completely private and utterly beautiful. She felt privileged that Ruby had invited her into this space, yet at the same time, a wave of unease washed over her. What did she need to tell her that required they come to this special place?

They sat in silence for a few minutes, enjoying the view and catching their breath. It was unlike Ruby to be so quiet. Iris tucked her hands under her legs to keep them still, surreptitiously glancing at her friend to make sure she was okay. Ruby's eyes seemed focused on the horizon— or somewhere beyond it, somewhere Iris couldn't see.

When the silence was shattered by a little sparrow squawking and darting after a red-tailed hawk, Ruby watched the birds cross the sky, nodded, and then began to speak.

"Did I ever tell you the place I grew up looks a lot like this?" she asked. Iris shook her head and said, "You've never told me much at all about where you grew up. Wisconsin, right?"

"Yeah. Up north. There were a lot of quarries around there, and farmland. Tons of cows." Flashing a grin, she added, "They don't call us cheese heads for nothing."

"My grandparents lived in an old farmhouse, but it wasn't a working farm anymore. They just loved the open space and having a place for all of us to come visit. We didn't live far, so we got to spend a lot of time there. My brothers and I loved staying there and going for hikes and stuff. My parents weren't farm types at all—my dad's a pediatrician, and my mom worked in his office. It was my grandparents who taught me about pitching a tent, boning a fish, and growing stuff."

Ruby pointed at a small white house on a far-off hillside. "See that house over there? That's about how far away my grandparents' house was from us. I could see it from my window. It was just like that, only it wasn't white . . . "

"It was red," Iris finished, the hair on her arms rising as she spoke.

Ruby turned to her right and nodded. She took several slow breaths, blowing the air out in a whoosh. "My brothers are always saying what a great childhood we had; only it wasn't . . . at least not for me."

Iris followed the line of her gaze, which seemed fixed on the surface of the lake below. She held her breath, not wanting to disturb whatever process was happening inside her friend's mind. Her own mind was seeing again the lines of the red house and the face of the little girl in the window. Ruby had told the medium there had been a fire. Had she been in the house when it happened? What hadn't been her fault? Iris turned up the collar on her coat, suddenly chilled, though the wind was calm.

"Craig and Frank were a few years older than me. They were teenagers when it happened. I was only ten, and nothing was ever the same. I hated everyone and made life miserable for the whole family. When my parents threatened me with boarding school when I was fourteen, I took them up on it. I ended up in Iowa, at the Hope School, and after graduation, I never went home again. I couldn't face them or that burned-out shell of a house. I especially couldn't face my grandparents."

The last bit came out so softly that Iris barely heard it. She scooted a bit closer, causing Ruby to look up. Her eyes were red but dry. "Were you there when the fire started?" Iris asked.

Ruby shook her head fiercely. "No, I was home. My dad and brothers went to help, and my mom sent me up to my room and told me not to worry. But I could see it. You see, my bedroom had a big window overlooking the valley where Gram and Gramps lived. I watched that red glow from the direction of their house grow bigger and bigger until, suddenly, it was gone. They lost the whole house and everything in it. Gram and Gramps escaped with nothing but their pajamas. They even lost Chance, th . . . their cat."

"So, if you weren't there, why did you blame yourself?"

Ruby rubbed her nose with the sleeve of her jacket, looking so young that she could have still been that little girl.

"You don't understand. If I hadn't been so stupid, they would have gotten there in time. When I came down to breakfast and saw my grandparents sitting at the kitchen table wearing my parents' clothes, it was clear something awful had happened. They didn't talk at first, I think maybe because I was there. I just stayed really quiet until finally they told us.

"It was a fire in the dryer vent, and it spread up the side of the house before they realized anything was wrong. They didn't have smoke detectors, and it spread so fast. They were just lucky it hadn't spread to the stairs yet. They could have died, and everyone knew it. Even me." Her voice cracked, and she drew her legs up, wrapping her arms around her knees, as if trying to hold onto all they lost that night.

"You don't have to keep going if you don't want to," Iris said. She could see Ruby's mind was focused on Wisconsin—not on the lake, not on her, not on today. Yet she could also sense her friend was somehow okay. She seemed to be drawing strength from the rocks, as she released her knees, placing her palms down on the stone and sitting up straighter.

Ruby shook her head firmly, like a horse shooing a fly, and wiped her eyes with both hands. "No, I'm okay. There's not much else to tell."

"But why was it your fault? You weren't even there."

When Ruby answered, she almost sounded like a different person; her voice so flat as to be unrecognizable. "I left the phone off the hook, so they couldn't get through to my dad in time. If they had, he could have gotten there sooner and at least saved Chance."

She started to interrupt, but Ruby put up a hand to stop her. "I saw my mom bring the phone out of the den that night, after my dad and the boys left. She didn't say a word to me about it—nobody ever did—which is why I was sure they blamed me for it. I was so stupid . . . "

"You were ten years old. You weren't stupid." Iris spoke slowly, deliberately, hoping her anger didn't show. How could they have let a little girl carry so much guilt with her all these years? Recalling the demonstration, she added, "The medium said it wasn't your fault, didn't she?" Ruby nodded. "Do you believe her, do you think?"

Ruby didn't answer right away.

Iris kept silent, unsure how—or if—to respond.

It was peaceful here, making it easy to forget that a town—and a life—lay below them. She never would have known Ruby carried such heartbreak inside her; but then again, she never spoke of her own losses, either. By some unspoken agreement, they had been friends for years yet never talked about the past. The sense things were changing was growing stronger, and she wasn't at all sure she liked it.

The tolling of a church bell seemed to draw Ruby out of her reverie.

"So, here I am," she said, "sitting on this ledge with my best friend, who I now know is my best friend for a reason. If it wasn't for you, there wouldn't have been that painting, and I wouldn't have gone to that demonstration. I wouldn't have heard it wasn't my fault." She stood up, reaching a hand back to Iris to help her to her feet. "And to answer your question: Yes, I believe it."

Later that day, Iris went out to the studio and lined up all the house paintings against one wall. They still were just houses, and the reason she drew them was still unknown. She sat there, staring at them until the light began to fade, repeating the question that had been running through her mind all afternoon. *Who do the rest of them belong to?*

CHAPTER 20

Iris was waiting for Ruby when she got off work. She'd picked up several books from Lucia's, and they weighed a ton. Since Ruby was coming over for dinner anyway, she decided to enlist her help carrying the heavy bags home.

Ruby grabbed one of the bags and staggered dramatically. "What on earth have you got in there?" she asked, as the handle snapped and the bag split open, scattering the books across the sidewalk.

"Books," Iris answered unnecessarily. "I couldn't decide which one was best, so I just bought everything Lucia recommended. What do you think?"

"Mediumship for Beginners." "How to Be a Psychic." Ruby read off the titles of the books as she gathered them up. "Planning a career change?"

"Not exactly." Iris laughed. "I just don't understand enough about this, and there is so much to know! I feel like I don't want to do anything else but learn." In fact, the feeling was so strong she'd barely slept that night. Her mind kept going over and over what she knew—and didn't know—hoping for answers in the quiet of the night. She hadn't felt this way since she'd first met Michael, and she wondered how this could feel so much like new love.

"So, do you think you're a medium then?" Ruby asked.

She shrugged, setting the second bag of books on a nearby bench as she sat down, motioning for Ruby to join her. "I really feel like I'm learning something new about myself, and I can't stop trying to learn more." She fingered the books and picked one up, staring for a moment at the ghostly image on the cover. "Do you think it's weird? I mean, do you think the whole medium thing is weird? Am I crazy or something?"

Ruby looked at the book, and then at Iris. "First of all, you are *not* crazy. But I'll be honest, this is all a bit weird. A few weeks ago, you and I had no idea what a medium even was. I thought when you died you just rotted—no heaven, no hell, just . . . nothing. But now . . . I don't know, I talked to Jeremy, and I really think it was my grandmother. And I *know* that's her house you painted. So to me, that makes you a medium just as much as anyone else." Her face grew serious, and she paused before adding, "Just promise me something, will you?"

"Sure, what?"

"Promise me you won't start looking like the creepy woman on the cover of your book. I like nice, normal Iris, thank you." She winked, her face splitting into a wide grin. They laughed, until Ruby again turned serious, her voice dropping to a whisper. "Do you think they watch us? The spirits?" She pointed to the sky as if that were where "they" were.

Iris shivered slightly, rubbing her arms to dispel the feeling. "Funny, I was thinking the same thing when I was writing in my journal the other day. I felt self-conscious—you know? Like someone was listening." The feeling had unnerved her for sure, and the memory of it brought back the same sense of unease.

"Well, Jeremy seems pretty normal," Ruby responded hopefully. "And I recognized a few of the people at that demonstration. They don't seem self-conscious at all, so maybe you get used to it after a while?"

"I hope so," Iris said. Her arms prickled with goosebumps as she realized she was self-conscious and probably looked it, too. "I never did get used to having a roommate in college, you know. I changed in the bathroom for half of freshman year."

"You didn't!" Ruby had begun to giggle. "Did you ever get over it?"

"Oh, sure—but at the time, I didn't know if I would make it through college. I was pretty much an only child growing up, so I never had to change in front of anyone. It wasn't until Michael came along that I got over it." She began flipping through one of the books, hoping to hide the tears that still prickled whenever she said his name.

Ruby didn't seem to notice. "Damn, I hope it isn't like having a roommate. That would be awful. You can't hide in the bathroom from a spirit." Her face flushed in a rare show of embarrassment. "Will you try to find out . . . I mean, just for research's sake . . . "

"Yeah. I think I better if I ever want to shower again!" She laughed, standing and gathering the books back into her arms. "Come on, help me get this home, will you?"

Ruby didn't get up right away, her usual buoyancy deflated. Iris offered her a hand up, and a look of concern. Ruby shrugged it off, then asked, "Hey, after we drop these off, wanna come over and grab a pizza? I'm not really in the mood to eat dinner alone tonight."

The room smelled of garlic and tomato, and the remnants of dinner lay scattered across the coffee table. They'd both been famished, so it hadn't really mattered what they ate, except the pizza was especially good tonight. All that remained were a few crusts. Iris sat back, enjoying the last of her wine, eyeing Ruby warily. She'd been unusually quiet all evening.

Iris needed to let her friend find the words, without interjecting her own to fill the silence. Their hunger had made the lack of conversation easy, but with food gone, there was no longer an excuse. Ruby drifted over to the window, gazing out over the town as the streetlights came on. After a few minutes, she squared her shoulders as if deciding something, and turned back around to sit down on the couch, reaching for her own glass of wine.

"Do you think my grandparents are watching me?" Ruby asked.

Iris's throat clenched in sympathy, and she reached a hand up over her chest, feeling Ruby's pain as if it were her own. "I don't know how to answer you. A few months ago, I would have said no way. But now, after all I've seen, I think maybe they could be." She shrugged helplessly, wishing for a better answer.

Ruby shrugged too, smiling weakly. "I know we're both just learning. It's only, I was wondering . . . " She took in a deep breath, letting it out in a whoosh. "When you saw the red house, did you see them too?"

The words came out so fast, Iris didn't catch them at first. Then suddenly she understood. "Them—you mean, your grandparents?" Ruby nodded, still smiling, but with a slight tremble in her lower lip.

She thought about the painting, trying to recall what she had felt when she was making it. She remembered the emotions, and the lost little girl, but no one else. Her mind searched for them, trying desperately to give Ruby the answer she thought she wanted.

"No," she finally said. "I didn't see them."

Ruby sat twisting her hands, staring off into the distance. Iris wasn't sure what she wanted—or needed—to hear, so she just started describing what she *had* noticed when she was painting.

"The house was sad as I was painting it. I know it's weird, but that's just the way it felt—sad." She recalled the little girl in the window, and also how she had painted over her at the last minute, thinking somehow, she wasn't meant to be there. There was no need to tell Ruby, she decided, knowing somehow, still, that face had been for her alone and not anything she needed to pass along.

"I remember after I finished, I thought about telling you, and it felt . . . exciting. Not me, I didn't feel excited . . . the house did." Seeing Ruby was listening, and not laughing, she continued. "Then there was this . . . love, I guess, and I remembered Michael and my parents, which made *me* sad.

"And then I panicked. It was just too much, so I hid it from you and everyone else." She hoped she wasn't making matters worse but didn't know how else to answer except by being honest. She felt terrible for hiding it from Ruby, knowing now what it represented.

"Iris, I don't blame you for hiding it. I think I would have done the same thing, or worse. I just think about it a lot, and I guess I'm a little jealous you might be seeing my grandparents when I can't." Ruby gazed down at her hands; her body curled forward protectively.

Iris hadn't realized Ruby was having such a hard time with it all. "I'm sorry," she said. "I wish I could go back and do it all again. I wish I'd shown it to you that day."

"When did you paint it?" Ruby asked.

"Last fall. I was trying to make you a Christmas present."

"Funny," Ruby said. "It was a present for me, just maybe it needed to wait a little bit."

She thought about this, realizing as she did so that Ruby might be right. Maybe there was something to the notion that things happen for a reason. She didn't always believe it, but in this case, maybe it was true. "More wine?" she offered, hoping to break the tension.

Ruby extended her glass, looking Iris straight in the eye. "Neither one of us would have known what to do with it last fall, so it's better it happened now, when Jeremy was around to help." She sat back on the couch but didn't look away. Iris, feeling uncomfortable with the attention, got up and went to the kitchen, returning with the box of cookies she'd brought. "Dessert?" she asked as she set them down in front of Ruby.

"Thanks," Ruby said, though she made no move to take one. "You mentioned the house made you think about Michael. I know he was your boyfriend, but it's funny—you never talk about him. I mean, I see his picture on the table, so I know he was cute, but you've never told me anything about him."

She felt like time had stopped, and Michael might walk right through the door. She had kept him back in New York in her mind, allowing him out only when Charlie was around. It was easier that way, almost as if he wasn't dead, just someone she left behind. She didn't want to change that, to talk about him now, but she could see what Ruby was doing—turning the tables, getting the focus off of her, and maybe finding a way to share their stories, and grief.

"He was great. He was a pediatrician. Or he was about to be one—he'd just finished his residency. He would have been a great one, too. He had these really gentle hands, like they could never hurt anything. And his voice was gentle, too—he didn't sound like a New Yorker at all—and kids just loved him. So did I."

She wished for a moment she was back in her own place. She wanted to see his picture, to study his face. Her mind was searching for the details, but time had dimmed them somewhat, as the softer memories faded like an old quilt.

"I love the picture you have in your living room. He was so young . . ." Ruby said, her voice trailing off.

The photo flashed in Iris's mind like she had just turned on the TV. Suddenly, she could see him as clearly as if he were sitting there, and not just as he was in the photo, but as he was in the moments before and after it was taken. They'd been in Central Park, checking out the spring flowers, and she'd made him pose for the picture in front of a blossoming pink cherry tree. He hated posing, but she'd made him laugh, promising he could pose her wherever he wanted for the next photo. The glint in his eye might be missed by others, but she knew it was his brain planning his next move. She had the photo he took of her, sitting among a flock of pigeons, to show for it.

It had been the last outing they'd taken together.

"Yeah. He was just getting started. It was all so unfair. And you know what the worst part of all of it was? Walking into church and seeing his parents sitting there. I know what it's like to bury a parent, but I will never forget what it was like to witness someone bury a child."

"I'm sorry, Iris. I didn't mean to drag up those awful memories. I can see why you never brought him up." Ruby handed her the box of tissues, snagging one for herself in the process.

They talked for a while longer, sharing stories of their families until finally Iris rose to leave. "This mediumship stuff sure stirs up a lot of feelings, doesn't it," she said. "I think I would have really liked your grandparents, and I know Michael would have loved you."

"He really sounds like an amazing guy. And he did bring you and Charlie together, which brought you here, so I have to say I'm grateful to him." She paused, as if something had just struck her. "You know, what we were talking about earlier—spirits and all that?"

Iris nodded, a shiver running up her spine.

"You think he can hear me?" Ruby asked, not waiting for a response. "Hey Michael, I'm sorry you didn't live to meet me, but thanks for sending me Iris. She's the best."

Iris pulled her friend into a fierce hug. "So are you," she said, before grabbing her coat and heading out the door. As she walked down the quiet street, she began to speak softly, hoping Ruby was right. "Have I got a story to tell you, Michael," she began, and by the time she was home, she'd let all of it out. As she crawled into bed, she felt lighter, and freer, and for the first time in a long time, no longer alone.

CHAPTER 21

Jeremy should be a poker player. Iris had been watching him for a while now, and she could read nothing from his face. She'd given him the sketches to see what he thought of them, and the waiting was killing her. He picked his head up, suddenly seeming to sense he was being watched. She looked away, but not quickly enough. Soon she could feel his eyes on her. Nervously, she reached for the pitcher of lemonade and refilled both their glasses.

"What is it you wanted to ask me?" Jeremy asked. He set the sketches down, reaching for his drink. He was no longer watching her, and the tension in her shoulders lessened as she sipped from her own glass. When he asked why she had shown him the drawings, her hand clenched so hard she thought the glass might break.

She stood and walked to the edge of the porch, her heart beating in her throat. The sun shimmered on the surface of the lake, and the breeze made the midsummer heat bearable. Taking a deep breath, she turned back to her guest.

"How do you do it? The medium stuff, I mean. When we were at that demonstration, you said you saw a guy who looked like Santa Claus. What do you mean by 'you saw him'? Was he standing there in the room with us?"

"Ah," he said, setting his glass back down. He sat for a moment, his steepled fingers held against his mouth. Then like the teacher he said he was, he answered her question with one of his own. "Why did you come to the demonstration?"

The question surprised and flustered her. "I don't know, really. The . . . I think it was the flyer . . . I don't know. Something about the picture made me want to go." Embarrassed, she paused, allowing the memory to come back to her. Then she recalled the lighthouse. "Oh yeah, I thought it was an art show. We had no idea until we got there." Heat rose into her face, and she turned away, hoping he hadn't noticed.

"What do you know about mediumship?" he asked, not seeming at all bothered by her embarrassment.

"Only what I've been reading, really. Ruby and I talked a bit after the demonstration. She said she talked to you?" He nodded silently. "Well, I was curious, so I picked up a bunch of books in town, but they're sort of hard to read. It's mostly stories about people that have died, and, well, to be honest, it's kinda depressing."

"Then I think maybe you haven't gotten to the good parts." He winked, displaying a hint of playfulness beneath his normally reserved demeanor.

"The good parts?" she asked as her mind scrolled through the stories she had been reading, of grieving families, and dying wishes, and lives upended by voices and visions and dreams.

"The parts about our spirits, or souls, and the fact they don't die when our bodies do. That's the good part," he said, with a smile that told her he believed every word he was speaking. "And that's where mediumship comes in. Mediums are literally the ones in the middle, between spirits and physical human beings. We provide the evidence so others can know our spirits live on."

There was an excitement to him as he spoke and, she thought, an eagerness to share his knowledge. She could understand why he had been brought here to teach.

"So, how does a person get to be a medium?" she asked. "You teach classes—is it like learning to be a teacher or something?"

"More like learning to play the piano, I think. There needs to be some innate ability there, even if it is only the ability to believe in oneself and try. What I do is help the student to recognize that ability, and then practice and help it grow. Some have stronger abilities than others, and it's my job to build their confidence and see how the abilities develop. Not all piano players become concert musicians, but if there is a strong talent and a will to put in the time, it can happen."

She thought about this, putting it in terms of her artistic abilities. She'd always been a doodler, so maybe that was the innate ability. When she had first moved here, Charlie had encouraged her to take classes at his gallery, as compensation for his not being able to pay her much to do his accounting. Once she had some guidance, her talent had flourished. She rubbed her arms to dispel the chill that had risen as she connected the dots to her apparent ability to communicate with spirits.

"So, how does a medium see someone? Is it like seeing me sitting here?" she asked while self-consciously scanning the room for ghosts.

"Not exactly," Jeremy said. "When I am allowing a spirit to show itself to me, I look off into space and see it in my mind."

Two things struck her. He said he allowed spirits to show themselves, so maybe there could be some control to this. Setting that aside for the moment, she focused on the mechanics. "You're saying you don't see people standing in the room with you, with your eyes?"

He shook his head. "Oh no; some mediums do, of course—but not me." Confusion must have shown in her face because he continued. "There are some mediums who see with their eyes and hear with their ears. But my experience is not like that. Everything for me happens in my head—like imagination."

"Oh," she said, feeling something suddenly click into place. "I think I get it. It's like you imagine what you tell everyone you see?" She paused as if for breath, the next question forming before she had even gotten all her words out. "So then how do you know it's not just your imagination? How do you know you aren't making it all up?"

He closed his eyes for a moment, sitting back in his chair as if he had been expecting the question. "I don't think those are the same thing, exactly," he said, pausing to make sure she was keeping up.

She ran her hands through her hair, holding onto her head as if that would help her mind to stop running from question to question. "I'm sorry, but isn't your imagination when you make something up?" she asked, unable to hide the frustration in her voice.

"When you use your imagination, you *are* making things up, but you are also letting your mind wander—it isn't always an active process. Think about when you dream. You aren't trying to imagine all the adventures you have in your dreams. Your mind just uses the imagination to work through your worries or hopes while you sleep."

She recalled the dreams she still had of Michael. She had always thought they were just her brain's way of helping her heal. A spark of hope flashed in her mind, followed by a vision of Michael, smiling. Maybe it was something more.

Jeremy was still speaking, and with a tinge of regret, she returned her attention to him. "Clairvoyance is like dreaming in a way. The pictures just come to you, and then when you share them with the person they are intended for, they become stories. That's when you know you didn't just make it up. Those images come together into something meaningful to someone who is not in your mind and whose story you don't know. You couldn't have made it up if you tried."

Any regret she had been feeling vanished in an instant. The air was alive with what he had said, with an air of expectancy hanging over them. They sat there in silence for several minutes, Jeremy once again seeming to know she needed time to process all he had said. She ran that last sentence—'you couldn't have made it up if you tried'—over and over in her head until she came to a decision. Rising from her chair, she said, "I've got something to show you," and rushed inside.

She held the sketchbook in her arms, clutching it to her chest protectively, as if she needed to hold her pounding heart inside. Jeremy raised an eyebrow but didn't say anything. She sat down across from him, willing her voice to not break.

"Do you remember I did some sketches of you the first day you were here?" she asked.

"How could I forget? You said I was awkward." He grinned, and some of the nervousness lifted.

"You looked uncomfortable, not awkward," she corrected, feeling about as confident as a freshman on the first day of school. "Anyway, I did other sketches based off the photos I took."

"Is that what you have there?" He pointed at the sketchbook.

"Yeah. Except when I was looking at those photos, I kept seeing other things." She paused to make sure he was following her. He quirked his head in question, so she tried again.

"I saw things that weren't in the photos, the same way I saw Ruby's grandmother's house. I didn't see these things on the paper, just . . . in my mind . . . like you said a medium sees. They were distracting, so I sketched them in a separate book so I could focus on your portrait without them bothering me."

He took the sketchbook from her and slowly flipped through the pages. She tried not to stare but couldn't help following along as he stopped to look at the various images. Her eyelid twitched annoyingly, and a bead of sweat dripped down her back. It was all she could do not to reach out and grab the book back from him. Finally, he stopped at one of the images, of an older-looking woman with a hat on her head and said, "Tell me about this one here."

She startled, regarding him suspiciously, not having expected that question at all. But as she thought about it, she realized she actually did have an answer. "She's an old Scottish lady. When I saw her, she was just standing there, hands on her hips, as if she disapproved of me—or what I was doing, maybe. She wasn't mean or anything; she just didn't like it."

Raising her hands in helpless surrender, she added, "I don't know how else to explain it."

Jeremy gave her a grim look, although there was a twinkle in his eye. "You're exactly right," he said. "She disapproved strongly of me."

"I'm sorry—what? Or, um, who?" she said, shaking her head slightly in confusion.

He laughed, kindly, seeming to enjoy her bewilderment. "That," he said, "is my mother-in-law, Mary. She's from Edinburgh, and she did not in any way approve of her daughter marrying me. She didn't approve when I was at the university, and it only got worse when I began to work as a medium. That is a perfect likeness of her, right down to the hands on her hips and the scowl on her face."

She was stunned, and her hand shook as she reached to take the notebook from him. But she was also now more curious than ever. She pointed to the image on the opposite page. "What about the dog? Is it yours, too?"

She should have known he wouldn't answer. Instead, he asked her to tell him why she drew the little dog. He wasn't getting the fact she didn't know why she did any of this. But once again, no sooner had the thought crossed her mind than she realized she did know why.

"He was just sitting there beside you in the picture," she said. "He wasn't doing much, but he wouldn't go away. There was something about him being sandy, so that's why I drew the little starfish. I thought maybe he was at the beach." As she picked up the drawing, she recalled something else. "He was really quiet, though. So, maybe the beach bit is wrong. He might have been sick or something," she added, as if the dog was right there in front of her and not some product of her imagination.

He grinned. "That is Sandy," he said. "Her name, I mean. And she was quite ill at the end. She was rather old and arthritic, and she used to sit at my feet for hours as I read. She was mine, but only in her later years. She belonged to my mother-in-law first and came to us after she died. She was never a very active dog, and even less so after we got her. I swear that dog actually mourned Mary's passing. She would sit by my feet and stare at the door as if old Mary would walk in again." He looked wistfully off into the distance, rocking gently in the chair.

"I didn't much care for my mother-in-law, but I decided maybe she wasn't all bad if she produced a daughter like my wife and raised a sweet dog like Sandy. I wonder if maybe Sandy wants to help me remember my mother-in-law more kindly." He stopped rocking, turning back in her direction. He didn't say anything else, seemingly waiting for Iris to continue.

She turned the page, nervously looking over the image she had there. She nodded, almost to herself, before turning the book around to face him. "Okay, I've got one more. It's one of the sketches I did of you, so there aren't any other people or animals on it. What's strange is when I drew it, I felt so strongly I needed to put this frame on it." The image was a simple sketch of his face, but around it was a border with scalloped edges, as if they had been notched out with a half-circle cutter.

"Okay, I know you will want to know why I drew this," she blurted, though he had made no move to ask her anything. "The thing is, I don't really know why. It was as if someone was encouraging me to, but I couldn't see what it meant—the weird frame." She paused, her own gaze now drifting out over the town. Suddenly, she drew in her breath, as something had suddenly become clear.

"You know, it feels like your mother-in-law is here—I see her. She's smiling—no, wait, she's laughing . . . and . . . and . . . clapping! She's applauding!" She clasped her own hands together, completely caught up in the scene she was seeing. It was as if she was right there in the room with them.

And then just as suddenly, the woman was gone.

Iris scanned the room, rubbing her arms to dispel the sense of not being sure where she was for a moment. She blinked a few times, swallowed, then turned her focus to Jeremy's smiling face. He looked at once like a proud parent, and a grieving child.

"What are you thinking?" she asked when she was able to again form words.

"That, Iris, looks to me like my face on an old postage stamp."

She peered at the framed edge and nodded in agreement. "Yes, that's it. But why?"

He smiled more broadly. "I think my mother-in-law is giving me a stamp of approval. I think she is trying to say, 'I disapproved of you once, but not anymore.' Maybe the dog has told her about me—told her I'm alright."

"All that from these sketches?" she asked.

"Not just the sketches. It's everything else you had with them, including the feelings you felt about Mary and Sandy. Then with the last one, you expanded on it, delivering the final piece. She is applauding for me. I always hoped she would come around one day. Thank you."

"Really? I did all that?" she asked, feeling quite pleased with herself. "So, do you think maybe I am a medium? Like you?" She tucked her trembling hands under her thighs, hoping he wouldn't notice.

"There is not a doubt in my mind—nor should there be in yours. But enough for today. Let this sink in for a while. It's a lot to take in."

A few weeks later, she was sitting out back, enjoying an unusually cool summer evening. Setting aside the book she was reading, her eyes were drawn to the big maple in the middle of the yard. She had planted it when she first moved in, and its size made her realize just how long it had been since she left New York. *How could time go so fast?*

She turned back to her book, one of the memoirs that famous mediums seemed so fond of writing. Yet again, the author described experiencing spirits as a child and sensing something different throughout her life. Another author had written about seeing his grandmother sitting on the bed every night when he was young. She reminded herself she had experienced none of that. Then with a pang, she realized it had been weeks since she had seen any houses.

What just moments before had been a small sliver of doubt rapidly swelled to a massive slice of fear. She must have done something wrong; otherwise, why would they have stopped? Looking over at the stack of books and the journals beside it, she began to feel foolish. *You're not a medium if it can just disappear.*

Chastising herself for wasting time on something as stupid as this, she gathered up the books, stuffed them in a bag, and tucked them away behind the couch. She had work to do.

A week later, she pulled the books back out, opened her journal, and began taking notes. The houses were back.

CHAPTER 22

Jeremy added a bit more tea to his cup, tasted it, added some sugar, and sipped it again. He broke off a bit of muffin, reached for the butter and jam, and slowly assembled a seemingly perfect snack to go along with the tea. He was stalling. She cleared her throat slightly, hoping to nudge him to answer her question. The longer he delayed, the more nervous she became. She was resisting the urge to tap her feet so strongly that her legs had started to cramp.

"What did you think?" she asked again. They were sitting in her studio, having just spent an hour looking over her paintings of the houses. He had seen them at the fair and been quite free with his opinions that day. But today, when he had begun looking through them, his reaction was different. He'd set them down, started to speak, then gone silent. They had definitely spooked him.

"I'm sorry," she said, breaking the silence for the third time.

He finally looked up. "No, Iris, I'm sorry. You asked a simple question, and I haven't answered it."

"Why not?" she asked. "Is there something wrong with the paintings?" Her knee began to bounce slightly, and she reached a hand down to stop it. She was close to tears and fighting fiercely to keep them at bay.

"There is nothing wrong with them at all, Iris. In fact, they are wonderful," he said. "I remember them from your show. I especially love the little details you put in, like flowers in the window or a toy in the garden." He flipped through the canvases and set a couple on the table. "Now these ones are lovely, but to most people, they would just be ordinary houses. You've already told me they aren't ordinary, and clearly, to Ruby, that farmhouse is not. Tell me about them, will you?"

Realizing she hadn't done anything wrong, she allowed her guard to drop. "Oh, I liked that house. It's full of memories—good ones, I think. It feels like it was always really busy, like the hub of the neighborhood. I remember painting it and being really happy."

"And the other?" he asked.

"I finished that one in about an hour. I have never painted anything so fast. Every time I stopped to clean my brush or put out more paint, I felt really impatient, like if I waited too long to draw it, everything would change." She turned away as the heat rose into her face, raising her hands to cover the flush she could feel in her cheeks. "Sorry," she said.

He stared patiently at her. "You've nothing to be sorry about. You've described these beautifully. And now that I'm looking at them as a psychic rather than an art lover, I can see what you are saying. It makes sense to me."

She closed her eyes, breathing in a deep and cleansing breath. It made sense. Months of thinking she might be losing her mind had taken a toll on her. For the first time in a long time, she felt safe enough to share what had been happening.

"Excuse me," she said, walking over to a closet in the back corner of the studio. She moved aside some supplies and a tarp, then pulled out another canvas, leaning it against a chair so they could both see it. "This one freaked me out—a lot—when I drew it. I stuck it back there to make sure I couldn't hear it anymore."

"Hear it?" he asked, cocking his head, then leaning closer to get a better look at it. She watched him, trying to gauge whether he was worried by what she had said. He seemed more interested than scared, which gave her the courage to tell him about it.

"When I painted that one, I kept smelling fresh grass . . . and manure . . . and I remember I saw a lot more than just the barn in my head. I saw a cow giving birth and . . . and I heard someone tell me it was going to be okay." Her voice dropped to almost a whisper at the end, and she bit her lip, hoping he hadn't noticed.

"Iris, there is another term we use for mediums, for those able to interact with the spirit world. We call ourselves 'sensitives.'" It is because to interact with spirit, we use our senses, only in extraordinary ways. The way you have described these images shows how sensitive you are. You described these houses as if you were describing people, and the most beautiful thing about it is you don't seem to realize you are doing it. It's a natural part of you, which is why it seems to have taken you a bit by surprise."

She opened her mouth to speak, but he put a hand up, one finger raised, asking her to give him a minute.

"Let me explain. You see, some mediums hear words in our heads, and we call it clairaudience. Most of us see things, spirits and such, and we call it clairvoyance. Mediums often feel things, too, like you've been doing here. That is called clairsentience. 'Clair' means clear. Clear hearing, clear seeing, clear feeling—all of these are the extraordinary senses mediums and psychics have. What you are describing to me are these ways of sensing. You even smell clearly!"

This struck her as funny for some reason, and she stifled a laugh, realizing laughter seemed out of place in the moment. He smiled back, and she relaxed again, no longer worried about what he was going to say. "Now this next bit is really important," he said. "How are you feeling right in this moment?"

She answered immediately, the feeling was so strong and clear. "I feel warm . . . and safe . . . and . . . I'm not worried anymore."

"Wonderful. That is your true response to what I told you. It feels beautiful because it is beautiful. Your heart knows what is right, and it knows this is good. You can feel that right now. Warm and safe. Remember how this feels, okay? Maybe write it down somewhere. Because you will have doubts sometimes . . . "

"Oh, I have those already!" she laughed.

"Well, now when you have them, remember how you felt today. Those feelings are your soul . . . your spirit . . . your heart, letting you know what I told you is true, and it is good." He placed his hand on his chest, the sincerity of his words mirrored in his face.

"Thank you. You have given me a lot to think about," she said as she walked him out front to his car. "I hope not too much," he said with a wink, as he pulled the door closed behind him.

She sat on the porch steps, watching him drive away. Filled with an overwhelming sense of contentment, she let her mind wander as she watched the breeze blow through the trees. She was still sitting there an hour later when she heard her best friend's unmistakable laugh.

"Anybody home?" Ruby teased. "I've been waving at you for half a block. Where are you?"

"Oh, I'm a million miles away, and right here, too. How was your day?"

C H A P T E R 23

Iris turned into the parking lot of Andre's restaurant, pulling up to drop the car with the valet this time. She and Ruby had been coming here for years, ever since Andre had moved up from Brooklyn to open it. It was Charlie who had convinced him to come, and the two of them had created an award-winning restaurant that could have passed for an art gallery.

Andre, looking elegant in his suit and tie, greeted them at the door, then walked them to their table in the corner. She waved to Charlie, who was sitting at the bar, his usual spot on a weekend evening. He raised a glass to her in greeting.

Jeremy arrived a few minutes later, looking uncharacteristically flustered.

"Did you find it okay?" Iris asked.

"I didn't need to. The taxi driver knew just where it was. My apologies for being late."

"You're fine," Ruby said. "But why the taxi? Something happen to your car?"

"Nothing that can't be fixed. It wouldn't start this afternoon, so the rental agency is swapping it out for a new one tomorrow." Looking uncharacteristically shy, he added, "Might I trouble one of you for a ride home this evening?"

"Of course!" Ruby answered, pointing at Iris with a wink. "She's driving, if that's okay." He laughed, and the two continued on for a bit, joking good-naturedly like old friends.

Iris listened quietly, laughing at the banter. She thought back on how differently things could have turned out had Jeremy not come into their lives. She shivered slightly, reaching for the breadbasket to hide her unease. Then Ruby started telling one of her stories, Jeremy grinning at the tale, and her fear lifted, replaced by wonder at all that had come into her life.

"So, who comes to your classes?" Iris asked. "Are they already mediums? Or are they trying to be mediums? Like, who thinks to go take one of your classes?"

"Oh, they come for all sorts of reasons. Some are curious because of something they heard, or they've been dragged there by a friend, or they've experienced something otherworldly," he said, nodding at the two women. "Some come looking for a new way to make money—there's always that aspect, unfortunately, but most come with lovely intentions, and equally lovely abilities."

They were interrupted by the arrival of their food, and Iris took the time to think about what he had said. She couldn't imagine ever being skilled enough to take money for this, although selling some of the paintings would be nice. But what would people think if she tried to sell them? Would she have to explain what they meant?

The worry must have begun to show on her face because all of a sudden, she realized Jeremy was watching her, eyebrows raised in question. Waving him off, she said, "You were telling us about the classes and why people come . . . "

"Right," he said, seeming to sense she was worrying. "Some people really have no idea what this is all about, and popular culture makes them afraid of it. They come to learn what it is, I think, hoping it will make them less frightened." She looked down at her plate, not wanting to meet his eye.

He continued gently, "Fear can be really hard to overcome at first, because it can be such a fierce barrier to enlightenment. Still, the fact that they are there at all means they are willing to overcome that fear, and most often they do."

Ruby coughed, reaching for her water as if something were caught in her throat. She set it down, looking sideways at Iris, before speaking. "Well, there was something we were talking about one day. I wanted to talk to you about it, but it felt silly asking. It might be related to that fierce barrier of enlightenment thing."

Iris jumped in. "I'm not afraid of it anymore, but I also don't really understand it."

"It still weirds me out a bit, to be honest," Ruby said. "Remember how you said we all have loved ones in spirit who are around us? Well . . . um . . . do they . . . uh . . . watch us? Can they see everything we're doing?" She held her glass in her hand, but didn't drink, waiting for his response.

Iris focused on her plate, nervously pushing the food around. "I might worry about it a bit too, to be honest," she said. Jeremy had the grace not to laugh, but the twinkle in his eye gave away the amusement he was trying to hide.

"The simple answer is yes, they are around you, but no, they are not watching you." He turned back to his dinner, pausing with his fork midway to his mouth to add, "You can shower in peace." Iris blushed, while Ruby laughed out loud.

"But seriously," Iris persisted. "If spirits can see us, then how do they not watch? Are there rules or something?" She'd been more bothered by this than she'd let on and silently thanked Ruby for bringing it up. She bit her lip, hoping he knew she wasn't kidding.

He set his fork down and wiped his mouth on his napkin, giving them his full attention. "We can't really know what it is like to live in the spirit world, of course, so I couldn't say if there are rules as we would know them. There is love, of course, and love would never hurt us, so that is enough to reassure me they don't do anything to make us uncomfortable."

"But—" Ruby interrupted.

Jeremy cut her off with a gentle wave. "Ruby, since spirits are no longer physical beings, I imagine they can't see like you or I do." He pointed at his own face. "No eyes and all that."

"Okay, so then how do they know where we are—so they can be near us?" Iris asked.

He stopped to take a sip of wine. "I'm told they know us by our light." He paused. "Beautiful concept, isn't it?"

It was starting to make sense. She thought about those who were blind—they recognized people by how they sounded and felt, she guessed. So maybe this wasn't so different. "So, our 'light' is different and identifiable then?"

"That's the way I understand it," he answered with a satisfied nod of his head.

She could almost see the gears working in Ruby's mind. She guessed her friend had a million questions floating around in there and no qualms about asking any of them.

"So, do you see spirits all the time, or just when you want to?" Ruby blurted out, as she sat back to let the server clear their plates away. Iris wondered what she thought of the conversation she had to be overhearing as she worked.

"Oh, just when I choose to be aware of them," he said. "I think of it like this. When I want to connect to the spirit world, I turn my attention to them. When I don't, I keep it focused on the physical world." Seeing their confusion, he offered an example. "See the table behind me, with the four women at it?" They nodded. "Try to listen to what they are saying for a moment."

Iris spoke first. "They're talking about their kids, I think."

Ruby nodded. "Teenagers, it sounds like!"

"Makes me glad I don't have any," Iris quipped.

Jeremy pointed back and forth to the two women. "Okay, and now you are listening to each other at this table, right?"

"Yes . . . "

"What you just did was turn your attention to their conversation instead of ours. Once you turned back to us, their conversation faded into the background." He surveyed the two blank faces, waiting to see if they understood.

Iris was the first to make the connection. "I see! It's like the spirit is sitting at the next table, and you turn your attention to it to receive information?" She turned expectantly to Jeremy.

"Exactly," he answered with a grin.

Ruby, just a step behind Iris, suddenly nodded knowingly. "Ah, that makes sense! So, unless you want to be rude to the people you are with, you stay 'tuned in' to us and not to the dead folks?"

Jeremy chuckled. "Yes—that's the best explanation I can give you. I'm glad it makes sense." He seemed relieved when the server returned to offer dessert and coffee. Iris hoped they hadn't pushed too much. She appreciated his kindness and promised herself she'd stick to ordinary things for the rest of the evening.

After the others placed their orders, she said to the server, "I've been smelling your lemon cake for the last ten minutes. I'll have some of that, please."

The woman answered patiently. "I'm sorry, we don't have any lemon cake on the menu."

"Oh, is it lemon pie then?" Iris asked.

"No, we have chocolate torte, ice cream, and a cheese plate. Nothing lemon at all. I'm sorry."

She cringed, stammering as she asked for the torte instead. "I'm sorry, that was weird," she said to her friends when they were alone. "I could swear I smelled something lemon baking. How strange is that!"

Ruby laughed, and Jeremy merely reached for his coffee, saying nothing. Iris kept to her silent promise and steered the conversation to anything other than mediumship for the rest of the evening.

Outside, after dinner, they waited for the valet to bring her car around. It was one of those evenings when the air was crisp enough to remind everyone autumn was coming. "I'm actually a little chilly!" Ruby remarked, and they got into the car with the windows closed, grateful for the warmth.

Iris wrinkled her nose in disgust. "I can't believe someone smoked in my car. I wish I had noticed before we got in. I wouldn't have given him that tip."

"Oh, don't be so hard on the guy. It can't be that bad. I don't even smell it," Ruby chided as they drove away.

CHAPTER 24

Iris didn't want the evening to end. She drove slowly, listening to her friends chatter as she navigated the winding roads through the hills around town. As she rounded the bend at the edge of town, her own house came into view first. She had left the porch light on, and the soft glow beckoned like a warm fire on a cold night. It didn't take much to convince the others to stay for a while.

Sound carries well at night, and as she walked through the living room with a tray of drinks in her hands, she could hear the conversation out on the porch. "You really didn't smell the cigarette smoke back there?" Jeremy asked.

Ruby chuckled softly, but not softly enough. "Not at all," she said. "Iris has the most sensitive nose I've ever seen. And for the record, I didn't smell the lemon cake, either." Ruby laughed again, and while Iris was sure it wasn't malicious, it still stung. She listened for an answering laugh from Jeremy, but fortunately there was none. Setting the tray down, she turned on the stereo, using the onset of some background music to announce her presence.

There was no sign of anything amiss when she pushed open the screen door, and Jeremy jumped up to take the tray from her. "Have you thought any more about taking a class?" he asked innocently. "I can help you find one if you'd like."

She took the pivot, happy to ignore what she had overheard. "Not yet. The books are good right now. Besides, I can just ask you, right?"

Jeremy laughed, taking the bait. "Alright, what questions do you still have tonight?"

Ruby jumped in before she had a chance to speak. "What do mediums do—I mean, besides the demonstrations like we saw. How do you make a living?"

"Well, some of us teach, like I do, and travel to places where we are invited. We get a fee, as well as the perks of traveling. Others work 'regular' jobs and do sittings—readings—on the side. Some mediums are good enough, and known enough, to make a living at it. But I promise you, none of us are getting rich."

"Then why do people do it?" Ruby asked. "It sounds like a lot of work to me."

"We do it to be of service—to others, those grieving, for example, and to those in the spirit world who want desperately to reach their loved ones. It is a real privilege to serve in this way. It's a calling, really— and a sacred one at that."

Ruby fumbled with the button on her jacket, her ears turning a deep shade of pink. Jeremy noticed, trying quickly to reassure her. "It's a fairly common question, you know. It's hard to envision someone living a life of service until it is you envisioning it for yourself. I don't know if my teenage self would have been happy knowing this was the life I would lead someday, but this middle-aged self most certainly is."

Iris cleared her throat, drawing two sets of eyes in her direction. "I've got a question. We talked about the clairs—clairvoyance and all. And it's just . . . well . . . I was wondering, have you ever heard of 'clairessence'?"

"I have," Jeremy said. "Where did you hear it?"

"I'm not sure." She looked around, as if trying to identify the source. "I just keep hearing it in my head—clairessence."

Jeremy seemed puzzled at first, and then suddenly his face turned wistful. "Iris, you said you heard this in your head—you didn't read it?"

She shook her head. "No. I never heard it before tonight. But I started hearing it after we left the restaurant. I kept hearing it as we drove home, and then again while we were sitting here. Why?"

"I think I know where it came from." His voice softened, and he paused, taking a sip of his drink after a moment. "Oh, I'm fine," he said, seeing the look of concern on her face. "Let me help you see something, okay?"

"What do you mean 'see something'?" she asked.

"Well, remember back at the restaurant when you expected lemon cake on the menu?" he asked.

She nodded and rolled her eyes, flushing in embarrassment.

"Tell me again why you expected it."

"I just smelled it. It was distinctive, like the smell you get when someone opens a box with a cake inside. It filled my nose." Recalling an earlier lesson, she added, "So do you think that was a spirit-smelling thing? Clair . . . "

"—alience," he finished. "It's the word I used for it when we were talking the other day. But another term for it is clairessence."

She made the next connection on her own. "The cigarette smoke in the car—do you think that was the same thing?"

"I am quite sure of it actually, and I believe the two might be related." He sat forward in his seat a bit, looking expectantly at Iris, as if she were the one with the answers.

"Then Iris was hearing the word to describe what was happening?" Ruby asked.

Jeremy nodded in agreement to Ruby. "Yes, I think so, but there is more to it." Turning once more to Iris, he asked, "Was there anything you sensed along with the word, or with any of the smells?"

She thought about it for a moment before answering, "The smells were just what I said, but when I was hearing the word, it seemed really important for some reason. That's why I asked about it. But it also felt . . . lovely . . . I guess. Like it was the most beautiful word in the world." She looked at Jeremy, who seemed suddenly a million miles away. After a moment, he snapped back to attention.

"Well done, Iris. Really well done," he said.

She gave him a quizzical look. What exactly had she done?

He leaned forward, eyes bright, a soft smile lighting his face. "I believe those two scents are from the same spirit, and it is related to that word—clairessence. I think what, or rather who, you have here is my wife. Her name is Clara, and she smoked from the time she was a teenager until she died of lung cancer at age fifty. And she always made me a lemon drizzle cake for my birthday, which, notably, is tomorrow."

Iris and Ruby didn't say a word, both surprised into silence.

"What you heard were actually two words, *Clara's scents*. The fact it sounds like the term for clear smelling makes it a fun play on words, which is something my wife loved to do when she was here. She smelled like both of those things all the time, and your describing the scents brought her to life for me as clearly as if she were sitting right here."

Her hands shook. She tucked them under her arms in an attempt to still the trembling. Ruby gave her a pointed look, one eyebrow raised. She looked away, then swallowed, and turned to Jeremy. "Your wife? I had no idea she wasn't alive. I thought she was back in England, being incredibly patient while you were over here. I thought the portrait was for her."

He bit his lip. "It is for her. I promised her, when she first got sick, I would get it done. It really did mean a lot to her. I have been dragging my feet for years, partly because it reminded me of her, and partly because, as I said, I hadn't found the right artist. Now I know why that artist was you."

She sat there quietly for some time. She couldn't believe she had received all that information without even trying. Finally, she asked, "But why did this happen without my seeking it out? I thought this was all in my control, like listening to the other table at the restaurant."

"Iris, I believe the spirit world did this to show you what you are capable of, while also providing me with a beautiful postcard from my wife. They will often do that, do two things at once, because it is efficient, and getting messages through can take a lot of work. And for me, the message from my wife coming from someone who couldn't have known anything about her makes it more evidential for me. If one of my friends had given me the same birthday gift, I might not have fully believed it since they would have already known all of it."

She didn't know what to think, other than she had so much more to learn. She told him as much, adding, "Will you teach me more?"

Now it was Jeremy who seemed to find his hands incredibly interesting. He cleared his throat before answering. "I wasn't going to ruin the evening for you, but since you asked, I need to tell you that I'm heading back to England at the end of next month. I've got things to take care of at home, and I'm booked into a bunch of workshops through the winter. I'm not sure when I'll be back. But I will be happy to talk any time you want. Or you can email . . . or write. I won't disappear. I promise."

She swallowed the lump in her throat, trying to appear unconcerned. "Of course, I knew you wouldn't be here forever. I'll be fine. I've still got all those books—they should tide me over for a while." She tried again to smile, but a sense of panic was growing stronger by the minute. How would she ever do this all on her own?

"I'm sorry, Iris," he said. "Remember what I've told you already. You are just beginning here, and development is a process, not a single point in time. Be patient with yourself, and trust you will find all the right teachers and experiences you need."

"But how will I know they're right?" she asked, cursing herself for sounding like a child.

"In all the ways I've told you. They will feel right, or there will be persistent signs, or something wonderful will pop up out of the blue. Learning to trust those signs is a process too. And it's okay to be nervous sometimes. Just don't make rash decisions when you're scared. Talk to a friend, or call me. But most of all, don't worry. You are doing fine. I promise."

They sat for another couple of hours, talking and sharing stories. Jeremy had a knack for storytelling, and the visit from his wife seemed to have loosened his reserve. Ruby continued with her questions, while Iris sat back, listening to the two of them. She had so many stories and questions of her own, but for tonight, she decided to hold them inside. So much had changed in such a short period of time.

Telling her not to worry was like telling a dog not to bark. She could do it for a few minutes, but inevitably the anxiety resurfaced. But the stories were soothing, and the fact Jeremy was such a normal and lovely person was calming. As she finally crawled into bed, her last thoughts were, *God, I hope he's right.*

CHAPTER 25

ris set down the book she had been reading, discouraged once again. She shouldn't compare herself to others but did it anyway. Ever since Jeremy had announced he would be going back to England, she'd been feeling uninspired and inadequate. He had told her this was natural, and likely would never go away completely, but still, it bothered her.

She turned her attention back to her book. The medium she had been reading about was also an artist. She was known for the clarity of her evidence, which often included portraits of the deceased person. *Now that would be pretty clear.*

She thought about the paintings of the houses. Those might be clear too, but what was she supposed to do with them? She could display them in a gallery and hope the intended recipient showed up, but that didn't seem very practical. Maybe it was all just a waste of time. They certainly weren't doing anyone any good sitting in a closet.

"Maybe you are supposed to paint spirit portraits too."

She jumped, eyes darting around the room as she tried to rub the goosebumps away.

She was alone. The initial surge of adrenaline eased, and she realized she hadn't heard the words spoken out loud. But they had come, unbidden, into her head. Tossing the book aside, she reached for her jacket. She needed to move, and she needed some air.

Stepping out onto the porch, she realized running away from a voice in her head was logically impossible. "This is nuts," she said to no one in particular, and then she heard from the sidewalk, "I know—isn't this traffic awful?"

She turned her head to see Lucia coming toward her, struggling with a load of boxes. It was windy, and her long black hair was whipping around as she struggled to move it out of her face with her shoulder.

Looking beyond her, Iris could see a line of cars extending as far as she could see in both directions. It was peak foliage time, and the leaf peepers were out in force. "Need a hand?" she asked as she hurried down the steps.

"*¡Gracias!* I've got my circle today, and I need to get there to set up. I can't be late, so I finally parked the car and just started walking."

Grateful for the interruption, she relieved Lucia of half of her burden. "Let me take those—I could use the walk," she said. "What did you mean by your 'circle'?"

"My spiritual development circle. We meet at my shop once a week. It's part book club, part meditation group, part learning and discovery. It's also a good excuse to get together to enjoy good company and conversation. You're welcome to join anytime."

"I'm not really into spirituality . . . " Iris began.

"You might be surprised. Spirituality is about the universe, and love. It's hard to explain, but I think you would understand if you saw it for yourself. And you said you were interested in mediumship, didn't you? We practice that, too."

She was intrigued, and if she was honest, a little excited, too. *Something* had gotten her off the couch just now, and a little company might be just what she needed. "Can anytime be now?" she asked, blushing at her own boldness.

"*¡Claro!*" Lucia said. "Trust spirit when it calls to you."

CHAPTER 26

She followed Lucia around to the back of the shop and up the outside staircase. "This is where I hold all of my workshops," Lucia called over her shoulder. "I think you'll like the space."

At the top of the stairs was a small deck that ran across the front of the building. It was just deep enough that the second story of the building wasn't visible from the street. It had large windows across the whole front wall, and French doors in the center. From here, she could see all the way across the lake to the trees beyond. They were afire with October color, the orange and yellow sharp against the sapphire blue sky.

Lucia followed her line of sight and echoed her thoughts. "I guess I can't blame them all for coming—it really is so beautiful. Come inside. The others will be here soon."

The room was a good-sized, wide-open space. Both the vaulted ceiling and the row of windows let in tons of light, making it bright and warm. The walls were painted a soft cream, and a large white rug filled the center of the room. Piles of pillows ran along one side of the room, with comfortable chairs lining the other walls. She breathed in, noting the smell of cinnamon coming from a large bowl of potpourri in the corner. A small windchime tinkled in the breeze from the open door. "What a great space!" she gushed. "It feels wonderful in here."

"I'm glad you like it!" Lucia grinned, clearly pleased at her response.

They she set about moving chairs and lighting some candles, chatting as they worked.

"We always start off with mingling as people arrive, but then we start promptly at five past the hour. I feel it is important to start and end on time out of respect for everyone's time. They all know it, so nobody will be late." Lucia turned on a small speaker, and the room filled with the sound of birdsong.

"So do you have something specific planned for today?" she asked. The beauty of the room was soothing, but she was still nervous. The quivering in her stomach was evidence of that.

"*¡Ay—Si!* We are having a meditation, and then I'm planning to talk about oracle cards. That's what is in these bags," Lucia answered as she placed the bags on the table.

Iris reached into one of the bags and pulled out a small box with a picture of a rose on the front. Opening the box, she found a set of cards, larger than playing cards, each with a beautiful picture and some words on the back. "These are pretty. What are they for?"

"They're for spiritual guidance. I'll explain a bit more when the others get here, but they're used as a way to receive answers or advice from spirit."

Lucia began putting a box of cards on each chair. Then, right on time, people began filing in, greeting one another, and taking seats around the circle. Lucia introduced her, and the warmth of their welcome put the last of her nerves to rest.

She recognized a couple of faces, thinking she had always thought of them as normal people. A flash of shame made her want to hide as she realized how that sounded, even to her own ears. *They are normal—just like you,* she reminded herself, hoping nobody had seen her blush.

A young man named Philip stepped up to guide the meditation. His voice was soft and sure, with a hint of a Southern accent. As she focused on breathing in and out, and following in her mind the journey he laid out, her body and mind relaxed. At the point where she felt she could stay in this state all day, Philip began to bring them all back to the room. Almost reluctantly, she let herself be aware of her feet on the ground and her body in the chair.

They turned their attention to Lucia, who had taken a set of cards out of the box, casually shuffling them in her hands. "We are going to start today with a basic single card reading. I know some of you might not have used cards before. Is that right?"

A couple of hands popped up.

Lucia took note of the raised hands. "No problem. The first thing you want to do before using any cards is settle your mind—that's why we did the meditation. Now, I want you to think of something you would like your spirit guides to help you with." The others nodded, obediently closing their eyes, or looking off into the distance.

Setting aside the question of what exactly a spirit guide was, Iris recalled what she had been worrying about when Lucia walked by the house. *I'd like to know what I'm supposed to be doing with all of this*, she thought, hoping that was the right kind of question to ask.

"Now trusting you will get the answer you need, start shuffling your cards. Mix them up well. Now turn to your neighbor . . . " Lucia paused, making sure everyone indeed had a partner. "Taking turns, take one card from your neighbor's deck and leave it face down in your lap. We'll wait until everyone has picked a card for themselves."

She turned to the woman next to her and quickly pulled the first card she saw. Her partner hesitated, taking her time with her selection. Iris stole a look around the room to see what others were doing. Some were taking their time, running their hands over the cards as if feeling them. Others were very quick to pick a card, and like Iris, did so seemingly without much thought. She wondered what those who were taking their time were doing, her list of questions growing longer.

Lucia looked around the circle, and seeing everyone had a card, announced, "Alright, now set the rest of the cards aside, and hold only the one you picked in your hand. Turn it over, and take a look at what is written on it. There will be an image and some words. What does it mean to you? Sit with it for a few minutes, make some notes on paper if you need to, and then we can talk about what you found."

Iris turned her card over, swallowing her nervousness about what she would find. The meditation had settled her for sure, but this was all still so new. Looking down, she saw an image of three roses. There was a soft pink rosebud, a larger yellow rose, and a big, fully open red rose. The words below it read:

Unfoldment
"This is a time of discovery for you. Your spiritual gifts are opening
up as beautifully as a rose coming into bloom.
Like the rose, your inner beauty will expand,
and you will bring joy and comfort to those you encounter.
Enjoy this lovely time of unfoldment."

She read the words again, just to be sure she understood them right. She hadn't heard the term "unfoldment" before, but the image of the rose opening up illustrated the concept so clearly, she was sure she understood it well. After a few minutes, Lucia asked them all to share their card with the group and any meaning they got from it.

As they went around the circle, Iris could see the cards were all quite different, and yet the meaning in them was consistently lovely. One man held up the image of a lion, with the word "courage" written below. He shared how he had recently left his job, one all seemed to know was a bad fit. He was trying to be patient, so he didn't jump into something worse out of fear. He said the courage card was nice reassurance he was doing the right thing.

Lucia showed her card as well, an image of a beautiful woman with wings, flying. Strange as the image was, it was also beautiful to imagine being free enough to fly like the birds. Her card had only the word "freedom" on it. "This is really empowering to me right now. Ever since my youngest moved out, we've been thinking of selling the big house and moving into someplace smaller. It would be so nice to not have to worry about all the upkeep that old place needs."

The older members nodded knowingly, while Iris was reminded of how she had felt when she bought the cottage. Free. She smiled widely at the memory.

"Iris, you seem to be happy with yours. What did you find?" Lucia asked.

Startled back to the present from her momentary daydream, she answered quickly, "Sorry—I was so caught up in yours I forgot I was next!" She turned the card so the others could see the image. "I'm new to all of this, so I have a lot to learn, but I think this card is reassurance it's okay. Does that make sense?"

"*¡Ay bendito!* It makes a lot of sense," Lucia answered, clapping her hands excitedly. "What a beautiful sign for you that everything is happening as it should. Opening up to spirit is such a beautiful experience. Enjoy it Iris, ask lots of questions, and trust in what feels lovely to you—that is the spirit guiding you."

CHAPTER 27

"What's a spirit guide?" Iris asked.

The question was met with silence.

"Jeremy, what's a spirit guide?" she repeated, giving him a nudge to get his attention. Earlier, she'd been showing Ruby a deck of oracle cards, explaining the exercise they had done at her first circle. She had tried to explain how to use them but didn't think she'd done a very good job of it. Now she had more questions than answers and needed some help.

Jeremy, meanwhile, had been engrossed in one of his books, seemingly oblivious to their conversation. "I beg your pardon?" he asked when she finally got his attention.

"I was asking about spirit guides," she sighed. "They talked about them in the circle as if everyone knew what they were, only I don't. Are they like angels?" She held up one of the cards, the one with the woman with wings, to illustrate her point.

"Well, yes and no," he said, taking his glasses off as he set the book aside. "You'll get different answers from different people, I think, but to me, a spirit guide is a kind of a helper. They help you find your way, find answers to questions, and ease your way if they can. I believe they are spirits, just like our loved ones, only they are tasked with accompanying us for a time."

She wasn't sure if she liked the idea of spirits leading her around. "Do they tell us what to do, like a guide on a tour does? Or do they just point the way and let us figure things out from there?" She imagined the ghost of Christmas future pointing the way to Ebenezer Scrooge's headstone, and she shivered, uneasy all of a sudden.

"Well, I believe it is somewhere in between those two extremes," he said. "A tour guide can't force you to do something. You can always leave the tour and make your own way, and you might be better for it. But the tour guide has been that way before and can suggest the best route, the best sights to see."

Ruby seemed skeptical. "But how can they know what's best? I hate being told what to do or where to go."

Iris covered her mouth to stifle a laugh. "She's right, you know," she said to Jeremy. "Ruby hates even asking directions. A spirit guide would be pretty frustrated trying to lead her around."

"Hey!" Ruby exclaimed, tossing a bit of cracker in her direction.

"Sorry," Iris laughed, "I'm just saying—"

Jeremy interrupted. "I'm sure Ruby's guides know her well enough to know just how to help her out . . . and when to let her find her own way, too." Ruby crossed her arms, nodding her head with a satisfied look that said, So there. It was Jeremy's turn to laugh. "Some of us are easier to guide than others, I imagine . . . "

Iris still had the image of Scrooge's ghosts in her head and was growing more confused by the minute. "Hold on. Are we led around, or aren't we? I like making decisions, but I like taking advice, too. So, are we on our own, or do they lead us?" she asked, hoping her frustration wasn't obvious.

"There are lots of images of ghosts and spirits in popular culture, Iris. Most of them aren't too pleasant, am I right?" She swallowed, nodding mutely in agreement. His ability to read her thoughts was still a bit shocking.

"Our brains and consciences are quite capable of leading us along in life. Nonetheless, our guides are there to help, if we want them to be. Personally, I believe they do a bit more than just point us in the right direction. I believe if we veer away from our goals or what makes us who we are, our helpers put up signs to get us back on track. And even then, we can still go our own way if we choose."

"Okay, so then what constitutes a sign?" Ruby asked.

"It can be anything, really, that gets your attention. Like that book you found over the summer. A repeated word, a series of numbers, even a song can be a sign. And what is a sign to me might be meaningless to you. They are personal, and only the one for whom they are intended usually sees them. Usually. I have had enough experiences to know sometimes spirit uses other people to get through to us when we are particularly dense."

Iris didn't think she was dense, per se, but she was having a really hard time conceptualizing what he was saying. She wanted something more concrete. Were these guides people, and would she see them or feel them? Could she hear them? Recalling the times she had heard voices in her head, she wondered if maybe that was one of her helpers. Trust them, she heard, and her heart skipped a beat. Trust them, she heard again, more insistently.

She took a deep breath, forcing herself to look her friends in the face. "So, I never told either of you this, but a couple of times, I have heard a voice in my own head, when I wasn't expecting to hear anything. I know I told you I heard something when I painted that barn, but it was when I was seeing a spirit image, so I figured it came from the connection I had. The thing is, sometimes it's not related to spirit at all. At least I don't think it is. I just . . . suddenly hear a voice in my head. One time I think I might have even heard it out loud."

She peeked shyly at her friends, as she looked down at her lap, wiping her hands on her jeans. "The other day, I was thinking about the houses, and I heard something like, 'Maybe you are supposed to paint portraits too.' I didn't know where it came from, and I didn't want to tell anyone because it sounded like something you shouldn't tell people is happening, but it did. Do you think maybe that was a spirit guide talking to me?"

Ruby poured a fresh cup of tea for Iris and handed it to her. She wrapped her hands around the mug, grateful for its warmth. After she had taken a sip, he answered her. "That sounds like it could be, Iris. But it also could be your own spirit speaking to you. We all have an inner voice, remember, and sometimes it speaks directly to us. For it to be so clear and unexpected tells me it could be either, but it likely wasn't something you made up. I know you are clairaudient, so I would expect your guides and helpers would speak directly to you sometimes."

She examined her hands, following the lines of the veins across the backs of them. "But how do I know it isn't just me talking to myself? Just now I heard, 'Trust them,' only it sounded like me. Does a spirit voice s-sound different?"

"Most people say spirit helpers sound like our own voices," Jeremy answered in the way he had of making the most extraordinary things sound perfectly normal.

"So how do I know the difference?" she asked, the need to know as strong as her need for water, or air.

"Because spirit voices will always be loving and make you feel safe," Jeremy said. "You were afraid to bring this up, and then heard reassuring words that made you feel comfortable sharing. That sounds to me like words from either your own soul, or from a spirit guide, because it was lovely, affirming, and trustworthy."

Her skin prickled as she thought ahead to what the alternative might feel like.

"Now let's say you had heard something like, 'Don't bring it up, or they won't understand.' How would that feel?" he asked.

She rubbed her arms to dispel the feeling. "Scary. Like I was getting ready to do something wrong." Mouth suddenly dry, she reached again for her tea, letting her mind work through what he had said, trying to connect the dots.

After a minute, she took a deep breath. "Okay. If I hadn't said anything, we wouldn't be having this conversation, right?" Jeremy nodded. "So, that means it would have been my ego trying to protect me—even though you haven't told me I've done anything wrong?"

"Yes." He grinned, seeming pleased with himself. "But all it would have protected you from is this conversation, which it sounds like is pretty consoling. That's why the ego isn't always the best voice to listen to. Your soul, spirit, heart, whatever you want to call it, is far wiser and will help you take good risks, because it knows there is love to be gained. But remember, sometimes you need to listen to the voice of caution, so it isn't always so straightforward. Life would be too easy if we didn't need to discern things for ourselves."

She started to ask another question, her mind already ten steps ahead. Jeremy put up a hand to stop her. "Iris, discernment is always difficult to understand. There are lots of books about it, and people spend their entire careers trying to help people understand how to do it well. You aren't going to understand all of it today. Try to remember spirit is loving, kind, and helpful. When you sense something or hear something, if it is all of those things, you can trust it."

She wanted to continue the conversation, but realized he was probably right. Her mind was already running in circles, and a pain was growing right between her eyes. She pinched her nose to dispel it, then reached for the plate of cookies, offering them as bit of a bribe. "Okay, just one last question, and I'll leave it be. Can we ask our guides for help, or do we just have to trust they will help us when they can?"

"Oh, of course you can ask them for help," he answered while lifting a cookie from the plate. "That's the best way to receive it. Ask for what you need, or what you long for in your heart, and they will help you to find it."

"Gosh, I am going to miss you," she blurted. "Are you sure you don't want to stay here in the States?"

"I would love to, Iris, but I really do need to get back. You know how to get hold of me, and I am happy to talk anytime. If you have a lot of questions, or just want me to have time to think about an answer, then write me an email. I promise to write back promptly. And I also promise to be back here in the spring."

"You better be!" Ruby scolded. "I can see the rabbit holes this mediumship is going to take us down. I'm already exhausted trying to figure it all out!" She winked, making it clear to Iris she didn't mind.

His expression softened as he absently stroked his throat with one finger. He seemed focused on something over her shoulder, as if there was someone behind her. Her own throat quivered a bit, unsure of what was going on. After a moment, his focus shifted back. "May I ask you a question, Iris?"

"Sure!"

"Do you know someone called Mike, or Michael, perhaps?"

Momentarily speechless, she took another sip of tea, acutely aware of the warmth as the liquid moved down her throat. She became aware of something else, too, a feeling as though something was leaning against her right shoulder. Finally, she answered, "I do know that name. Why?"

"Well, there is a gentleman that has been at the edge of my awareness for the last half hour. He's got short red hair, and he's dressed like one of those doctors on television: blue scrubs and a white jacket. He's quite young, too."

She was powerless to stop the tears that sprang instantly into her eyes. "I know him. It's my f-friend, Michael. He was a d-doctor." She reached for a napkin, her hand shaking along with her voice.

Jeremy's face relaxed into understanding. "Ah, that explains it. I wasn't sure who he was here for, but as soon as I asked you, he moved in closer. He's sitting right beside you now."

She nodded, tears now fully falling. "I know. I can feel him."

"He's just shown me a small key. Do you understand that?"

She nodded, reaching unconsciously for the pendant that still hung around her neck. She lifted it out, showing her friends the precious gift from Michael that was always hidden from view.

"He said he already gave you the answer you seek."

She frowned in confusion, trying to focus on what Jeremy was saying. "The key is the answer?" she asked. "I don't understand. Did he say anything else?"

"No. I'm sorry I can't explain it for you. Give it some time, and it should make sense. Sometimes the understanding will come when you least expect it. In the meantime, take his visit as a lovely way of letting you know you aren't going to be alone in this. I think he really just wanted you to know he is here."

She rose and planted a kiss on Jeremy's cheek. "Thank you for that. It—and he—meant the world to me."

CHAPTER 28

Jeremy headed back to England, and Iris settled back into a more normal routine. December would be here soon, and she had commissions needing to be finished before the holidays. Charlie was looking for a few new paintings to hang in his gallery, and she had prints to be made that he could sell in the gift shop. There was little time for reading—or worrying—about spirits. The only exception was the circle at Lucia's. She had made it a point to carve out that time for herself, and so far, she hadn't missed a meeting.

She headed up the stairs above the shop, pausing on the balcony to take in the view. The trees had long since gone bare, and the hills stood stark and grey in the distance. Shivering, she pulled her hood up, not ready to go inside just yet. "It's beautiful, isn't it?" she heard from over her shoulder. She turned to see Lucia step out the door to join her.

"It is," Iris said. She loved this time of year, the pause between the busyness of the tourist season and the holidays. She took a deep breath in, feeling the cold air fill her lungs. "I never get tired of the views around here. Do you?"

Lucia chuckled. "The views, no. The cold, yes. I don't think I'll ever get used to it." Gesturing toward the open door, she nudged Iris to come inside. "Come on. I've got hot tea and cake. We're doing something different today."

Intrigued, she followed inside, leaving her coat on one of the hooks by the door. The tea was soothing and warm, and she sat quietly, enjoying the peace and stillness. Soon the others had filtered in, and Lucia opened the circle.

"Alright everyone, I have a question. How many of you think when you give your sitter evidence, if the evidence is true, it will be recognized?" They all raised their hands. "Why do you say that?" she asked.

"Well, because spirit is intelligent, and so they won't give information the sitter wouldn't understand," Alex answered.

"And if we are doing it right, the evidence is from the spirit, so it should be recognized," Philip added, smiling confidently.

"And spirit wouldn't show us something that isn't true, would they?" Iris asked. She had read spirit doesn't lie, and she believed it, trusting the houses she drew were real places, somewhere. She drew her mug of tea in closer to her body, letting the steam rise up under her chin, needing to feel its warmth.

"I wanted to tell you a story. A friend of mine recently came back from a weeklong class on mediumship, and she had an interesting experience." Lucia set her own mug aside, leaning forward as she told the story, making eye contact with each one of them as she spoke.

"There was someone on the course who had a bit of an attitude. Maybe he was just overconfident, but my friend didn't really like him. She's not confident at all yet, so that probably contributed to how she felt about him. Anyway, on the last day, they did a sort of speed-dating type exercise. They had five minutes to give a reading to someone before moving on to the next person." She stopped, grinning at the open-mouthed members of her circle. "Scary, huh?" she said.

"So, my friend gets to this guy, and he just blurts out something about a soldier. She doesn't know any soldiers, and she tells him so. Well, he won't give up. He tells her this guy never came home, and he never got to say goodbye. Only my friend has no idea who he's talking about. The five minutes ends, and they move on to someone else. She has a good laugh with another friend at this guy's expense, and that's the end of it."

Iris thought about what she had said, that spirit doesn't lie. Now she wondered do they maybe make mistakes? Looking around, she could see the others fidgeting nervously, and a couple were whispering to each other. Lucia cleared her throat to get their attention.

"Now I didn't tell you this to make you feel bad, or to worry you. That guy was probably scared to death of having to work so fast. And my friend telling him she didn't recognize any of it I'm sure only added to his nervousness. I'm telling you this because the story wasn't over that day."

"When my friend came home, she stopped by her parents' house to pick up her dog. When she got out of the car, she noticed the flag hanging from the neighbor's porch. It was one of those POW-MIA flags from the Vietnam war. She couldn't remember a time when it wasn't hanging there, and so she had stopped noticing it." Lucia paused, allowing everyone to begin to put the pieces together.

"The soldier . . . " Alex said, his eyes wide.

Iris realized her own mouth was open, and she covered it with her trembling hand. The guy had been right. "So, what does that mean?" she asked. "Should your friend have accepted what he told her even though she didn't recognize it?"

"No, that's not the message here. First of all, you won't normally be so tight for time. That was a stressful exercise, so both of them weren't at their best, I think. But what I want you to remember is, sometimes the evidence won't be recognized, and yet it will still be true. It's important that you, as mediums, don't force anything on your sitter, or worse, try to make it fit so they do accept it." She stopped, letting her words sink in. Her face was serious, and Iris could tell she wanted them to see that.

"But it's also important to remember you might not recognize the evidence a medium gives you. Or your sitter won't recognize what you are giving them. Remember, spirit is profoundly intelligent and knows how to get the evidence across. If the medium has received and shared the information accurately and it is not recognized, spirit will find a way to get it across to that person. That's what happened here. She saw the flag, and the evidence made sense."

Iris raised her hand. "I think I understand, but why would they . . . er . . . the spirits tell your friend something about someone she didn't even know? The Vietnam war was decades ago."

Lucia's seriousness evaporated. She grinned at Iris, nodding like a teacher pleased her student has finally understood the concept she has been explaining. "That wasn't the end of the story. A couple of weeks later, my friend was back at her parents' house, helping them clean out the attic. She found some old photo albums, and in them was a picture of a bunch of kids hamming it up for the camera.

"She was just a baby but recognized her older siblings and some of the kids from the neighborhood. And standing in the middle of all of them was this tall, skinny kid in old jeans and a striped shirt. He was laughing, and the other kids seemed to all be looking up at him.

"It was the soldier. She probably wouldn't have paid it any mind, had it not been for that reading she'd gotten in class. Because she had, she noticed him and decided to take the picture next door to his parents. They had never seen it and were so thrilled she had remembered him enough to bring it by." Lucia looked pointedly at Iris. "Never underestimate the love that is behind what we are doing. And never doubt that great healing can come from it too."

An awesome weight of responsibility settled on Iris. If spirits were counting on *her* to prove they were real, then she needed to make sure she was doing this right. Her thoughts drifted to the houses again and what she was meant to do with them, but before she could get too distracted, Lucia reminded them they had practicing to do.

The instructions were simple. They were to find a partner, then decide who should give evidence first. That person should close their eyes and allow the spirit communicator to give them whatever evidence they had. The recipient would remain silent and tap once on the medium's knee if the evidence was recognized, twice if it wasn't.

"What if we aren't sure?" someone asked.

"*Ay,* good question. If you aren't sure, do nothing. Those of you getting a contact should take no response as an indication you need clarity in your evidence. Remember, focus on what the spirit is giving you, not on who your sitter is. Let the evidence come as it is, without judgment."

Iris paired up with Philip, offering to go first. She closed her eyes, turning her attention to the area behind her eyes, her so-called "third eye," and waited to see what images or feelings appeared. Sure enough, almost immediately, she saw an image of a sunflower, which then became a field of sunflowers, surrounded by a split-rail fence.

She described it to Philip, and he tapped once on her knee. Confidence building, she described an organic smell, and said she could feel the sun warm on her face.

Tap.

She began to see a figure appear in the distance. As he came closer, she described him as wearing a suit and a hat, like the type men wore in the 1960s.

Tap.

"I feel like he is a very strong man, but very sad as well," she said.

Tap.

"I think he might be related to you."

Tap. Tap.

Her cheeks burned in response. Wrong then. Recalling what she had been taught about unrecognized evidence, she turned back to the man she saw and asked him to clarify. It worked. "I'm sorry," she said. "He isn't related to you; but he is close to you—like a family friend."

Tap.

From there, things went smoothly. She felt the man's energy and was able to relay the message he wanted to convey. He had been the caretaker at their family farm in Pennsylvania, and he told Philip he was still looking after all of them. When she had finished, Philip explained that his family back home was struggling to make ends meet and had recently decided to try growing sunflowers, hoping it would attract tourists in the late summer and open up new opportunities beyond selling potatoes and corn. "Thanks, Iris," he said. "That was good and meaningful, too!"

She took a deep, satisfied breath, feeling the tension ease as she exhaled. The hard part was over. Now it was Philip's turn. She sat back, waiting for him to be ready, eager to see what he could do.

It started out well. "I have a woman here, older, but not elderly. Maybe sixty? I'm hearing the word 'mother,' so this is either your mother or a mother figure."

He paused for a moment, and Iris reached over and tapped once on his knee. She rolled her eyes at the same time, thinking sixty is not old at all, but Philip was only about twenty-five, so to him, her mother must seem ancient.

"I see her wearing casual clothes, jeans, and sneakers, and she has long hair, tied back."

She remembered how her mother couldn't wait for the weekends, when she didn't have to wear her formal work clothes and could spend time working in the yard or walking in the park. This was how she remembered her mom best. She tapped his knee again, once.

The next piece of evidence didn't fit at all.

"I get the sense this woman, your mom, was very laid back and informal in the work she did."

Iris tapped twice.

"Hmm. Let me see if she can be clearer." After a moment of silence, he added, "I think there is someone else who is very casual in her work. She may be telling me about you as a way to indicate she is still around you."

Even though it wasn't really evidence of her mother, it did describe Iris very well, and so after a moment's hesitation, she tapped once. Philip seemed pleased and continued on.

"I get the sense you are worrying about something, and she wants you to know she is aware of it. She is showing me another woman, who stands right beside you. Do you have a sister by any chance?"

She tapped once. She did have an older sister, Alice, though they were far apart in age, and she hadn't seen her in years. Suddenly, her stomach clenched as she wondered if her sister might have died, and this was how she was going to learn of it. Breaking the rules of the exercise she said, "But my sister isn't dead."

"Oh. Okay," he said. "Well, she's standing right next to you. I get the sense there is a tension here. Are you and your sister estranged?"

She didn't consider herself estranged from Alice, just not close. Swallowing her growing unease and forgetting Lucia's directive to say nothing if she wasn't sure, she reluctantly tapped once.

She wished Philip could see her face. He would see she was upset, but with his eyes closed, he simply took her tap as affirming he was doing a great job. She thought about interrupting him, but before she had a chance to, he spouted out what he must have thought was a lovely message.

"I think your mother is here because of that estrangement. I see her picking up a phone now, so I think she is encouraging you to call your sister. It seems to be the message she is conveying. I can see her smiling now, so that tells me I got the message right. She says she loves you very much and hopes you can make amends with your sister."

He opened his eyes, looking expectantly at Iris. He needed some feedback, but she needed air. The worry rising inside threatened to overwhelm her. She hoped her sister was okay. *Was she sick . . . or dying?* The look on Philip's face brought her back to the room for the moment. He was so excited, like a young puppy waiting for a pat on the head. Not wanting to discourage him, she tried to emphasize the positive.

"I think that was my mother, and she did like to dress casually on the weekends. But she worked in a law firm during the week, so that part of her life was pretty formal."

"Did the message make sense?" he asked.

Stifling her better instincts, she answered, "I'm not sure. I need to check a couple of things. But thank you for giving it to me." She spoke as reassuringly as she could, hopefully hiding the wreck she was inside.

As the circle broke up, Lucia approached her. "Are you alright?" she asked. "You look a little worried."

"Oh, it's fine," she said. "My mom came through, and I hadn't expected that. I just need to process what was said." Not wanting to discuss it further, she quickly added, "Sorry, but I have to run. I have an appointment after this." She grabbed her coat and headed out the door, not bothering to say goodbye to anyone else.

CHAPTER 29

Everything was not, in fact, fine. Iris grew increasingly worried as she walked. She so rarely spoke with her sister, but she was certain Alice would have let her know if she was sick. Iris took it to mean something sudden might have happened, and her worry for her sister grew. There couldn't be any other reason her mother would have wanted them to be in touch. She had known they lived separate lives, and the whole family had always been fine with it. But Philip had called it an estrangement, and Iris began to see maybe it was.

She tried to recall the last time she had called her sister just for the heck of it. Nothing came to mind. She tried to remember something fun they had done when they were younger, and again she came up empty. Guilt began to consume her, and any doubts she had had about Philip's reading began to fade. *He must have been right*, she decided. This was followed by another thought. *If she's fine, she'll think I'm an idiot. If she's not fine . . .* That brought on another wave of fear, enough so that the last thing Iris could imagine doing right now was calling her sister.

On some level, she knew it would solve the problem, but she was paralyzed by the thought it might not. Rational ideas seemed to have slipped beyond her grasp, and she spent the next couple of hours sitting on the couch staring at the phone, willing it to ring.

Unsure what else to do, Iris decided to go for a walk to try to distract her from her worrying. She should just call her sister and get to the bottom of things, but the dreaded possibility of something really being wrong gripped her so tightly she couldn't make the call. It was a gloomy November afternoon, but she didn't care. She threw an old sweatshirt over her jeans and headed toward the hills outside of town.

Needing to hear her own voice, she started to speak aloud to her mom. "Why did you tell me to contact Alice? What is going on? Is she okay?" The questions kept coming, and Iris began to imagine she was hearing the answers. *Alice is hurt. Alice is sick. Alice is dying.* She walked faster and faster, her steps keeping pace with her words, hoping the answers would change.

Eventually, they did. She reached the top of a hill and paused. *Call her.* The words were strong and clear. She took several slow deep breaths, letting the cool evening air fill her lungs as clarity filled her mind. The only way to get the truth was to call her sister, even if it did mean giving in to what Philip had said. Reluctantly she reached for her phone, only to realize she must have left it at home on the table. She froze. Looking around, she realized just how far she had come. It was going to be a long walk home, and her fear was back in full force.

As if to echo her darkening mood, it had begun to drizzle. Just as she got back into town, it began to pour. Iris was drenched by the time she stepped onto her porch, the raindrops mingling with her tears. Stepping into the front hall, she kicked off her shoes and jacket and headed straight for the phone.

The call was answered on the third ring.

"Hello?"

It was Alice. Ignoring her soaking wet clothes, Iris dropped down on the couch and let out a bit of the breath she was holding. *Alive then.* The thought surprised her. Even Philip had said she wasn't dead.

"Iris, is that you?" Iris realized she was holding the phone in front of her, staring at it as if it were Alice herself. Putting the phone back up to her ear, she tried to still the fear enough to speak calmly. "It's me, Alice. How are you?"

"I'm fine, Iris—what's up? You don't usually call on a weekday."

"Everything's fine," Iris answered unconvincingly. She wasn't sure where to begin, having neglected in the last day to give any thought to explaining her worries to her sister. "I just . . . we haven't talked in a while, and I was thinking about you—that's all."

"We talked on my birthday, didn't we? Iris, I'm happy to hear from you, but you seem upset. What's going on?"

Iris took another deep breath and wiped the dripping strands of hair out of her eyes. She didn't know how to explain why she was calling and reached for the explanation that most closely resembled the truth.

"I had a bad dream last night, that's all. I dreamed something happened to you. I wanted to make sure you were alright."

"I'm fine, Iris. Really. Nothing is wrong at all. But while we might not talk a lot, I do know you're a terrible liar. Your voice cracks any time you do it. So tell me, what's the real reason you are calling?"

Realizing lying clearly wasn't going to fly with Alice, she reminded herself, *Tell the truth, even if it's not all of it.*

"I'm sorry, Alice. The truth is, I saw a medium yesterday—do you know what that is?"

"I do." She could hear the scorn in Alice's voice and imagined the look she was giving her right now.

"This guy, this medium, told me Mom wanted me to call you because something was wrong. He said you were standing next to Mom, so I thought something had happened to you. He also said we were estranged."

Alice snorted in amusement.

"Gosh, that sounds stupid now that I say it." Iris had started pacing the room as she spoke, her nerves getting the better of her. But when Alice laughed, she sat down on the floor, depleted all of a sudden.

"I wouldn't call it stupid," Alice said. "You know I hate that word—but I would call it ridiculous. I'm fine, and we're not estranged. But honestly, what are you doing visiting mediums?"

"I don't know. I've met a few recently, and it's cool to hear what they have to say." She tried, and failed, to sound unbothered by the whole thing.

"Cool, huh? I can hear how upset you are, Iris, and obviously what this guy told you wasn't true. I'm fine. And Mom isn't coming to you from the beyond, telling you she's upset or worried. Please, Iris, stay away from those folks, okay? No good can come from that stuff."

The relief at hearing her sister's voice evaporated in an instant. *No good can come from this,* she repeated to herself. With a start, she realized she was dripping wet and freezing, and she was starting to shiver. She couldn't let Alice know what a mess she actually was.

"I'm sorry for being such an idiot. I shouldn't have listened to him." She stood up, hoping that would help her to sound confident and sane.

"You're not an idiot. Mediums like to prey on nice people like you.

They're just looking to make a buck, and they don't care who gets hurt along the way. I'm sorry you were so worried."

"So am I," Iris answered with as much pep as she could muster. "It was nice talking to you anyway."

"You can call me anytime, you know. I don't bite," Alice said.

"I know, me neither." She hesitated for a second before adding, "Love you—I'll call you next week."

Iris hung up the phone, feeling relieved in a way, but now thoroughly confused and utterly terrified. She repeated Alice's words, "No good can come of that," over and over in her head like a mantra. Thinking back over the last twenty-four hours, she decided Alice was right. No good *was* coming from this, and not only had Iris been hurt by it, but she had also upset her sister. Who would be the next one to get hurt?

She thought about Philip, and the message he had given her. Her anger flared. He shouldn't be doing this—why is he even allowed to be in the circle? Then she thought about herself. She didn't always get everything right when she practiced. Far from it sometimes. What if one of those times it really hurt someone? Could she live with herself? Maybe her sister was right that nothing good could come of it.

Her thoughts drifted back to her paintings, the red house, and Ruby's reaction to it. What had come of that was good, at least as far as she could tell, but what if it hadn't been? With a start, she realized how differently it all could have gone. Ruby could have been furious. What if she had dredged up something even more traumatic that wasn't meant to be remembered?

In an instant, her imagination had conjured up a different unfolding of events at the fair. She imagined Ruby angry and unforgiving. She saw her storm away, never to be heard from again. A wrenching stab of grief filled her chest, and she moved to the window, staring woefully out at her studio. Grief turned suddenly to anger, and anger to resolve. *Enough.*

Acting quickly, before she changed her mind, she gathered up her oracle cards, the sketchbook, and the journal she had been using for practice, stuffing them all in a box. She opened the back door, intending to head up to the studio, determined to erase any hint of mediumship.

She would paint over those houses once and for all and forget any of this had happened. The blank canvases would be her way of starting over, a sign for herself in a way.

But the rain was coming down sideways, with a wind so biting it made her pull the door closed in a hurry. Her teeth chattered, and she hugged herself, realizing with a grimace she was still wearing her rain-soaked clothes. She chastised herself once again, this time for letting this stupid spirit stuff distract her from the basics of staying safe. She'd end up sick if she didn't cut this out.

Tomorrow then. She had planned to do some shopping in Great Barrington anyway. She'd pick up some fresh primer while she was there and have those paintings erased by the end of the day.

CHAPTER 30

Ruby sat staring out the window. The red of the traffic light was reflected in the drops of rain on the windowpane. The rush of cars going by suddenly stopped, further evidence the light out front had changed. In the sudden silence, her attention turned to the other sounds around her. She could hear the drumbeat of raindrops on the roof, the sound of her neighbor downstairs running the vacuum, and the sudden thump as the cat jumped down from the shelf in the closet and ambled over to Ruby for a scratch. Spellbound for a moment, she silently wished it could stay like this forever. But then the raindrops glowed green, the hum of traffic resumed, and the spell was broken.

Sighing, she returned to the task at hand. She picked up her pen, determined to put words on paper. *She had delayed long enough,* she thought, and smiled wryly at how great an understatement that was. It had been five months since she had seen Iris's painting. Five months since the demonstration. And twenty-five years since the fire.

She had thought about it every day since June, processing with her adult mind what she had been unable to process as a preteen. The demonstration, and the reassurance from her grandmother, had helped Ruby to realize just how much guilt she had been holding onto.

She wondered if this is what therapy would have uncovered, had she ever gone that route. Small-town Wisconsin was not a place where therapists thrived, especially all those years ago, and then life had settled into a routine, and Ruby had contentedly forgotten the summer she turned ten.

The only sign she had borne any of the feelings about that night into her adult life was the fact she had refused to return home for any reason at all. Her family had come to her; she just hadn't wanted to be there. Eventually they had stopped asking why she wouldn't come home. She figured they must know there was some reason but was grateful they had let it be. It was left as an unspoken fact, tucked away and never discussed. Only now it suddenly mattered, and Ruby knew she needed to talk.

It had gotten dark in the room as the rain grew stronger, and she reached to turn on the lamp. There was a chill in the air, and she realized in a few more weeks it would be snow, not rain, she would be watching come down. Ruby's mind wandered to what that would mean—thinking of the holiday crowds that would come through and the town events she would need to attend. She always felt somewhat trapped once the holidays set in.

Sighing, she finally put the pen down. Clearly this letter to her parents was not going to get written today. She wished she had said something years ago, because then this difficult task would be behind her. But she hadn't, and it wasn't, and she was terrified of what opening the door on the past would do.

Getting up, Ruby slipped on her boots, grabbed an umbrella, and set out for a walk. She was procrastinating, but a sudden longing for hot soup and a sandwich gave her an excuse to set the letter aside.

She started to cut across the green, then noticed the rain was easing up. She could feel the storm was passing and noticed a small patch of blue sky beginning to be visible above the treetops. The air smelled of mud and wet leaves and wood-burning stoves. So instead of heading straight for the store, she decided to loop around the lake before heading into town.

Other people were starting to venture out as well, and Ruby greeted her neighbors as they passed. An hour later, she was back at the green, and it was as if the storm had never happened. Lucia had her door open and was rolling up the awning. The smell of lavender wafted out into the street. Ruby waved as she passed by.

There was only one other person in line at the diner, so Ruby didn't have long to wait. By now the sun was shining brightly, and the owner had set the chairs and tables out on the sidewalk, hoping to capitalize on the sunshine as long as it lasted. Feeling content and hungry, Ruby sat down at a table at the end, where she could easily watch the people going by. She loved this town. She loved everything about it, including the autumn tourists. She loved showing her family around when they came to visit, and she loved the friends she had made.

She thought of Iris and offered a quick prayer of gratitude the two of them had each wandered into this town and found each other. And as she sat there thinking about how great her life was, she suddenly felt an overwhelming desire to see her family. She just couldn't keep this all to herself any longer. And a letter wasn't going to cut it. A plane flying overhead caught her attention, and with that, she made her decision. An hour later, she had a flight booked and was on the phone with her dad. "I've got some time off. I'm coming home."

CHAPTER 31

Iris woke exhausted. She hadn't really slept for any stretch of time, and when she had, her dreams had been vivid and disturbing. She shuddered as she recalled the one that had woken her this morning. She'd been back in high school, up in front of an auditorium full of people. In the front row sat her parents, Michael, Ruby, and Charlie. She had a row of easels behind her, each one covered in a black cloth. As she pulled the cloths off the canvases one by one, her loved ones stood and walked out, leaving Iris alone on stage, facing a barrage of boos and insults. When she turned around to see why they were booing, she'd woken up.

It was still dark outside, and she could hear the rain hitting the bedroom window. She grabbed her old flannel shirt and threw it on over her pajamas, stumbling downstairs for some tea. The heat hadn't kicked on for the morning, and it was cold in the house. She thought of climbing back into bed, and the idea of sleep was enticing. The thought of that dream coming back was not.

Cupping the hot mug of tea in her hands, she curled up on the couch, pulling the fleece blanket up and around her. She sipped the tea, allowing the sense of foreboding to begin to ease, as the warmth spread down her throat. The only sound was the rain, the rest of the world still asleep, and the road outside silent and empty. After a few minutes, she reached for her journal.

She wanted to write down what she remembered from the dream, hoping to find some meaning to it. Somewhere she had read you needed to be calm in order to understand your dreams correctly. The sound of the rain was soothing, and the tea had warmed her up. Figuring this was as calm as she was going to get, she began to write down everything she could remember.

She didn't get much past the people sitting in the front row. As she recalled the easels covered in black cloths, her heart began to beat faster, and she was suddenly nauseous. Fear began to rise like a pot of water boiling over, and within seconds, the peace of the morning had vanished.

The dream was a sign. It had to be. In her dreams of Michael, he was always happy . . . and loving. Never had he turned his back on her. And Ruby and Charlie, her closest friends, had never turned their backs either. They all turned away when she took the covers off the paintings—even her parents. That had to be it. She was right—those paintings needed to be destroyed. If anyone saw them, she'd lose every friend she had. No good was going to come of this at all.

It took longer than she'd expected to take all the paintings down. Even though she had determined she would destroy them, she still needed to examine each one as she took it off the wall. The happy little cottage Jeremy had liked brought tears to her eyes. She lingered with it a bit, wishing he were here right now, knowing she could just call, yet at the same time, she couldn't. She was ashamed by what she was feeling, embarrassed she was falling apart, and terrified of what would come next.

She pulled the last few down in a rush and tossed them on top of the pile in the corner.

It normally took no more than a half hour to get to Great Barrington, and nothing would be open for a few hours, but she desperately needed to get out of her studio, out of her house, and away from these paintings. With an urgency verging on panic, she grabbed her jacket and bag, tossed them in the car, and headed out past the still dark houses and shops of her little town.

The highway beckoned, but since there was time to kill, she continued on the smaller roads, letting the GPS lead her. The rain made driving difficult, and the usually scenic roads proved more hazardous than she had expected. After skidding on a patch of wet leaves as she rounded a sharp turn, she pulled into a gas station to let her nerves settle. She needed gas anyway. This station had a convenience store attached to it. Suddenly hungry, she stepped inside to find a snack and maybe a suggestion of a better route to take than the one she was on.

The clerk eyed her knowingly. "Not from around here?" he asked.

Embarrassed, she lied, just a little. "No, I'm from New York. I was over in Lakeview last night. The GPS doesn't know it's raining, and I don't want to get onto another little road that's even worse."

He grinned, with a kindness in his eyes that reminded her of Michael. "Turn right, then left at the next intersection. Route 7 is about a mile down the road," he said as he bagged the snacks she had picked up.

She blushed, realizing she should have known if she'd just thought about it for a minute. "Thanks," she said as she rushed back out into the rain. It was still early. The sky was brighter, so she knew the sun was up, but it would be hours before the art store opened, or anything else for that matter. Approaching the highway, she made a decision. Rather than follow the signs to Great Barrington, she took the next turn, towards New York. If she couldn't go home to Lakeview, maybe she could go home to Manhattan.

CHAPTER 32

The rain began to let up by the time she hit the New York border. She found her old classic rock station and let the music and brightening skies lift her spirits. A sense of purpose had taken hold, along with a sense of determination. It had been a long time since she'd been to the city. A visit with old friends would be just what she needed. She pulled over at a rest stop and called to make a reservation at the little hotel she had always recommended in her old neighborhood. When they told her they had a room at a great price, she took it as yet another sign.

The good feelings were short-lived.

It had, in fact, been years since she had been to Manhattan, and even longer since she had meaningful contact with her old friends. They still exchanged Christmas cards, but as she realized once she began running through these friends in her mind, she wasn't even sure she had anyone's number. She pulled up to the hotel, feeling defeated before she even began.

It was only then she realized what should have been obvious. She had no bag, no change of clothes, not even a hairbrush. It would be hours before she could check into her room, and she was utterly and completely alone. *You're an idiot—a freakin' idiot.*

A long honk, followed by a couple short beeps, made her jump. "What?" she yelled, raising her hands above her shoulders and turning to look at the offending honker. She was greeted with another blast of horns and a colorful series of phrases from the cab driver behind her. He pointed to the sign she had neglected to read, indicating she was in a loading zone. With a grrr, she put the car in gear and sped off.

Her inability to find street parking did little to lighten her mood, and when she finally gave up and pulled into a garage, she was fit to be tied. Then, realizing she at least had some privacy now, she let her guard down, bursting into tears. She didn't know what she was doing, why she was here, or what she was supposed to do next. Finally, she pulled out the blanket she kept in the trunk, crawled into the back seat, and fell asleep.

Predictably, she awoke cold and hungry, and she looked like she had slept in her car. This was not what she had planned at all. Who was she kidding? She hadn't planned anything. *Some psychic you are,* she scolded. Before she could find something to eat, she slipped into a quirky old thrift shop a few blocks from the hotel. It was tucked in between a dry cleaner and the police station, a surprisingly good location for such a store. She made quick work of finding a couple of outfits, including an old dress that would double as a nightgown.

She was at the counter paying when a sign on the wall caught her attention. *Psychic Readings, No Appointment Needed. $40.* "She's really good," the clerk said. "Predicts all sorts of things for people. She helps people around here all the time. You interested?"

Iris shook her head. "I'm all set," she said while gathering up her bag. Pulling it into her arms, she heard a clink as something hit the floor. "I'm sorry," she said as she reached down to retrieve the small metal disc that had landed at her feet. She turned it over, revealing the word 'believe' stamped onto the surface.

She stood there for a moment, eyes fixed on the little silver charm. It had to be a sign, but of what? Was she supposed to visit the psychic? Her sister's warning to stay away from people like that echoed in her head. But the charm was warm in her hand, its message insistent in its simplicity. Quickly, before she changed her mind, she handed two twenties to the cashier for the reading and another dollar for the silver disc she slipped into the pocket of her jeans.

CHAPTER 33

She was directed down a narrow hallway lined with boxes of what she presumed were donations. The floor felt gritty, as if it hadn't been swept in months. The heavy metal door at the end of the hall was ajar, and the sign read, "Enter here for Madame Celeste." Swallowing her unease, she pushed the door open.

The room felt nothing like where her circle met. Whereas Lucia's space was filled with light and the soft scent of lavender, this space was cold, a bit damp, and smelled strongly of sage. Normally she loved that smell, but in here it was doing a poor job of covering up the smell of damp cardboard and old clothes, making her gag.

It was so dimly lit that she didn't even see the woman at first. As her eyes adjusted, she could see the outline of a figure seated at a small table, an antique lamp casting an amber glow over the room. Simple bookshelves lined the wall, and crystals hung from the ceiling. She hesitated, wondering if this had been a bad idea. But then the woman spoke, in a voice as soft as butter, saying, "Don't worry, I don't bite. My name is Celeste. Come, sit down. It's alright."

She moved closer, sitting down in the soft chair across the table from the woman, silently trying to reassure herself. If she didn't relax, this would be pointless. "Give me your hand, dear," Celeste said, and Iris pushed aside the sense she was in some two-bit sideshow from the 1800s.

"I'd rather . . . I mean . . . do you need to hold my hand? Can't I just sit here?" Her hands had been grasping the arms of the chair, but now she shoved them in her pockets protectively. Her fingers brushed against the silver disc she'd bought. 'Believe,' it had said. She took a deep breath, trying not to cringe at the stench. *Alright*, she thought, extending her hand. *I'll believe.*

"You're worried about something," the psychic began. "I can tell it's something major—is that right?"

"Yeah," Iris gulped. "It's pretty major." Her voice quivered annoyingly. She took another deep breath, willing herself to calm down. *Please let this not be like Philip,* she silently prayed as she fought the urge to pull her hand back again.

Madame Celeste continued, "I get the sense you've been looking for something, and that is why you've come to see me." From there, she spent the next few minutes fishing for information. She was conversational and friendly, and Iris felt herself reluctantly drawn into the conversation, revealing that her worries were not about children or a spouse, nor were they about politics or world events. When the woman asked if it had to do with her work, Iris flinched.

"Ah," the woman said. "Your work has been worrying you, I see. You are worried about retiring, aren't you." Not waiting for a response, she added, "You are young. Don't waste your time on such worries. Retirement will come when it comes."

Iris tried to make sense of what she was hearing. She was thinking of retiring in a way, at least from mediumship. And it had been worrying her. If Madame Celeste was seeing it, did that mean she was supposed to quit? Destroy the paintings and abandon the work?

The next words made her break out in a cold sweat. "You're being given a blank slate," the woman said. "Take the opportunity presented to you by it. Your fortune is about to change."

Iris sat forward, expectantly, to better hear what came next. Only the woman seemed to have nothing else to say. "Tell me about the blank slate. What does that mean? What am I supposed to do with it?" Iris asked. "And what do you mean by fortune?"

"It's not for me to say," the woman replied, releasing Iris's hand. She sat back in her chair and crossed her arms over her chest. Iris waited, hoping for more advice, but the woman remained silent, gazing dismissively down her nose at her.

"Is that all?" Iris asked. "Is that all you're going to tell me?" She was nearly frantic inside, needing to know what this all meant. The woman didn't answer but instead reached into her robe and produced a card, which appeared to be an advertisement for more sessions. After handing it to Iris, she said simply, "Thank you. Please come again," and rolled her chair backwards, disappearing into the curtains.

Outside, the sky had cleared, and the sun was bright, blinding her as she walked out into it. She began to walk, hoping the movement would stop the feeling that she might quite literally fall apart, right there on the street. She needed to get to her hotel, to be alone, inside, and away from the commotion of the Manhattan streets.

She tried to recall the things Jeremy and Lucia had taught her, remembering that psychics merely read your energy—they don't communicate with spirits as a medium does. The fishing for answers had been irritating but not particularly harmful. It was the rest that was bothering her.

She was worried the psychic had been correct, and she was trying to find out what she should do next. The problem was the whole 'blank slate' thing. What did that even mean? Did she mean the paintings she was planning on painting over? Did it mean she was doing the right thing? And what about the opportunity and good fortune part? Maybe the spirits were telling her it was the right decision.

Trying to focus on the positive, she thought about what it might mean to be given a blank slate. What might there be for her if she did let go of the mediumship? Had it been a distraction from something else, perhaps? Maybe that something else was the opportunity and good fortune Celeste had been talking about.

Setting aside the sense she had that the psychic had been a bit of a charlatan, she began to feel maybe coming to New York had been a good idea after all. Turning the corner, she stumbled upon a little pizza joint she remembered from her college years. Her stomach grumbled, reminding her all she'd had to eat since breakfast was a candy bar.

The pizza proved to be a mistake. It tasted as good as she remembered, dripping with cheese and just the right amount of sauce. But as she sat at a little table in the corner beside an old pinball machine, memories of Michael came flooding back. He'd loved playing pinball, and since he had so little money during medical school, many of their dates had been to places just like this. They'd sit and eat a slice or two, then play pinball until the quarters ran out.

What am I supposed to do, Michael? She asked it in her head, somehow trusting he would answer. She turned her attention to her mind's eye, trying to picture Michael there. She could see his face, but only dimly. She heard nothing but the pinball machine behind her, pinging as a couple of kids took a turn at it. With a sigh, she picked up her bags and headed back to the hotel, hoping they'd have her room ready by now.

Disappointed in her inability to bring Michael's spirit to mind at will, she returned to the idea of the blank slate. For some reason, she couldn't get it out of her mind. A fresh start must be what she needed. But how many do-overs did you get in life? Hadn't she left these very streets to find out who she was? Who was she, anyway? Maybe she wasn't meant to be an artist after all.

No, that wasn't right. It couldn't be right. Her gut clenched at the thought of giving up her studio, her clients, her brushes and paints and . . . canvases. She had to give up those canvases. She had to paint them over. And if that meant giving up her career completely, well, she'd done that. She could do it again. Good fortune awaited her, isn't that what the psychic had said?

The storm clouds had come in with the sunset, and a downpour soon followed. Even with the streetlights and traffic signals, the streets felt dark and foreboding. She ducked into a corner bodega, hoping to grab an umbrella, a toothbrush, and some crackers to settle her stomach. *Maybe a hot cup of coffee too*, she thought, as she lowered her hood, shivering as the raindrops hit the floor.

Behind the register, the display of magazines she expected had been replaced by rows of scratch-off tickets and lottery machines. A wave of nostalgia washed over her. So much had changed since she'd left New York. Most importantly, it wasn't home anymore. She thought of the little sandwich shop in Lakeview and the bench on the hill above town, hoping it would still be the refuge it always had been once she walked away from the mediumship. Would Lucia still be her friend? Would Ruby ever forgive her? She rubbed her arms, hoping to dispel the chill that had settled in.

A gentle cough from the cashier reminded her of what she was doing. "Sorry, just these," she said as she pushed her items across the counter. Her mind returned to what Madame Celeste had said about good fortune and opportunity *Maybe she would be okay,* she thought, as she stuck her card into the little machine.

As she waited for it to process, she stared mindlessly at the rows of scratch-off tickets. The cashier noticed, asking if she would like some of those too. "Cash only," he added impatiently.

Her stomach lurched again, and a shiver ran up the back of her neck. Maybe that was what the psychic had meant. Here she was, with an opportunity for good fortune right in front of her. Hadn't she just been hoping things would be okay? Why else would she have come in here? If she won, maybe she could give up painting altogether, and that would take care of the houses for good.

"I'll take one of each," she said firmly, reaching again for her wallet. She accepted the pile with a shaky hand, stuffing the stack in her bag. This was exciting. She never gambled, and maybe lottery tickets weren't serious gambling, but it was something new. She needed something new, and these tickets might be just the . . . ticket.

She would later try to blame it on tiredness. The drive had been long, and the nap in her car insufficient. She hadn't had enough water, the pizza wasn't very good, and it was raining. She didn't want to blame herself for being stupid, so she blamed everything else. Even— especially—Madame Celeste. Sitting on the bed in the hotel room, surrounded by dozens of losing lottery tickets, she began to cry. She felt like a fool. Nothing she was doing was making any sense anymore. If she couldn't even recognize a bad psychic, what business did she have being a medium? She just wanted to go home.

She pulled up in front of the small white house, the light in the living room a welcoming beacon in the dark. She waited a moment—just long enough to see Alice walk by a window—before getting out of the car. She hadn't been here since their mom had died. The house was exactly the same, right down to the crooked mailbox to the right of the door. Her fingers trembled as she reached for the bell, and her face begin to quiver. It took all the effort she had to freeze it into some sort of a smile as she waited for her sister to answer.

"Iris?" Alice asked, pulling the door open wide. "Are you alright?"

She couldn't hold the tears back any longer, collapsing into her sister's arms the second she crossed the threshold. All of a sudden, it was all too much for her to handle. She wanted her mom, and Alice was the closest thing she had to her.

She'd always hated how much her sister had tried to mother her. She'd rebelled against it strongly and had even thought she hated her sometimes. She definitely resented being told what to do. But now, sitting on the couch in her mother's old living room, a cup of hot chocolate in her hands, and her grandmother's old quilt over her shoulders, Iris realized she'd been wrong to keep Alice at arm's length.

"Do you want to tell me about it?" Alice asked, so softly that she almost didn't hear her. She didn't want to, especially after she'd been told not to trust psychics and then had gone right ahead and done so, but she knew she'd feel better if she did.

"I didn't listen to you; I'm sorry. And I feel so stupid." Alice didn't react, didn't criticize, so she kept going, explaining about the psychic and the lottery tickets.

"So, how much did you blow on those tickets?" Alice asked.

"About two hundred dollars," she answered, feeling her face flush. What a waste. She'd need that money if she quit painting, and she had absolutely nothing to show for it. "I'm sorry," she added, not knowing why she was apologizing for it.

Alice merely nodded, staring into her own mug for what felt like a very long time. "Was it fun?" she finally asked. Iris flinched. Of course it hadn't been fun. "The scratching off the tickets, I mean. Was it fun hoping you'd won a lot of money? I always thought that would be, but I'm too much like Dad—too much of a cheapskate."

She thought about it. She had been excited, especially with the million-dollar ones. "Yeah, I guess," she answered, her mouth twitching as she remembered how she pictured everything she'd buy when she struck it rich. It had been fun in the moment. "I'd never bought a lottery ticket before, either, you know. I guess Dad's influence runs deep."

There was a photo of her parents on the coffee table. It was at some party when she was young. They were laughing at something and looked exactly as she most liked to remember them. She picked it up, examining their faces and recalling the sound of their laughter. Alice reached for the photo, and then, as if in echo of Iris's thoughts, said, "I miss hearing them laugh."

"Me too," she said. "You remind me of Mom when you smile, you know. Your forehead crinkles like hers did." Alice feigned insult at the reference to her age, looking down her nose at Iris in anger. She couldn't hold it, though, and the tension in the room broke as the two dissolved in laughter.

They'd talked for a while after that. She didn't tell her everything, especially not about the paintings or the practicing she'd been doing. But she had been scared, and lonely, and missing her parents and Michael so strongly since it started. She would have thought she'd be missing them less now that she knew spirits were real, but the opposite was true. She missed them more.

It was nice being back in the house her mother had lived in for so many years, even though it was now full of Alice's stuff. There were little things of her parents around, like the mug she was drinking out of, but it wasn't until she went up to her old bedroom that she saw the old house as she remembered it.

"You kept it like it was!" she cried as she walked in and sat on the bed. She could remember lying in this bed, her mother sitting beside her until she fell asleep, tears of grief still wet on her cheeks. The photos on the wall reminded her of happier times, too, when she'd stayed there on visits after moving away. Over the dresser hung one of her first paintings, of the view from the back porch of the bridges over Long Island Sound.

"There was no reason to change it," Alice said. "Nobody ever stays in here, and I figured maybe someday you'd come visit." There was a hitch in her voice that made Iris look up. Her sister had aged, and she seemed smaller, somehow, than she ever had before.

"I'm sorry. I don't know why I never did. I just . . . got busy, I guess." She shrugged helplessly, then motioned for Alice to sit down beside her. "I just wanted to be my own person, and being up in Lakeview let me do that. I should have come down. I really am sorry."

"Things change when you get older, Iris. I've never come to see you either, have I," Alice said. "I'd like to, if that's okay."

Iris felt safe for the first time in days. "I'd like that too," she said. "Maybe in the spring, once I've cleared out some things, so you have a place to stay." The thought of clearing out reminded her of her original errand, and she shivered. There would be work to do when she got home.

They spent another day together, going through old photos and catching up on so much of what they'd missed in the last few years. She hadn't realized how much she missed being taken care of by someone. When she packed up to leave, she felt a surprising regret she couldn't stay longer.

The ride home was far more pleasant than the ride down had been, but it was also far more time to be alone with her thoughts than she needed. She thought of her sister, already older than her dad had ever been, and the idea of hurting her caused a renewed surge of grief and worry over what could have been.

When she reached the turn for Great Barrington, she hesitated for a split second before putting on her blinker and turning off the highway. There was a parking spot in front of the art supply store. With grim determination, she bought what she needed and got back on the road toward home.

CHAPTER 34

Ruby sat looking at her phone, willing it to give her a sign that Iris was okay. She had called her as soon as she made the reservation but had gotten no answer. When two days later she still hadn't heard back, she went by the house to check. It was closed up tight. It wasn't like Iris to just up and leave without a word.

She was excited to finally be going home, but that excitement was dampened by her increasing worry something had happened to Iris. That worry only increased when she ran into Lucia.

"Have you heard from Iris?" Ruby asked. "She's usually good about returning calls, but I haven't heard from her in a couple of days. Has she been by your place at all?"

She hadn't been, and when Lucia's face began to mirror her own growing concern, it was clear something must have happened. "She's not home, and it's just not like her to take off without saying anything . . ."

Lucia didn't respond right away. She bit her lip, looking off to the side with a frown. Something had definitely happened. Ruby resisted the urge to grab her arm and shake her into responding. "Lucia, what happened? Why do you look like you did something wrong?"

Lucia snapped her head back around, looking at Ruby directly. "Nobody did anything wrong, at least not that I know of. It's just, well, she was a little bothered when she left here the other day. I was going to ask her about it next week."

"What do you mean, bothered?" Ruby asked, her eyes narrowing as she clenched her fists.

Lucia fingered her necklace nervously. "Oh, I'm sure it was nothing! She just seemed quiet . . . or . . . worried when she left. But I didn't see anything unusual happen. It probably has nothing to do with that at all."

Ruby thought it was likely it had everything to do with what had happened there, and now she was more worried than ever. "Let me know if you hear from her," she called as she turned to head back to Iris's place.

Rounding the corner, she was relieved to see a light on in the kitchen. *She's back. Thank God.* She closed her eyes, took a deep breath, and allowed some of tension she had been holding to release.

As she waited for her friend to answer the door, she tried to look relaxed, swallowing the lingering worry still residing in her gut.

"Hey, Ruby. Come on in," Iris said, quickly turning her back as she walked back into the kitchen. She sounded flat, resigned, and tired. It was as if the spark in her had gone dim.

"Are you okay?" Ruby asked, peering around the room, hoping for some sign of what was upsetting her friend. "You didn't return my calls, and I saw your car was gone. Everything alright?"

"It's fine. I just needed some supplies and to clear my head," Iris answered while walking away again, this time into the living room. She curled up on the couch, pulling a blanket up over her knees. Even from the doorway Ruby could see the dark circles under her eyes, stark against her pale skin.

The concern Ruby was feeling must have been evident on her face because Iris shook her head as if clearing away cobwebs, then added in a stronger voice, "I'm fine, Ruby. Really, I am."

She even smiled, though it didn't quite reach her eyes.

"Iris . . . " she started to say, but stopped when Iris bristled, putting up a hand as if to say, *enough.* Ruby focused on her hands, unsure of what to do next. She didn't want to push, but clearly Iris was hurting. *What on earth was going on?* she wondered.

Iris cleared her throat, seeming to realize she was being rude. Her face softened just a bit. Ruby hesitated, unsure how to respond without driving her friend back into whatever this mood she was in was. What the heck was going on?

"Come on," Iris said, getting up from the couch, "Help me get this stuff up to the studio, and I'll make a pot of tea for the two of us, okay?"

She accepted the deflection and reached for the box nearest the door. "What's in here?" she grunted as the weight of the box stopped her short.

"Primer—sorry, I should have warned you!" Iris exclaimed. "There's two gallons in there. Be careful."

"What are you gonna do—paint the whole house over?" Ruby gasped as she picked up a can in each hand.

"Something like that," Iris murmured.

She stiffened, the cans of paint suddenly feeling even heavier. What did *that* mean? Something was still up. "What did you say?" she asked, instantly regretting that she sounded like a scolding old schoolmarm.

Iris flinched. Her voice cracked as she answered, her eyes shaded once again. "I said, yes—the studio needs a refresh." Then she reached for one of the cans of paint, grabbed the brown bag of supplies in the other, and headed out the back door without a look back.

Following Iris into the studio, Ruby immediately noticed the box by the door filled with sketchbooks and several empty spots on the wall. With an ache, she realized what was missing. The houses, which Iris had been openly displaying for weeks, were gone. And there in the corner, as if thrown there hastily, was a pile of canvases.

Ruby's attention moved from the pile to the blank spots on the wall, then to the cans she was still holding in her hands. Primer. She set them down gently.

Iris turned away and began unpacking her supplies, keeping her back to Ruby.

"Iris," Ruby said.

There was no response. Iris stood there, trembling ever so slightly.

"Iris, look at me. Please."

Iris thought she had a firm hold on herself and on the decision she had made over the past few days. She would cover over the houses and get rid of the sketches and anything else related to mediumship. That last word carried a painful energy, and she fought to hold back the tears that rose with it. She glanced around nervously before turning to face Ruby.

"I'm done. Done. With all of it. I'm going back to my normal life and normal friends. I had a g-good time in New York, and it reminded me life is more than lakes and mountains, and it's a lot more than imaginary buildings and imaginary encounters with dead people." She avoided Ruby's eyes, afraid if she looked her in the eye, she would lose what little composure she had managed to muster.

"N-none of it is real," she added, her voice cracking once again. "And none of it is good. I just want to be normal again, okay?" Her eyes swept the room, looking for anything to settle on other than the concerned face of her best friend.

Ruby listened and tried to find a piece of what Iris had said to start with first. She didn't know where any of this was coming from. Worse, there was a creeping dread her grandmother's house and the events that had unfolded since Iris had painted it put her soundly into the category of "not-normal" things.

"Am I a normal friend?" she asked, the weight of the question heavy in her chest.

Iris flinched.

Her heart sank. She was right. She was one of the things to be done with. Time seemed to slow down as she waited, powerless to change what Iris was thinking.

"It's not you," Iris finally explained, "But you are a part of it—like it or not. This mediumship stuff is nonsense, and it's dangerous. I mean it. I'm not going to play around with something that might get someone hurt. I won't do it. I'm too sensitive, and my imagination gets out of control. I was stupid to think this was something good."

Ruby's mind scrambled to make sense of what she was hearing. "Wait a minute. Are you telling me you think Jeremy's a bad guy? Or Lucia? You think *they're* doing something wrong?" She shook her head as if that would make Iris's words settle into something understandable. "I don't get it."

Iris ran her hands through her hair and let out a long sigh, her eyes distant, as if focused on something far away. "I don't get it either," she admitted, seeming to waver a bit. "They're both great. It's just . . . mediumship isn't something to play around with, and that's what I've been doing—playing." She returned her attention to the room as she added, "And when you play with fire, someone will get burned."

"Who got burned, Iris? What happened?" Ruby could feel her pulse quickening, the urge to help her friend—or pummel whoever hurt her—rising up like a pot about to boil over. "Did *you* get hurt?"

Iris put her hands over her face and slowly slid to the floor, her back against the wall. Unsure of what else to do, Ruby sat down across from her and let her cry.

After a few minutes, Iris sat up, adjusting her sweater and wiping her face. She gave Ruby a weak smile and reached out a hand, squeezing it in reassurance.

"Do you want to tell me what happened?"

Iris nodded, then began evenly enough, recounting what had happened in the circle and her phone call with Alice. She seemed to be deliberately trying to keep her voice light, but every so often, a bit of tremulousness intruded, shattering the façade she'd crafted.

Ruby didn't interrupt, just nodded at appropriate times, letting her compassion show on her face. It was only when Iris told her about the phone call with her sister that she began to lose her composure. She slapped her hand over her mouth to try to contain what was clearly an inappropriate reaction.

She wasn't fast enough. Iris's eyes widened in horror as she asked, "Are you laughing?"

She tried to lie, but the muffled "no" came out like a snort. She turned away, taking a deep breath to try to calm the eruption of laughter threatening to burst forth. When she turned back, Iris was staring at her, beet red and clearly furious.

"Ruby, it's not funny. I was really scared!" Suddenly Iris was on her feet, heading straight for the box Ruby had seen by the door. She picked it up and turned it over, cards and sketchbooks scattering across the floor. "I'm not kidding about this," she shouted, her voice reverberating in the small space. "I should have listened to Alice in the first place and never gotten mixed up in this stuff!"

She kicked the box, a bit too hard, and it skittered across the floor, striking Ruby in the side. "Ow!" she muttered, rubbing her arm a little more than it needed. Iris stood by the door, hands over her face in horror. "I'm so sorry—are you okay?"

"I'm fine, but what the heck is going on? I'm sorry for laughing—I didn't mean to upset you. It's just you're always telling me what a scold your sister is. You say she acts like she's your mother. You never listen to her. It just struck me as funny you would let her get under your skin so much about this." She could see she was getting through. Iris was listening.

"How is it you let her convince you this time? This has all been so beautiful, and exciting, and affirming, hasn't it? Why does her opinion matter so much now?"

Iris sighed and came back over to sit on the floor. "It's what Philip said, I guess. He told me my mom wanted me to call Alice. He said she was happy I understood. Only Alice was fine, and I felt like an idiot. And I realized this is not some game—real people can get really hurt. And I just don't ever want to be the cause of that—for anyone."

"Come on. You could never hurt anyone, especially not on purpose." She paused, making sure Iris was listening. "And I don't know Philip, but I imagine he wasn't trying to hurt you either."

"That's just it. I still got hurt." Iris reached for a tissue and wiped her nose. "And I didn't even tell you about New York yet."

Oh God, what now? Not wanting to upset Iris further, she joked, "Let me guess, you decided self-flagellation was the answer, so you went to see your sister."

Iris wiped her hands on her jeans and cleared her throat. "Well, I did go see her, but that wasn't the bad part." She paused, as if deciding whether to continue. "The bad part was I blew a couple hundred dollars on lottery tickets . . . after I went to see a sketchy psychic."

"You what?" Ruby exclaimed, not sure if she should laugh or cry. The friend she knew didn't even like buying raffle tickets from the Boy Scouts. "Did you win anything?" she asked, thinking it the most obvious question.

Iris fidgeted with her bracelet as she answered softly, "I didn't even win a dollar. I mean, how is that even possible? Everyone wins a dollar sometimes, don't they?" Her voice trailed off as she slouched down a bit more, still not looking up.

Ruby didn't know what to say. Even by the standard of all the strange things they'd experienced in the past six months, this was odd. She was the impulsive one, not Iris. Iris was always so levelheaded and calm. She held her breath, waiting for the other shoe to drop.

"The thing is," Iris said. "I was so sure I was going to win. There was this psychic, and she told me I'd have good fortune." She handed Ruby the silver disc, explaining how it all seemed like a sign. Only it wasn't. "She told me I was a blank slate, or I was going to find a blank slate, or something like that. But she wouldn't tell me anything else when I asked her to explain."

"I'm confused," Ruby said. "You were all upset about what Philip said, so then you went to some psychic in Manhattan and followed her advice? Why would you do that? I thought what he said scared you."

Iris closed her eyes, rubbing a finger between them. "I was scared," she said, her mouth barely moving. "I guess I just thought maybe spirit was trying to help, and I should listen to all these signs. I thought the blank slate meant I should paint over the houses, and maybe stop painting altogether." She opened her eyes, pleading for understanding.

"When I realized I had just blown all that money on nothing, I got even more scared. I finally decided being alone wasn't helping, and so I drove out to see Alice. She was great—honest," she added. "And then I drove home, stopping only to get those paint supplies we brought up here."

Something was nagging at Ruby's brain. There was something Jeremy had told her last summer that might be helpful, only she couldn't quite bring it to mind.

"It's too risky," Iris said. "Alice was right. There are people out there using this stuff to take advantage of people, and that really scares me. But was scares me more is I could have hurt you if things had turned out differently with the painting. And that would kill me—to hurt someone I care so much about."

That was it. Fear. He'd told her if she was afraid, her perception might be off, like it was in those first days after the medium told her about her grandmother. Iris was clearly terrified.

"But you didn't hurt me, I promise." She took a deep breath, hoping she would remember this right and not cause more harm than good. "Jeremy said you shouldn't make decisions when you're scared. Do you think that might be what happened in New York? Because none of the things you're telling me about this psychic make much sense. I don't think a blank slate means what you think it does, and I've seen those little silver discs in every gift shop in the Berkshires. And I wonder if she says those things to a lot of people. It all sounds pretty generic to me."

She could see something was getting through. Iris had stopped fidgeting and was paying attention. "You didn't do anything wrong, Iris. You were scared and looking for answers, I think. Only you looked in the wrong place. I wish you had come to talk to me. I think I could have saved you some grief. You see, the reason I came over was to tell you I'm going to Wisconsin, to see my parents. It will be my first time back since high school, thanks to you."

The change in Iris was almost instant. She sat up straighter, her eyes brightening, a smile spreading across her face. "Oh, Ruby, that's wonderful . . . right?"

Ruby stood up, reaching a hand down to Iris to pull her to her feet.

"I promise you, Iris. It's a good thing. And you are a good person. Okay?"

Iris sagged, looking up to the sky. "I don't know about that . . . "

Grabbing Iris by the shoulders, she pulled her into a hug. "You are the kindest, smartest, best person I know. I promise." When they stepped back from each other, Iris seemed happier, her tired face a bit brighter.

"What are you going to do now?" she asked, with a motion toward the pile of canvases in the corner.

"Don't worry. I won't destroy them . . . " Iris said, her voice trailing off as she reached the door, holding it open so they could both walk through.

The hesitation in Iris's voice told Ruby they weren't through this yet. "Will you give Jeremy a call, or talk to Lucia about what happened at least? I just don't know enough to really help."

Iris nodded. "Hey, you have helped, thank you. I'll go see Lucia. She's probably wondering why I didn't show up to circle last time. When are you leaving?"

"Tomorrow," she answered. "I was afraid I'd chicken out, so I booked a flight for Friday."

"That's good, Ruby. I'm really happy for you. And thank you—for everything. I couldn't ask for a better, or more normal, friend."

CHAPTER 35

The next day, Iris sat in her studio, gazing at the spots on the wall where the paintings once hung. She tried to keep her conversation with Ruby in mind but instead kept coming back to what Alice had said, and what had happened in New York. What if it was a sign? What if she wasn't meant to be doing this stuff?

Suddenly, she was right back into the vicious mind-circle of questioning herself. For every "it's a good thing," she slapped right back with, "someone could get hurt." There were two sides warring in her head. She wanted so much to believe it was as good as it had been until last week, except last week had happened, and she was still worried.

She needed to stop looking at the pile of paintings in the corner. She also needed to stop sitting around worrying. There were plenty of old boxes in the garage. She grabbed a couple, piled the house paintings inside, and dragged them into the closet, setting the two cans of paint on top. Maybe out of sight would be out of mind.

It was now late afternoon as Iris headed out into her garden. The November sun was low in the sky, and the light through the trees created a pattern on the grass that called to mind the lake and the day she and Ruby had sat on the cliff talking about her childhood as the sun danced off the water below. Ruby had been so comforted by the message she had received from her grandmother. The memory lifted her spirits, and she smiled, only to have a cold breeze bring her uncomfortably back to the present.

Looking up at the sky, she suddenly shouted in frustration, "God, what do you want me to do with this?" A blue jay hiding in a nearby bush startled at the noise, flapping furiously as it flew up to a safer perch in the oak tree. She glanced over her shoulder, hoping no one else had heard. Feeling chastened, she spoke again, this time in a normal tone of voice, "I don't have it in me to always wonder if I will help or hurt someone, God." Finally, she whispered, "Please, help me to know what to do."

The last rays of sun disappeared behind the hills. Shivering at the darkness, she headed inside, left her key on the table by the door, and curled up on the couch. On the wall was the painting she had done of the church, with the light glowing from within. As she gazed at it, a warmth spread through her body. Comforted, she reached for a blanket and closed her eyes.

Before she could fall asleep, the phone rang. It was Charlie. She hadn't heard from him in months, but the sound of his voice always lifted her up.

"It's been a while," she began. "What's going on?"

"Well, Andre is out in the kitchen making dinner, and I've got the evening off, a fire in the wood stove, and a dog at my feet." She could hear the joy in his voice. They had been married less than a year, and she had never seen him happier.

"You're making me jealous here. What a life you two have got!" She laughed when Charlie didn't argue with her, then added, "Do you ever wonder what Michael would make of all this?"

"He'd be flabbergasted," Charlie said. "He was always trying to reassure me the world was changing, and that I'd find love one day. I didn't believe him. Well, I believed him about the love part. I had enough crushes to know I *could* love—just not about the marriage part. He never saw the roadblocks I did."

"It's funny. He never saw them for me either. He was always so optimistic." She wondered briefly what he'd say about the house paintings and how scared she was these days, but she kept it to herself, instead adding, "I sometimes wonder where I'd be if he hadn't died. I like to imagine him here in this house sometimes, but at the same time, it's hard to see it, you know?"

Charlie laughed softly. "Yeah. I've been thinking about him too, for some reason. I was cleaning out some papers and found this postcard he sent me one summer. As I read, it was as if he were right here talking to me again. God, I miss him."

Iris swallowed the lump that rose suddenly in her throat. "Yeah. Me too."

"So that's why I called. I was thinking about him, realized we haven't talked in a while, and wanted to check in. How are you?"

She pinched the bridge of her nose, grateful this wasn't a video call. She really didn't want to talk about herself right now. "I'm fine. Just painting and trying to pay the bills. You know, usual stuff, nothing special." Usually, she was much more skillful at steering conversations and would have turned it back to Charlie. Today she was still too rattled.

He tried again. "So, who was that guy with you and Ruby at the restaurant last summer?"

At first, she couldn't recall what he was talking about, then her mind found the memory. "Wow. We really haven't talked in a while! His name's Jeremy. I met him at the fair last summer. He was in town for a few months, and we got to be friends. He . . . "

She paused, not sure how, or if, to continue. She didn't even want to talk about herself, much less get into the whole issue of mediumship and spirits. When her voice trailed off, Charlie jumped to the wrong conclusion.

"Good friends, huh? You keeping something from me, Iris?"

"It's not like that. Honest." She hoped he didn't notice the whine in her voice.

"So why the hesitation? What's up with this guy?" Charlie could be stubborn and wasn't going to let up on this line of questioning. Still unsure how to answer, she paced slowly around the room, stopping in front of a table covered with pictures. She picked up the one of Michael, taken the year before he died.

Charlie kept pressing, but gently. "Let me guess. He's Ruby's boyfriend, and you're jealous."

Iris laughed. "Ha! No. That's not it."

The glass in the frame was filthy, and she slid the photo out so she could clean it. As she did, a scrap of paper fluttered to the floor. She picked it up and set it on the table next to her keys, only then noticing the words standing out like a neon sign: *Be who you are.* Michael's card.

Holding the card in her hand, she realized Charlie was still talking.

" . . . take you out to dinner next week?"

"I'm sorry, what did you say?" Iris asked.

"I was asking if I can take you out to dinner next week. I hate talking on the phone because I can't see what you're doing when you don't answer. Are you okay?"

"Yeah. I'm fine, just distracted. That sounds great. I do have something I want to tell you, and it will be much easier in person." She was smiling now, no longer interested in cocooning on the couch.

"Great. I'll pick you up Wednesday at seven," Charlie finished before wishing her goodnight.

As she hung up the phone, it occurred to her that Charlie might just be a bit psychic too.

Back in the kitchen, she picked up the pile of mail she had left there earlier. It was mostly ads, as usual, but one caught her attention. It was for the Sanctuary, the retreat center where Jeremy had worked. These ads came from time to time, but she had never paid them much mind. Today, something about it made her take a closer look. As she read through the brochure, it suddenly became clear what she needed to do. She called the number on the back, threw some clothes into a bag, and within an hour, was gone.

CHAPTER 36

The parking lot of the Sanctuary was long and narrow, wrapping around the building that rose above it on the crest of the hill. The lights from the windows glowed warmly above, beckoning her to come inside. Her decision to drive up here had been made so quickly that she needed to take a couple of minutes to settle herself before actually walking in the door. The image on the cover of the brochure featured a stone archway, with a valley shining in the light of the setting sun visible on the other side. The image was what had called to Iris as she imagined herself walking into something light-filled and beautiful.

But it was the title of the workshop that really grabbed her attention. "Moments of Grace." There was that word again—grace. It came to her just when she needed it, every time. It had felt like an answer to her whispered prayer.

The promised stone archway stood just to the side of the main entrance. Though the sun had long since set, the sky was a deep, inky blue. The reception area was quiet, and empty. She craned her neck to peek around the corner, hoping this had not been another mistake. In the next room, a young woman sat at a small table, eating dinner. She jumped up, hastily wiping her mouth on a napkin as she apologized.

"Oh, sorry—I wasn't expecting anyone else," she said.

Iris apologized, explaining about the last-minute decision and late registration. Dinner had already begun, and the guests were in the dining room. She was directed down the hall and encouraged to eat before heading to her room. "Meals are communal here, so if you don't go now, you'll have to wait until breakfast."

The room was noisy with conversation, the tables fully occupied, save for one. A woman waved her over to the empty chair beside her at a table by the window. The other seats were taken by two young couples energetically chatting away. They paused long enough to say hello, then turned back to one another. A young man sitting alone at the end of the table tipped his head kindly in greeting but didn't say a word.

There was a meeting after dinner—an orientation of sorts—and as they introduced themselves, she learned the guests were a mix of ages and backgrounds, some seeking inspiration and others simple peace. When asked to introduce herself, she held up the brochure and told them she came to see what was on the other side of the archway, keeping the rest of her reasons to herself.

"The structure of this weekend will be a mix of formality and ease," the host announced. "Each morning, we will have a guided meditation, and I ask all of you to please attend. It will help you to enter into the day fully present to what is here for you. Afterwards, you are free to sit longer in meditation, take walks on the many trails outside, nap, read—whatever seems to draw you in. I will be offering opportunities to talk about what you are experiencing, and I will be leading a couple of mindful hikes on both Saturday and Sunday mornings."

Iris had never done anything like this, but the man's soothing voice and the idea of a mindful hike had her both intrigued and incredibly relaxed. The next bit confirmed her sense this weekend was meant to be.

"The goal of this workshop, as you might have guessed, is finding moments of grace. More precisely, it is about making space for those moments to appear. I ask you to be open to what comes, allow yourselves to do what feels right inside of you, and above all else, take care of yourselves. This weekend is about *you* and taking care of *you*. I think we can all agree that is something we don't do often enough." There was murmured agreement and a spattering of laughter through the room. Iris willed herself to relax and take it all in, but her fidgeting fingers made clear she was both nervous and excited for what the weekend would bring.

She went up to her room and was pleased to see the crescent moon rising just outside her window. The window was impressive, reaching almost to the floor. She realized that with the lights out, she could even see the stars from where she sat. As she meditated on the view, her thoughts returned to the paintings and the mediumship work in general. She just didn't know what to do, and every option she thought of made her feel terrible. Discouraged yet feeling strangely peaceful, she climbed into the large, comfy bed and was asleep in minutes.

The next morning, Iris arrived early to the meditation room and found a seat in the back. Feeling rested and with her thoughts clearer, she reflected on the talk the night before. "Be open to what comes," he had said—and "take care of yourself," too. That last bit seemed more important for some reason, and she resolved to listen. It was a relief to be in a place where everything was provided, and all she had to do was be. She offered a silent prayer of thanks for the brochure that had appeared so fortuitously.

They had guided meditations in Lucia's circle, and she expected this to be much the same. In fact, it was quite similar, although much longer, and by the time the hour was up, a deep inner calm and sense of wellbeing had settled in. The biggest difference was whenever they meditated in the circle, it was in preparation for practice communicating with the spirit world.

When this meditation ended and there was nothing more asked other than to spend her day as she wished, she was almost giddy. With a start, she realized that this time, the meditation was for her and not for anyone else. The sense of being hugged returned, and she allowed the feeling to move through her. It was as if she was being wrapped in a warm blanket. She recalled the previous day when she had curled up on the couch in need of comfort. This was so much better.

The mindfulness walks turned out to be a nice break. As they walked, they were encouraged to pay attention to what was around them, noticing every sound and sight, with the intention of keeping memories of the past and worries about the future at bay. It took some work, but each time she reached a state of complete lack of concern about anything other than the world in front of her, the relief was like falling into a cloud of feathers.

Returning from the riverside path, she rounded the corner at the entrance to the property, stopping to take in the view. The building was made of large granite stones, with archways formed above the windows and doors. Out in front, the gardens had not yet been cleared, and the last of the perennials were trying to hold on for another day. She moved closer, sitting down on a bench by the side door. As she had been taught, she moved through her five senses, trying to be mindful of everything around her.

Resisting the temptation to imagine the garden as it must have been in the summer, she marveled at what was still in bloom. The roses were the biggest surprise. They were brilliant red and as fresh as they must have been in June.

Listening, she could hear the rustle of critters in the leaves covering the ground. One particularly brave squirrel stopped in front of her, as if showing off the acorn in his mouth. They sat there, eyes fixed on each other for a long time, until in a flash, he skittered away.

The sun was warm on the back of her neck, even as the wind made her wish she had grabbed a hat. That same wind carried with it the smell of winter. Someone had a fire going somewhere, and she could just catch the smell of rotting apples from the orchard across the way.

Wanting to see if the rose still held its scent, she reached quickly to bring one toward her. Her hand recoiled automatically as her finger was pierced by a thorn. *Well, I guess that takes care of all five*, she thought as she sucked the injured digit, noting the metallic taste of blood.

She headed inside to tend to her finger, thinking there just might be something to this mindfulness thing. She hadn't realized how much her brain needed the rest until she got to the end of the day and noticed she hadn't thought about mediumship or home at all. At dinner, the others at the table spoke softly to themselves, leaving Iris and the young man to eat their meal in silence. Surprising herself, she didn't feel left out but rather grateful to be left alone. *I could get used to this*, she thought, savoring each bite of the gourmet meal.

Sitting in her room on Sunday morning, she gazed out over the hills, marveling at the deep pinks and purples of the sunrise. Being present had its benefits. She was calmer than she'd been in days. Still, she had a decision to make and knew she couldn't put it aside completely.

Setting her shoulders as if for battle, she took out her journal and wrote "Mediumship" across the top of the page, then drew a single line from top to bottom. On one side she wrote "What Is Good," and on the other, "What Is Bad." She had resolved to solve this problem like she used to, using logic and lists. Now she'd see what her bottom line would be.

She stared at the page for a few minutes, feeling the unease begin to creep up her spine. *This won't do.* She ripped the page out and tossed it in the trash. *Start from the premise that it is good.* It was something Jeremy had taught her once about discernment. Starting from the expectation everything is good takes fear out of the equation. She started again. "Reasons to Continue" and "Reasons to Quit." This was more objective, and she began to fill in the lists.

The reasons to continue began as a list of people: Jeremy, Lucia, Ruby. She added joy when someone is recognized and excitement at bringing someone peace. Wonder. That sense of awe at what she saw, and what she created, and what others understood from what she was seeing. Ruby again—and how she had been able to open up about and begin to heal from her past. Recalling what had happened at home the other day, she added Michael to the list.

On the quit side were also some names: Philip and Alice. She added fear, worry, stress, and doubt. Doubt was a big one, because it made the other things worse. When she began to remember why she was afraid, a trembling started deep inside. As her breath began to come faster, she turned to the mindfulness lessons she had learned and focused her eyes on the beam of sunlight shining on the middle of the walnut floor. Feeling calmer almost immediately, she sat back and examined the list.

Okay, Jeremy had told her to think about how she felt with each option. She read over the reasons to continue, and at first, she was filled with a sense of serenity, and love. But when she thought of the people on the list, she was filled with sadness thinking about how hurt they would be if she quit and also how terrible she would feel if she said something to hurt any of them. The sadness was stronger than the serenity, so she ascribed the former to this list and wrote "sadness" at the bottom of the column.

Turning to the quit list, she was again filled with sadness as she read through the names and the worries. But then she remembered to breathe, and the act of letting go left her feeling strangely happy. It was as if a weight were lifted, and she could breathe again. "Peace" she wrote below the second column. Closing her book, she set out for one last walk before dinner, trying not to think about what awaited her at home tomorrow.

When she sat down to dinner, her silent tablemate suddenly found his voice. She hadn't gotten two bites into her dinner before she heard, "You've decided something, haven't you."

"I beg your pardon?" she said, looking at the young man and wondering if he was talking to someone else. He sat there, calmly looking at Iris as if they had known each other for years. Without hesitating or looking the least bit uncomfortable, he continued. "So, what is it? What did you decide?"

Though initially taken aback by his directness, she answered him truthfully. "I'm a m-medium . . . or I'm becoming one . . . or . . . something like that, but I've changed my mind. I've decided to give it up and just go back to being an artist."

"And is it a good thing?" he asked. "I mean, are you happy? Because you seem decided, but that's not the same as being happy."

She didn't know what to make of this suddenly inquisitive and oddly intimate conversation, but rather than end it, she found herself engaging. For some reason, she believed she could be open with him.

"To be honest, I feel like I've lost a part of who I am." As she spoke the words, she realized just how true they were. Afraid she would begin to cry, she bit the inside of her cheek while reaching for the basket of bread, seemingly intent on selecting the perfect roll.

He continued to look at her, not saying a word. Feeling his gaze upon her, she began speaking to fill the space. "I thought this was a good decision—I worked so hard all day to make it." Seeing the kindness in his face, she decided to show him her journal and the table she had made. He glanced at it patiently, as one would with a small child's schoolwork, and said, "So your table there helped you make this decision?"

She was beginning to wonder where this was going, but nodded.

"Tell me how you feel again?" he asked, his face a genuine mask of compassion and understanding.

"I feel lost, or like I've lost something. But it doesn't make sense." She pointed again at her list. "The reasons for quitting are so much stronger than the reasons for continuing. I don't know why I feel this way. The thing is, it has been so nice being taken care of this weekend. I didn't have to worry about anyone getting hurt, and there weren't any houses or faces or voices cluttering up my brain."

"You had a break, then?"

"Well, yeah, I guess." Her lips twitching in amusement.

"It sounds to me like you needed one," he said, his eyes serious. "Tell me again what you decided."

Across the room was the large window facing the fields. It was fully dark now, so she couldn't see anything but the reflection of the room in the glass. She knew there were walking paths out there, which called to mind the painting she had done when she first met Jeremy. She could see the mountains and the traveler on the road, and its meaning suddenly became clear. It was she who was on this journey.

Feeling the light fill her heart, she allowed it to show in her face. "I'm not gonna quit," she said. "It's who I am, and I could no sooner give this up than give up my name or my identity." She leaned back, pleased at the sound of her own words.

"Now how do you feel?" her persistent new friend asked.

"Really lovely—like everything is right with the world."

And as she said it, she knew it was true. And what Jeremy had taught her about discernment suddenly made sense. This feeling, the immediate one she expressed because this strange young man had asked her so unexpectedly, was the true one. Everything else came after. He was smiling at her now.

"Just remember to take some breaks when you need them, okay?"

"Thank you," she said.

Then, as if his work was done, the young man turned back to his meal and didn't utter another word. He waved kindly at her as she got up to leave, and she walked away realizing she had never even gotten his name.

CHAPTER 37

"Do you believe in angels?"

Charlie paused, the bread in his hand halfway to his open mouth. Setting it back down, he reached for his glass of wine instead. Iris focused on her own roll, carefully spreading the butter as if she were being judged on how precisely she did so. She could feel his eyes on her as she waited for his response.

"You mean like the angels in the Christmas story? The heavenly host and all that?"

"Well, yes and no," she answered. "I mean, like actual angels, right here with us. Do you think that's a real thing?"

"I've never really thought about it, I guess. But if they existed two thousand years ago, why not now?" He peered at her over the top of his glass, eyes kind but curious.

She nodded. "That's what I was thinking too. It's logical, right? If you believe the stories in the Bible, I mean." She took a sip of her own wine, savoring the taste of it for a moment. Charlie seemed to sense she was still talking and waited.

"You know I was raised Catholic, right?" she asked.

"Sure. I mean, Mike used to go to mass, so I figured you did too." He paused for a moment, seeming to be remember something. "You stopped going after he died, right?"

"You remembered," she gulped. She wondered if the grief was as clear on her face as it was on his. Michael was on both of their minds tonight, and painfully so from what she could see. "It didn't make sense to me to go. I hated it all so much after the funeral. And then once I lost the habit, I never went back."

"Is that what you wanted to talk about? Church?" He sat back, narrowing his eyes and looking straight into her own.

"Not church exactly," she said. "It's just that you're the only person I know who still goes to mass, and since I don't know any priests anymore, you're the closest thing to one."

He cleared his throat uncomfortably but held his tongue. He was listening, and she was grateful she had decided to talk to him. He was her oldest friend, and she trusted him completely. They each took a bite of bread, letting the act of eating cover up the long stretch of silence.

"What do you think happens when we die?" she finally asked.

He shrugged. "We go to heaven."

"I'm sorry. I know you believe that. I guess what I'm asking is, do you think that when people die, their souls hang around us? Do you think Michael—or my parents—are still here?" She waved her hands around in a circle as if stirring the air.

"Absolutely."

She was momentarily stunned at the certainty in his voice. "You're that sure?"

"Of course. I've always believed in heaven. Haven't you?" He seemed genuinely surprised she was asking.

She took a deep breath, hoping she wasn't pushing too hard on a topic known to cause not just arguments, but wars. "I don't know. Sort of, I guess. I know it's what we learned growing up, but for a long time, I didn't believe it at all. And then, last summer, something changed."

He raised an eyebrow in question, but the dinner arrived, and she had to wait to respond. Grateful for the distraction of the meal, she let the conversation drift into other things until Charlie brought it back to where it began. "So tell me, what changed last summer?" he finally asked.

Over the course of the next hour, she recounted everything that had happened, up to and including the retreat and the mysterious young man who had helped her.

"Your angel," he said.

"Do you really think so? I mean, there was something about him that was different for sure. But an angel?"

"Well, why not?" he asked. "Like I said, if we believe it happened back when the Bible was written, then why not now? I don't think God stopped talking to us somewhere along the way. It sounds pretty smart to me, to use someone unexpected to deliver you such a helpful message."

Hope began to rise within her like the steam from a warm bath. Setting down her coffee, she asked, "Then you think this is a good thing?"

"Mediumship, you mean?"

"Yeah. I mean, sometimes I think I'm nuts to believe in it. And then, well, take the other day. Just before you called, I was yelling at God, asking what I was supposed to be doing. I was just doing it because I was so frustrated and scared, but then you called. And Michael's note fell out of the frame, and I found that flyer, and the angel guy was there . . ." She stopped when he put a hand gently on her forearm.

"And so maybe God did answer you," Charlie said, so softly it was almost a whisper.

She kept her eyes focused on her hands, fiddling with the napkin in her lap. "Maybe?"

"Let me tell you a story. I think it will help." He leaned forward, setting his plate aside and folding his hands on the table in front of him. She sat back, eyes focused on his face, her heartbeat slowing in peaceful curiosity.

"When I started at college, I was supposed to be an engineer. My family was really supportive, and I had it all planned out. I wanted to work for NASA and build rockets. Only by junior year, I was so bored, I started skipping classes—the second week. The thought of doing that work for the rest of my life was beginning to feel like a prison sentence.

"But I had signed up for this art history class as an elective, and everything changed. I adored the class and thought the professor was the most amazing person I had ever met. By the second semester, I had signed up for five art classes and changed my major. I had to do an extra year, but to me, it was worth it.

"When I was making the change, I needed some advice. I couldn't talk to my parents. They were so proud of the engineering stuff. So I went to see Fr. Paul, one of the theology professors, instead. My faith was really important to me, even then, and I wanted to know if he thought I was doing what God wanted me to do. He asked me, 'Charlie, is this choice to pursue art bringing you closer to God or turning you away from God?'

"I thought of the time I was spending in galleries and museums and in studying the works of artists like Michelangelo. I was outside in nature or sitting in art galleries any time I wasn't studying, and I was just so happy. I felt closer to God than ever before. What Fr. Paul said next is something I will never forget . . . "

"Don't keep me waiting; what did he say?" Iris quipped.

"He said, 'Then it's good,' just like that. 'Then it's good.'"

"Really? He was that certain?" she asked.

"Yup. As simple as that. He didn't hesitate for a second, and I knew he was right. Now, Iris, I will ask you the same thing. Is mediumship bringing you closer to God or drawing you away?"

She thought of the little church in town, and "Amazing Grace," and the retreat house. She recalled her conversation with Ruby up on the rocks above the lake and the joy she saw on Jeremy's face when she told him his wife was beside him. "Closer, without a doubt."

"Then I'd say continue with it. It sounds like you are doing a lot of good for people. If you keep your heart fixed on what is good—what feels like love—then you'll know you are using these gifts you have in the way they were intended."

He sat back, his fingers forming a steeple over his mouth, the edges of a smile peeking out. "Thanks," she said, reaching across to squeeze his hand. "A priest couldn't have said it better."

CHAPTER 38

Lucia was in the window of the shop setting up a Christmas display when Iris approached. She had been hoping to find Lucia there early, before the shop opened. The retreat and visit with Charlie had taken the worst of the uncertainty away, but there was still the matter of what had happened that day in the circle. As much as she felt reassured she was doing something good and worthwhile, she *had* been hurt, and she *had* made some bad choices because of it.

She tapped on the window, and Lucia jumped, turning around with her hand over her heart. Her face was tight in anger or surprise but softened instantly when Iris gave a gentle wave of greeting. She moved to the door as Lucia climbed down, motioning for her to come inside.

Another layer of fear melted away as she allowed Lucia to pull her into a warm hug. The store smelled of cinnamon and pine trees, her friend of coffee and peppermint. She breathed in, letting the scents fill her nose, bringing with them feelings of home and holidays and love.

She pulled back, but Lucia held onto her shoulders, holding her at arm's length and looking straight in her eyes. "How are you?" she asked, making clear this was more than just a greeting.

"I'm good," she answered as firmly as possible, hoping Lucia wouldn't notice how nervous she was. Pulling away, she began to finger some of the pretty items laid out on the counter.

"We missed you last week. Were you sick?" Lucia asked, in a tone suggesting she was a fragile piece of china, likely to break if she spoke too sharply.

Iris shook her head, turning back around to face her friend, determined to get through this. "I had decided not to continue, Lucia. I'm sorry. I should have called."

Lucia raised her eyebrows but otherwise maintained her air of openness and calm. "Is this because of something that happened the last time we met? You seemed bothered when you left."

So much had happened since then that she didn't know where to begin, and instead stood there, helpless in the face of the enormity of it all. Lucia smiled warmly, touching her on the arm. "Come, sit down, and let's talk."

As they walked to the back of the store, the familiar scents of lavender and sage rose from the various bowls scattered among the shelves. She took a deep breath and felt herself calm just a bit. "Let me make us both a quick cup of tea," Lucia offered as she disappeared into the office. When she returned, she lit a couple of candles on the table, handed Iris a steaming mug of tea, and sat down beside her.

"*Dime*, Iris. Tell me. What happened the other day? I know I can help."

She nodded and proceeded to explain what had transpired during the circle that day. The lavender and chamomile were having the desired effect, and she was able to calmly recount everything Philip had said. Then, at the end, she added, "I called my sister last week to make sure she was okay."

Lucia raised an eyebrow in question.

"Oh, she's fine—there was nothing wrong at all." She tried to look convincing. The concern on Lucia's face told her she hadn't succeeded.

"Ruby came by looking for you last week," Lucia said. "She was worried about you."

"I know she was." Iris poured herself a bit more tea, intently watching the liquid swirl around in the cup. "I saw her when I got back from New York, just before she went away. We talked about what happened, and I'm a lot better. But I hadn't been sleeping well, and I just didn't know what I was supposed to be doing. I'm really sorry I didn't come." She looked up, eyes pleading for understanding.

Lucia met her gaze and held it for a moment. "Listen to me," she said, waiting for her to nod in agreement. "It sounds like after talking to your sister, you realized what Philip told you wasn't accurate. Am I correct?"

She nodded half-heartedly, looking off to the side with a shrug. Her anger at Philip had dissipated, but it was not completely gone. "I don't know. I mean, I know he was wrong, but I don't understand why he said what he said. Some of it must have been true. He wouldn't just make it all up, would he?"

Lucia took a sip of her tea, then set the mug down. "No," she said. "Philip is a good kid, and he wouldn't intentionally make something up. I remember how happy he was, so I do think he thought he did a good job."

Iris knew her friend was trying to help, but for some reason, this was making her feel less settled, not more. She gripped the warm mug in both hands, staring into its depths, trying to keep the fear at bay. He had been happy? Couldn't he tell she'd been a mess? Why did spirit let this happen? She wanted to run, to get out of the store, away from the feelings rising up inside; but a gentle hand on her knee made her stay.

"Iris, listen to me. This is important. Spirits, our loved ones, and our helpers, won't ever tell us anything to scare us or hurt us or make us feel bad about ourselves. They won't ever do that—they love us too much. They are love, and love doesn't try to hurt people, okay?" Iris nodded, sipping her tea. She was listening.

"Now, the things Philip told you about your mom, did all of them make sense?"

She shook her head. "No, he had it wrong about what she did for work, and I told him so. Then he said my sister was beside me, which didn't make sense because she doesn't live near here. We hadn't seen each other in person in years."

"Did he describe your sister to you or just say she was your sister?" Lucia asked, her face beginning to brighten into understanding.

"He asked me if I had a sister. He said there was a woman standing beside me. When I said I did but she was living, he began to talk about our estrangement. I hadn't thought of it that way, though. We get along fine; we just aren't close because of the big difference in our ages."

Lucia was now nodding softly to herself. "What did he say to you next?" she asked.

"He gave me a message from my mom. He said she wanted me to call my sister. He said she was happy he had given me the message." Iris lifted her hand helplessly, acknowledging in the gesture both her uncertainty with what he had said and her lack of understanding of how she could have responded differently.

Lucia sighed. "Iris, do you remember when we talked about the difference between an evidential reading and a psychic one?"

"I think so. A psychic reading is when the medium connects with the sitter's energy, and an evidential reading is when they connect with spirit, right?"

Lucia nodded. "Yes, and with any medium, it can be easy to slip into a psychic reading when the evidential reading feels like it has gone cold. You told me Philip got the information about your mom's work wrong, and you told him so?" Iris nodded. "And you told him your sister was living, too?"

"Yes," Iris answered, understanding starting to blossom. "But I didn't want him to feel bad, so I tried to accept what he was telling me. You think it wasn't really my mom, then?"

"Oh, I think he had your mom there. The first evidence he gave you made sense." Lucia gave her a reassuring look. The tension she had been holding eased a bit.

"I think he may have begun to read psychically when you told him you couldn't take some of the evidence. He is relatively new at this, and it happens when someone gets nervous. They let their mind enter into the reading, and they pick up energy from the sitter, and sometimes it can end up creating a whole narrative that isn't accurate. Were you upset when he mentioned your sister?"

She stiffened as she recalled how she had thought her sister might be dead. *Damn, it was painful.* "What I don't understand is why he saw Alice if she's alive," she asked.

"Well, first of all, I'm not convinced he saw your sister at all. Second, I think he may have picked up on your fear and misinterpreted it as having something to do with your mother and the connection he had. I think he took that and began to try to interpret your energy and mixed it up."

Iris shivered, setting her tea down with a shaky hand.

"He wasn't trying to hurt you at all," Lucia said quickly. "I'm sure of it. But I do think he was trying to make what he was seeing make sense. And he even imagined a smile on your mother's face as a way to validate to himself he had done a good thing. Only he hadn't. Sometimes a medium will see a living person, but that doesn't mean they are dead or dying. And there should be a reason they are being seen. A good medium will give you that reason."

Iris was struggling to take all of this in. "So in other words, he wasn't seeing we were estranged at all, which is why the message wasn't true either?"

"Exactly. I don't think anything after the woman at your side appeared was accurate. My advice to you would be to let it all go. Tell yourself it wasn't accurate, because it wasn't."

Now she wanted desperately to know why her mother had been there. Did she have something she wanted to say? Anger flared again at the sense that Philip had not only terrified her, but he'd kept her from hearing from her mother—the person she wanted more than anyone to be there right now.

"Iris, is it okay if I do a reading for you now to see if we can make sense of this?" Lucia asked, seeming to read her mind.

She fairly melted with relief. "Yes, please."

They sat quietly for a moment, then Lucia nodded to herself and began to speak. "Okay, I see two people here, and I get the sense they are together. The man is quite young, maybe only about forty, and the woman is maybe twenty years older than him. They are holding hands, so I do think they are a couple. He tells me you look just like him, so I believe these are your parents. Does that make sense to you based on what I described?"

She nodded. "Yes, those are my parents. My dad died young." Lucia held up her hand to stop her from saying anything more. "Don't feed the medium, remember?" Iris laughed, feeling the energy lift as she did so.

"They are showing me a woman now, but she doesn't seem to belong to them. What I mean is, they are holding hands and clearly together, but she is standing off in the distance. I can't see her face clearly, but they are both looking right at her and smiling. I think she is important to them, just not family. Now I see the woman, and she is up on a cliff of some sort, just sitting and looking really peaceful. That's the only way I can describe it—she is just peaceful and very happy."

The recognition was instantaneous. "That's Ruby! I know exactly where she is. But why are they showing me her if she is alive? You said there would need to be a reason for it?"

"*¡Claro!* Of course! Let me see why they are showing her to me." She paused momentarily, eyes focused off in the distance.

"Your mom is handing me a gift, wrapped up in a red bow. I asked if the gift was for you, and she seems to be saying yes, and now I'm seeing Ruby again. Something beautiful is happening—she has this gorgeous warm light around her."

The excitement in Lucia's voice was contagious. The energy, too. The warmth Lucia was describing spread through her body, leaving the impression they were truly not alone there.

"I'm hearing your dad say, 'It's a gift.' No . . . wait, let me clarify, '*You are a gift,*' he is saying. It has something to do with Ruby. I think that's why they are showing her to me. Does this make sense?"

She wiped tears from her cheeks and cleared her throat. "Yes, it makes so much sense. Ruby's been right beside me since this whole mediumship journey began." She thought about where Ruby was right now, allowing a surge of hope to surface. Maybe what had happened really was bringing healing to her friend. "I think the gift is the mediumship, but also Ruby, and maybe . . . even me?"

Lucia clapped her hands together, clearly delighted. "I think you have it exactly right, Iris. You *are* a gift to others, and mediumship is a true gift that will help so many people, if you let it continue to unfold. Now, how does this reading make you feel?"

"It feels wonderful—lovely and comforting." She would almost swear she could feel her parents there with her, the love was so strong.

"Which is exactly how you know this one came from the spirit world. You feel lovely and comforted, which is how it will always be when spirit speaks to you. If you ever get a reading that makes you afraid or edgy or uncomfortable, it means it's not from spirit. Forget about it. It's going to happen sometimes. It's why we practice—to learn when it does. If you don't mind, I'd like to talk with Philip and explain this to him so he can learn from it, too."

Iris exhaled in relief. "Please do. He was so sweet about it and so excited when he thought he had gotten the message through. Make sure he knows I am not upset with him, will you?"

"*¡Claro!* Now give me a hug so I can get back to my window and get this store open on time."

CHAPTER 39

Ruby pulled onto the street where her childhood home still stood, and the memories come rushing back. It had been years, yet the neighborhood hadn't changed much at all. Houses lined one side of the road, and open fields ran along the other side, sloping down to the river below.

She stopped to gaze out over the valley, getting out of the car to get a better look. She was at once excited to be back, yet nervous at seeing it all again. Her stomach fluttered, and she realized it really did feel like butterflies were flying around inside. She thought of Iris. *Excitement and fear really do feel the same.* Still, between the landscape and the memories of her childhood, Ruby knew it was more excitement than anything else.

On the far side of the river, farms stretched out, their farmhouses visible in the distance. The fields lay fallow for the winter, yet they were beautiful in their tidy, tucked-in appearance. They would be as ready as they could be for spring planting next year.

With a deliberate effort, she located the farthest house from view, the one just across the little green bridge over the river. It was where her grandparents' house had once stood. Even though there was a new house and barn on the property, Ruby's vision was suddenly filled with an image of red flames in the night. She wondered if it had been wise to return.

Yes, it was wise. You are ready for this, she told herself. She thought back to the painting and the mediumship demonstration and found comfort in the healing she had found through those things. "And you can't change what was, but you can change how you live now, and how you see the future."

"Wise words, sis."

Not realizing she had spoken out loud, she turned to see her brother Craig stepping up onto the roadway. Long accustomed to spending time in the woods, he moved almost silently through the brush. He grinned at his sister, pleased to still be able to surprise her, and she laughed. As he leaned down to give her a hug, she realized she had forgotten how tall he was. His hair was just starting to go gray, and she noticed he still kept it very short to keep it from catching in the leaves as he prowled the woods.

"Where did you come from?" she asked.

Smiling, he pointed down the hill. "My place is just around the bend there, up a ways from the river. You knew that, right?"

Embarrassed at her failure to realize the address was so close to their old neighborhood, she shook her head. "I never made the connection. Sorry."

Thankfully, Craig didn't tease her for it, seeming to sense how fragile her emotions were. Instead, he asked about her flight, and they got caught up in recent goings-on in both their lives. While she had not been home since high school, she hadn't been out of touch, so it was remarkably easy to settle back into their old patterns of banter.

Pointing at her hiking shoes, he said, "Those should last you about an hour in the woods around here. Guess we'll have to let you borrow some boots."

"You think I'm going walking in the woods with you? You'll have me up and down the hills, pulling bugs out of trees all day." She pointed toward the house. "I'm staying inside where it's warm."

"Oh no, you're not! Frank and I have plans for the week. You'll see! And I wasn't kidding about the boots."

She scuffed her feet nervously, feeling suddenly like a fish out of water.

"Hey, sis, don't worry. Sophia's boots will fit you fine. Come on."

Craig climbed in the car with her for the short drive to the house. As they pulled into her parents' driveway, a wave of nostalgia washed over her so strongly that her hands shook as she set the handbrake. Craig reached over and gave her a kiss on the cheek. "Don't worry—it will be like you never left. Mom's so excited. Once you get inside, it will all feel a lot better."

He was right, as he always was. She marveled at how sensitive her brother was beneath his rugged outdoorsman exterior of steel-toe boots and a flannel shirt. She was grateful he had met her before she got to the house. It allowed her to ease into it all and made the last bit easier to handle.

"Well, look at you!" her dad said as she walked up onto the porch. "Looks like you never left the place." She looked down self-consciously, taking in the jeans and heavy sweater. Despite the apparently inadequate shoes, maybe she did look like she belonged there.

"It feels like I never left, but also like a lifetime ago." She stood with her hands in her pockets, staring at the floor, feeling every bit like the teenager she was when she last stood in here. "I'm sorry I never came back."

She still wouldn't look up, but when the tears began, seeing them roll down her own cheeks was simply too much. She gazed into her mother's now swimming eyes and, in an instant, found herself solidly wrapped in her parents' warm embrace. They held each other for a long time.

"Come on, there is coffee on the stove," her mom said. "You must be tired from the trip."

In a matter of minutes, she found herself snuggled onto the couch, steaming coffee in hand, muffins on the table, and a warm fire at her feet. Frank had arrived, and his kids and their cousins sat on the floor, with toys and games scattered around. It was good to be home.

CHAPTER 40

"Here Mom, need a hand?" Ruby reached down to help her step up onto the rocky ledge, but her mother batted her away.

"I'm not an old woman yet!" her mom exclaimed. "I've been walking around these quarries for forty years, Ruby. I know them better than you." As evidence, she neatly stepped around the rock ledge, using well-worn steps Ruby hadn't even seen.

"Well-played!" she laughed.

They had come to the park Ruby had so loved as a kid. Trails wound around and through the woods, following a river and climbing up to a large quarry lake. It had been their swimming hole in the summer and a skating pond in winter. Seeing it now, Ruby realized with a start how similar this place was to the rocks around the lake back at home. "I didn't realize how much I missed this."

They stopped at a viewpoint, and her mother sat down on a large rock. She patted the seat next to her, encouraging Ruby to join her. "Isn't it beautiful? A month ago it was gorgeous, with the aspens and maples in full color. But I love the way it looks now. There's still a touch of color on the oaks, and with all the other trees bare, you get to really see the landscape." Pointing off to her right, she indicated a rundown old building. "See that? That's where the quarry office was when I was a kid. It closed long before you were born, but when I was a kid, this was nothing like it is now. Did I ever tell you?"

"You did, Mom, when I was little. Gram used to tell us about it too. I remember coming up here sometimes. She'd show us how they used to transport the stones down the river." A wave of longing rushed over her, and she added, "Gosh, I miss her and Gramps."

The two were quiet for a bit, the only sound the rustling of the wind through the old oak leaves and the occasional hiker going by on the path behind them.

"I've really missed this place," Ruby said again.

"Then why haven't you ever come back?"

The question hung in the air between them. Rather than answer, she picked up a handful of rocks and walked to the edge of the ledge. She began tossing them into the lake below, one by one. *Come on*, she said to herself, *you've come this far. Just say it.* And yet the words stayed fixed in her throat.

Grabbing the branch of a tree growing out the side of the cliff, she slid down the little worn path to the ledge below. The next rock she tossed landed just a bit away from the edge, making an unsatisfying clunk on the rocks. The second one was better, landing with a little splash further out. Suddenly, she heard a loud plunk and saw a small geyser splash up far out in the lake. She jerked her head up just in time to see a second stone soar over her head and land in the same spot.

"I told you," her mother called. "I've been coming here a long time. Nobody's better at tossing stones in that lake than me. You clearly need practice."

"I'll have to work on it," she said as her mom climbed down and took a seat next to her. A hawk flew overhead, and she heard the screech of its mate calling from across the lake.

"I'm sorry, Mom."

"I'm sorry, too, for whatever made you feel so bad."

They sat again in silence, neither wanting to break the spell. Up here, where they were invisible to all but the geese and eagles, it was almost as if time had stopped.

"Do you ever wish you could go back and fix something you did wrong? To make it so it never happened?" She stared out over the water, seeing not the rocks of the quarry but the glow of flames in the valley. This was proving to be even harder than she had expected.

"All the time," her mom replied. "I wish I could bring my parents back. Do you know they were the same age I am now when they died? And I was only a few years older than you?"

She turned to look at her mom, thinking how young she appeared. "I never realized that. They were always old to me."

"To a child they were, but to me, they were just getting to the point where they were really living their lives. Your gramps was getting comfortable letting go of the farm, and Gram had convinced him to take her to Europe. She never thought she'd convince him, but she did."

Ruby cocked her head, thinking. "It's funny. I don't remember that trip. Where did they go?"

"They didn't. My dad got sick, and the cancer took him fast. Then I think it just took a toll on her. She stopped living, in a way, and then after the stroke, she just gave up. Can you imagine, giving up at sixty?" She put her hand up to shield her eyes from the sun, looking around at the landscape around them. Like Ruby, she seemed to be seeing what wasn't there.

"I was too young to be alone. My parents had died, and I wasn't ready for it. But I had your dad, and you and your brothers, which made me happy. So, I decided I wouldn't let anything stop me, or you, from living life the way we wanted." She paused and pointed to a deer walking up on the ridge. "I never regretted letting you go, Ruby. I missed you, but I never regretted letting you go."

Ruby stood up, suddenly needing to move. The stillness was suffocating, and she needed air. Her mom caught up to her at the next overhang, standing and staring off into the distance.

"What did I say?" she asked. "Aren't you glad I let you go? I thought I did the right thing."

She sighed. "It's not that, Mom. You couldn't have kept me here if you tried. I couldn't stand it, seeing their old farm just sitting there rotting in the snow. It was just too hard." She picked up another handful of stones and started tossing them into the water, not aiming at anything in particular, but hitting the same rotting log several times.

Her mother reached out, touching the sleeve of Ruby's jacket. "What are you seeing? Tell me, please." Ruby blinked, and breathed, and turned to face her mother.

"The fire, Mom. I look out at those trees and all I can see is the fire." She stopped, took a deep breath, and continued. "Did you know I was able to see it from my room?"

Her mom turned away, steadying herself on a rocky outcrop. "I didn't know that, sweetheart. I had no idea. I'm so sorry. I never knew." When Ruby didn't respond, she continued. "I'm sorry. I'm sorry we never talked about what happened. You were so young, and we thought it was better to just let you forget about it." Turning back to face her daughter, she added, "I think maybe we were wrong."

"You weren't wrong, Mom. I don't think I would have talked about it anyway. I was so afraid of how angry you would be with me. And then you never were. You never got mad—at least not about that night. And I never understood why. I deserved it—why weren't you mad?"

Ruby was moving again. Being so close to her mom, and recalling those days, was more than she could take. She climbed higher. When her mother found her, she was seated on the ground, her back against a large tree.

She hadn't thought to bring any Kleenex, and her sleeve was now wet from wiping the tears from her face. For a moment, she felt just like a lost and scared ten-year-old again. Her mom seemed to see it too and sat down across from her saying simply, "Tell me." And then she waited.

"That night, Mom, I watched the whole thing. I could see the fire from my bedroom, but I knew Dad and Gramps were there. I was sure they would take care of everything. Only they didn't. They couldn't. Dad didn't get there in time . . . " Ruby snapped the stick she had in her hands in half. Her mother jumped.

"I heard Gramps say the phone was busy." She turned her face to her mom, allowing the shame she felt to show. "He couldn't get through, and it was my fault! I left the phone off the hook on the porch, and they couldn't get through. The neighbors needed to come get him, and it took time. I was so stupid, and because of me, they lost everything. How come you never yelled at me for it? Why?"

Ruby watched her mother closely through her tears. She seemed to be holding her breath, her hand over her chest, and for a moment, Ruby worried she was having a heart attack. But then she seemed to come to a decision, as if she wasn't going to let herself lose control. She took several deep breaths, and Ruby could see the change as she relaxed just enough.

"There's something I need to tell you about that night, sweetie, but I want you to promise me you will listen to everything I have to say before you interrupt me. I've been holding this in a long time, and I want you to hear all of it." Ruby sat still, willing herself not to look away.

"Absolutely, without a doubt, this is *not* your fault." She had taken hold of Ruby's hands as she spoke, and she held them firmly as she looked directly in her eyes.

Ruby was listening. These were the words she had heard back in Lakeview, and she had tried to believe them then. Oh, how she wanted to believe them now.

"You were ten years old. Ten. Like Craig's little girl. You were not to blame, and I never did blame you. That's why I never got angry. There was nothing to be angry about."

"But the phone," Ruby said. "I saw you hang it up before I went back upstairs. You knew I had left it on the porch."

Her mother started to roll her eyes but caught herself. "You left that phone all over the house, all the time. Sometimes it was on the couch, or in a closet, or on the porch. Your brothers did the same thing. It was my routine, every night, to find it and put it back where it belonged. I learned from the boys not to waste my breath scolding—it was easier to just do it myself. But the night of the fire, I forgot. I was reading and got tired and just forgot. If anyone was to blame, it was me, not you. Ruby, you were ten." She reached out to lift Ruby's chin up, as if to make sure she was paying attention.

"That guilt stuck with me for a really long time. I didn't know how I could have been so stupid. And then one day, a few months after the fire, I told your dad. I was so embarrassed, and just like you, I thought he would be angry with me. Only he wasn't angry. I think maybe you need to hear what he told me too."

Ruby leaned forward, her eyes sharp, barely breathing.

"I can still remember it, as if it were yesterday. He said, 'Elaine, don't be ridiculous!'"

Ruby was caught off guard. "You're kidding," she said. "He called you ridiculous?"

"Yes. That was his exact word. It made me mad, but then it also made me laugh. Which was good. I stopped being afraid and was able to listen to him. The fire started in the dryer vent. You know that part, right?" Ruby nodded. "They didn't have any smoke detectors, so by the time

Gram and Gramps realized there was a fire, the whole basement was in flames, and it had spread up the outside walls of the house. The only things that saved them were their bedroom being right at the top of the stairs and the dryer on the opposite side of the house.

"They managed to get out just before the fire came through the floor. Then they had to get to the neighbor's house down the road to use a phone. There were fire boxes on the telephone poles back then too, so they were able to pull one of those at least, to get the fire department there. But by the time they got to the Carvers to call us, the house was pretty much gone. Your dad couldn't have saved it even if they had gotten through. It was just too fast, Ruby. It was an old farmhouse on a cold night. Nothing could have saved it."

Ruby was seeing the fire again in her mind. She saw her grandparents, sitting there in her parents' clothes, because they had barely gotten out alive. She saw her mother quietly hanging up the phone. Suddenly, she saw it all as it had been, not as she had imagined it was. "It wasn't my fault then?"

"Nor mine. It was an accident, Ruby; nothing else. And I am so, so sorry you have carried that with you all these years. I just didn't see it. I'm sorry."

CHAPTER 41

It was an hour's drive home from the airport, and despite the cold, Ruby opened the windows of the taxi in order to feel the air on her face after a long day spent on planes and in airports. She reflected on just how far away northern Wisconsin was but didn't let it dampen her resolve to go back as soon as she could.

It had been a wonderful trip. After her talk with her mom, the strain had lifted, and she had been able to relax and enjoy everyone's company. Craig had made good on the offer of hiking boots to wear, and then had dragged her on a trek to see the most beautiful waterfall in the world. They had also seen numerous birds, an owl, and a fox den. He was her big brother again, leading his little sister around in the woods, and she happily followed along.

Frank had a new baby, and Ruby spent a large part of her visit sitting and holding him for his grateful mother. Gracie, the six-year-old named after her great-grandmother, was a very proud big sister and insisted on showing Ruby everything she knew about babies. This mostly consisted of knowing if they cried, they needed either food, a clean diaper, or a pacifier. She was very good at providing the last. Ruby had loved every minute of it.

As the taxi pulled up in front of her house, Ruby realized she had nothing in the house to eat and thought about calling to order a pizza. Stepping inside, she smelled garlic. On the kitchen table was a bottle of wine and a note. *Welcome home! Lasagna is in the oven keeping warm. Call me when you are ready. Iris.*

CHAPTER 42

"So, your mom thought it was her fault, you thought it was yours, and none of you ever talked about it?" Iris had listened intently to Ruby's account of her time in Wisconsin.

"I know—now it seems so ridiculous, but she was trying to protect me, and I was so guilt-ridden that I couldn't talk to her. It's sad, really, that we couldn't have talked back when I was ten. It makes me wonder how my life would have turned out. I might never have left home, you know."

"But then you might never have come here and met me!" Iris joked. "Isn't it funny how life can turn out so differently based on the choices we make?"

Ruby plucked a few bits of lint off her sweater, letting them float to the ground. "It makes you wonder how anyone could ever dream of predicting the future," she said. "Do you think anyone could have seen how this all turned out?"

"Gosh, Ruby. I don't know. Here, help me with this. It's heavier than I thought." She was halfway in the closet, trying to get a grip on one of the boxes of paintings she had stuffed there before she went away. Ruby grabbed the other end, and together they lifted it up into the bench.

"Have you thought about what you want to do with these, Iris? Other than hang them back up here?" Ruby was laying the paintings out on the table, admiring them as she went. "I mean, look at them. This house looks like it's way out in the woods somewhere, but then this other is clearly in the middle of a big city, and it's still beautiful. Do you know anything else about them? Any clues as to who they might be for?"

"That's just it," she said, her eyes still wandering over the array of images on the table. "Lucia and Jeremy and even Charlie all keep telling me this is a gift I have, meant to help others. It got me thinking about the houses, and you, and . . . " She shrugged. "I don't know who they are for, but I was thinking there are some clues. Some of the houses have real feelings, you know?"

Ruby shook her head, the puzzled look on her face indicating she clearly didn't know.

Iris picked up a painting of an old brick house, its windows shaded and dark with the exception of a single light downstairs. "When I painted this one, it felt really lonely, but then when it was finished, it had become hopeful. I know that sounds weird, but it's true. And I'm thinking if I share it somehow, I'll be able to match it with the person it was meant for."

Taking the painting from her, Ruby examined closely, then closed her eyes as she held it in her arms. "Nope, I don't feel anything." Sighing, she set it back down with a wink. "But I know you do. I think you're onto something. We need to find out who this painting is for. Just like me, someone needs to see it." She sat down in one of the chairs by the window and motioned for Iris to join her. "So how do we make it happen?"

"We?" Iris asked as she sat down. "You want to do this with me?"

"Of course, I do! Let me finish telling you about my trip, and you'll understand why."

Iris watched her friend speak, seeing how painful it still was, but at the same time noting a strength in Ruby she hadn't seen there before. She shook her head slightly, trying to put into words what she was seeing. Suddenly, she realized what it was. "You're not afraid anymore, are you," she said.

Ruby shook her head. "I'm not. And the funny thing is, I hadn't realized how scared I was until I started talking about what happened. I had decided years ago to just lock everything away, and if I never went back home, I would never be reminded of it again. I was wrong, obviously. Even though I moved away, and ended up here, fear was still far too powerful in my life. I thought it was all about hope—you know, the name of my school and all— and it was, but it was also fear. I'm so glad I got to talk to my mother. She won't be here forever, and had I lost that chance, I never would have gotten the answers I needed."

This was not the same Ruby who laughed off everything and boldly stomped around town in a raincoat while the sun shined. Iris had never seen her so introspective. A now familiar shiver ran up her spine as she listened, marveling at the transformation.

"I thought working with plants and things would be enough to ground me in something living. It wasn't. I thought working at town hall, seeing people all around me all day, would also help me forget the people I lost when I left home. It did, but it wasn't enough either. I want more, Iris. I just need to figure out what more is. And for now, helping you find the owners of these paintings feels like a pretty good place to start."

They sat there in silence for a few minutes, each lost in her own thoughts. Eventually, Iris stood and wandered over to the wall at the back of the studio. "Let's take everything down and hang the houses here. I want to be able to sit and look at them. Hopefully I'll get some sense of where they're meant to go."

Working together, they made short work of hanging the paintings. Standing side by side, they admired the display. "It's as if they're a bunch of windows looking out on the world," Ruby said.

Iris touched the edge of one of the paintings gently, as one would touch something precious and rare. "I wonder what they will tell us now that they are out where they can be seen." She wrapped her arms around her torso, trying to contain the excitement growing inside. Then, with equal reverence, she pulled her comfortable chair and a small table over in front of the display. She would sit with them, as often as necessary, and see what they had to tell her.

CHAPTER 43

The midwinter wind howled down the road, and Iris pulled her hood up, turning her back to the worst of it as she did. Ruby pulled the door to the store closed behind her, carefully balancing two bags of groceries in her arms. There was a storm coming, and Iris had suggested getting snowed in at her place. They'd managed to grab every bit of comfort food they could think of from the grocery before it closed.

She'd stopped at the hardware store on her way to meet Ruby, and her own bag was heavy with extra batteries and candles. The scents of cinnamon and pine escaped the bag as she lifted it up into her arms. The store had apparently had to dip into their leftover Christmas supplies to satisfy the rush of customers.

Yelping as another blast of frigid air lifted the edge of her coat, she began to hurry along the sidewalk. "Did you hear they've upped the estimate to two feet?" she called over her shoulder.

"Oh, I heard it, just before I left work. Everyone else heard it too. I still can't believe that kid shoved me out of the way to get the last jar of peanut butter!" Ruby quipped, shifting the two large bags in her arms to get a better handle on them. "It makes me laugh. They'll be back in there the day after the storm is over, wonder why the shelves are empty, and complain about it. The day after that, it'll be back to normal, like always."

Fortunately, it was a quick walk to her place. The snow was just beginning, but there'd be no slowing this storm down. It was starting to stick to the pavement, and the wind, already fierce, was picking up.

Once inside, Ruby got the fire going while Iris put together some snacks in the kitchen. She walked back into the living room just as Ruby settled into one of the cozy chairs, her eyes fixed on the nascent fire. There was something different about her—a serenity, maybe. Seeming to sense she was being watched, Ruby turned, one brow raised in question.

"Sorry. I was just thinking you look different," Iris said. Ruby frowned, touching her hair self-consciously. "Oh, no—not like that. I mean . . . there wasn't anything wrong with how you were before, it's just . . . well . . . something's changed. In a good way." She added with a grin.

Ruby leaned back, relaxing into the soft cushions. Accepting the glass of wine Iris offered, she said, "Honestly, everything's changed. Ever since I learned what happened with my grandparents, I just feel different. I never used to think I deserved to be loved. And so I worked really hard to earn it, I guess." She paused, staring into the flames, the glass of wine untouched in her hand. "I realized when I was home, they never stopped loving me, and I guess it helped me to stop trying to fill every second with noise, to prevent someone from turning on me. I'm okay with a few minutes of silence these days."

Iris sat down by the fire, reaching for her own glass. She sipped slowly, savoring both the aroma and flavor, grateful for the silence as well. Ruby's words had peeled a little of the scab off the memories of those painful days in November, and she needed a moment to calm the thoughts, which if left unchecked, might send her emotions tumbling off a cliff.

"One of the things I was so worried about last fall was hurting you," she finally said. "I didn't know how things would settle out, and I was so scared you would hate me for what I did." Resisting the urge to look away, she focused on Ruby's face, hoping she wasn't in fact hurting her now for bringing it up.

"Why would you ever think I'd be mad?" Ruby asked. Then, seeming to recall she *had* in fact been angry at first, added, "I'm sorry. That's not fair. I was—angry, I mean—but not once we talked. I was curious more than anything else, and confused, I guess, but not anymore. There's no reason at all to be angry with you, and there wasn't then either."

Setting her glass down, she began to rub her hands, joint by joint, studying them as if trying to divine something from the callouses and bits of dried paint. Ruby gently nudged her knee until she looked up.

"Hey. What you did was open a door into the past, which helped me to see what I hadn't been able to see, and what had kept me from knowing I was safe and loved. Please don't ever regret what you did,"

Ruby said. "You gave me the best gift in the world."

Iris thought of the wall of paintings in her studio, wondering who else out there needed the same sort of gift. It was daunting, the idea they could mean something to someone she had never met. She had been hoping someone would come into the studio, another friend perhaps, and recognize one of them as Ruby had. But in the couple of months since they'd been hanging there, they'd received barely a comment from anyone.

"So, what should we do with the rest of them?" she asked.

Ruby wrinkled her brow in confusion, not being privy to Iris's wandering mind. "The rest of what?" she asked as she rose to add a log to the fire.

"The houses. I've been thinking they might belong to someone like you, and if so, it's not fair to those people to keep them hidden away in my studio." She was also running out of space. She "saw" a new house every month or so, and there was no place to put the last couple she'd done. She still needed to earn a living and couldn't give up any more wall space for them.

Ruby sat back on her heels, staring into the fire, slowly tapping one finger on her knee. She stood and pulled the screen back over the fireplace, grabbed some crackers and cheese, and curled back up on the couch. "We need to go public with them," she said, as if it were the most natural thing in the world.

Iris took a bit too large of a sip of wine, grimacing as the bolus hit the back of her throat. She coughed, heading to the kitchen to grab a glass of water. Her heart was pounding. When she sat back down in front of the fire, Ruby gave her a look of calm determination. There was a notebook and pen in her lap, and Iris realized there would be no going back now.

"Public, huh?" she asked. "How exactly are we going to do that? It's not like we have any idea at all where the . . . owners . . . or targets . . . of these pieces live. Where would we even begin?" She thought about the many galleries in the area, realizing she might have to approach each one to see if they'd hang her works. But how would she decide what went where? What if she got it wrong? She could feel her mind getting ahead of her and stopped, taking a deep breath and stretching her cold hands out toward the fire.

She took a look at the notebook in Ruby's hand. The page was half-filled before she had even finished talking. Ruby was in full-on project manager mode, and she knew from experience to let it play out. Some words stood out enough to be seen from where she sat. Words like website, blog, and gallery were followed by lists and arrows and doodles. She grinned as she watched Ruby's mind play out on paper.

Suddenly, they were interrupted by the unmistakable sound of a car having trouble getting up the hill outside. The whir of spinning tires grew louder, followed by a sudden flash of headlights through the front window. They both jumped up to see what was happening, arriving at the window in time to see a small white sedan skid sideways down the hill, spin around backwards, and come to rest against the curb.

Grabbing their coats, they went out to see if everyone was okay. The driver's side of the door was partially blocked by a telephone pole the car had just barely missed hitting. Ruby pulled open the passenger side door, peering inside. She pulled her head out, motioning for Iris to take a look. "Oh no. Are you okay?" Iris asked, reaching for her phone.

Lucia, looking sheepish in an oversized hat dripping with melted snow waved her off. "I'm fine. I thought I could make it home. I got caught up at the store and lost track of time. I didn't realize the roads had gotten so bad."

"Well, come on in and get warm," Iris ordered. "You can call your husband from inside. I don't think you're going anywhere tonight."

After setting Lucia up with some warm clothes and a hot shower, Iris joined Ruby in the kitchen. Soon they had a pizza in the oven and a pot of hot chocolate simmering on the stove. Lucia came down a few minutes later, looking warm and cozy in her borrowed pajamas. "*¡Bendito!*" she cried, clasping her hands in joy. "I haven't had a sleepover in years! My kids would be so jealous if they saw me!"

There was a soft chair by the fire with a wool blanket draped across. Lucia curled up there, gratefully pulling the blanket up around her. "Paulo says to thank you for taking me in for the night. I think he's relieved he didn't have to come out and get me. He hates the snow, you know. We've been living up here since we got married, but he's never gotten used to our winters." She laughed, and then, with a wink, added, "I think it was only when I showed him how much fun it was to stay warm that he decided to stay."

"He'd be a fool to let someone as wonderful as you go," Iris said, thinking about all the times she had been on the receiving end of her friend's kindness. She set the pizza on the coffee table and offered a choice of cocoa or wine to go with it.

"Oh, wine! Please! I'm cold, but my nerves are shot from my skid down the hill." Lucia held out a hand so they could see the tremor that was still there. "Thank you again for rescuing me!"

"Lucia, you said your husband isn't used to the cold. He's not from New England then?" Ruby asked.

She shook her head as she hurried to finish her mouthful of food. "He's from Miami, but his family is Dominican. He never even saw snow until he was in college. That's where we met, and we've been here ever since."

"Is he on board with your plans to downsize?" Iris asked.

"Not completely, no. He's an engineer, and so proud of our house. He helped design it when we first had it built. But he's getting tired of the work, and I think this storm might be just the thing that pushes him to let me start finding us a little condo." Lucia's eyes sparkled as she spoke of her husband, their love clearly visible on her face. Paulo was a lucky man.

"Is he into mediumship too?" Iris questioned as she reached for a slice of pizza.

Lucia began to laugh. "*¡Ay Dios mío!* Not at all!" She set her plate down, clearly finding the idea hilarious. They laughed along with her, but Iris wasn't feeling it. *Was he just not into mediumship, or did he not believe in it at all?* she wondered.

"Iris, you've never met my husband, have you?"

She thought about it, then shook her head. She didn't even know what he looked like.

"Most people in town haven't, unless they come to church with us. He's always working, and he never comes in my shop. I've had people tell me they didn't know I was married because they never see me with anyone. I'll tell you, the first time I heard those words, it stung. I love my husband, and I never thought how others saw us."

She stopped, taking a sip of her drink, thinking about her next words. "You see, Paulo has always supported me in my work, because it matters to me. But that doesn't mean he believes in it. He loves me. He supports me. And that's okay. Truly."

"But it must be so hard," Iris said, "to know your husband doesn't support something so important to you. How do you get past it?"

"*Ay*, I didn't say he doesn't support me; I said he doesn't believe in mediumship, which is different. The thing is, Paulo prefers to go to church and believes heaven is some place we all will end up some day. He can't accept that heaven is all around us and our loved ones are right here. Believe me, I've tried to convince him. My point is, not everyone is going to believe in what we do, and that's okay too."

Iris thought about it. Maybe this was how she could explain this all to Alice when the time came. She couldn't keep it from her forever, though it still made her nauseous to even think about trying to explain everything.

"Save your energy for the real conflicts," Lucia said, "because you'll get those too. Don't worry about what everyone around you thinks. You know what is true, and maybe someday they'll see it too. And if they don't, remember, that's okay. It's a big world, and we won't always agree on how the unseen part of it works."

They sat for a moment or two, each lost in thought. A shower of sparks rose from the fire as the logs readjusted, and Ruby rose to tend to it. Sighing, Iris picked up the now empty wine glasses and headed for the kitchen. "Come on," she called over her shoulder. "We still have time to get some cookies in the oven before it gets too late."

She started pulling ingredients out of the cupboard as Ruby set up the mixer and turned on the oven. They'd done this so many times that they moved around each other effortlessly. As the cookies baked, the conversation worked its way back around to mediumship.

"I have one more question, and then I'll stop with my worrying," Iris said. Ruby chuckled, sharing a knowing glance with Lucia. Iris cleared her throat with mock outrage.

"Ahem. My question is, do you think this ever goes away?" Seeing the blank stares before her, she clarified, "The mediumship. Do you think it ever fades?"

"You mean like a rash or something?" Ruby asked.

"I mean like a talent you don't use. Will the mediumship just disappear if I don't use it?" She blushed, knowing it was probably another dumb question, but she had to ask.

Lucia thought about it for a second and then said, "I don't think so. I think you might lose the ability to understand what you're sensing, but the sensing itself I think will always be a part of you. Like a muscle, if you use it, it will get stronger, but if you don't, it will weaken in time. Is that what you mean?"

Iris tipped her head down, a little embarrassed by the question. "Well, yes and no. The reason I'm asking is I was thinking back to some of what happened last year. With the paintings and everything. When it was happening, it all felt like . . . magic. It was amazing, and exciting, and, well, lately it all feels kind of . . . ordinary to me."

Ruby coughed, choking on the cookie in her mouth. Lucia didn't say anything, but she did put a hand up to cover her mouth. Iris glanced from one to the other and finally said, "What? What's so funny?"

"Ordinary?" Ruby asked. "Painting houses of dead people you've never seen before feels ordinary? Iris, I think maybe this is even more a part of you than you realized. That certainly wouldn't feel ordinary to me. Besides, I don't think life is ever going to feel like magic all the time. Just sometimes . . . like tonight."

The next morning, the three friends stood on the front porch admiring the beauty of the snowfall before getting to the unpleasant task of digging out from under it all. The evergreens bent low to the ground, some not even recognizable as trees. The early morning sun cast a golden glow over the landscape, the snow sparkling as the rays of sunlight caught each flake. The day promised to be cold and clear, the sky a stunning azure blue. They didn't speak at first, reveling in the glorious silence of a snow-muffled town.

It was Iris who broke the silence. "It's like a fantasy world, isn't it? I don't even want to step off the porch and disturb it, you know?"

"It used to be like this all the time where I grew up," Ruby said. "Sometimes the road wouldn't get plowed for a couple of days, and we'd be snowed in at home. My brothers and I could take a sled down to my grandparents. I don't think we'd come inside for hours the day after a storm like this."

"I remember when my kids were little. There was no way we could keep it pristine for more than a few minutes after the sun was up. They'd pull on their snow pants as soon as they got up. But it was so much fun, especially when they'd make Paulo come out and play. He learned to make a pretty mean snow fort after a while!"

Iris admired the beauty she had found herself in, thinking about how different her life was from when she grew up. "There was nothing pristine about snow in the city, but I can remember one time we had this huge storm, and the plows didn't get to my street all day. The kids all went out and played in the middle of the road, and we had an epic snowball fight. Even Alice joined in, and she was in college by then. It was one of those magical days you never for—"

The snowball striking her back stopped the rest of the thought. She turned just in time to see Ruby forming the next one before handing it to Lucia. "Oh no . . . " she said, running her hand along the railing to grab her own handful of snow. "You don't know what you're starting . . . "

Ruby grinned, and Iris was so focused on her she that missed Lucia stepping down off the porch. The snowballs started flying fast and furious, Iris taking advantage of the high ground after Ruby joined Lucia by the curb. Their squeals punctured the silence of the morning, and before long, they were red-faced and soaked, the shovels forgotten by the front door. After a break to warm up inside, they finally got to work on the cars and sidewalk before finishing the morning where they had ended the evening before—in front of the fire with mugs of cocoa in hand.

"Oh my gosh," Iris laughed. I haven't done that in ages!"

"You've got a pretty good arm there, Iris—I think you maybe had more snowstorms in New York than you let on," Ruby grinned.

"I'm gonna pay for this tomorrow," Lucia groaned. You two are a lot younger than me . . . but boy was that fun!" She swung her feet up on the footstool and closed her eyes in bliss. "What was it you were saying about magic last night, Iris? Something about there not being enough of it?"

Iris laughed. "Yeah. Go figure." Looking up, she added, "Thanks universe!" bringing on another round of giggles. Seeing her friends and feeling the love in the room, she held out her mug in a mock toast, "Magic indeed!"

few days later, Iris was in her kitchen when she heard a soft knock on the front door. Opening it, she was greeted by a very large bouquet of flowers, completely obscuring the person holding them. She gasped at their beauty and rushed to take them, only then seeing Lucia smiling from behind the blooms. "*¡Gracias, mi amiga!*" she said, her smile growing broader. .

She motioned her friend inside, and Lucia followed her into the kitchen. It was early, and the tea kettle was just beginning to whistle. She poured a cup for each of them, sure Lucia would want to chat for a bit. She wasn't mistaken.

"These are from Paulo and me," she said. "I told him he should come by himself to meet you, but he had an early meeting this morning." She winked at Iris over the teacup. "He'll stay mysterious, I guess!"

"Thank you, Lucia. They're gorgeous," she said, trimming the stems and setting them into a vase of water. "Do you mind moving that painting?" she asked, motioning to the canvas covering the kitchen table. "Just lean it against the couch—I'll get it hung later." It was the painting of the barn. Iris had decided this one was for her for some reason, so she had moved it inside the day before.

Lucia admired the painting as she set it down. "I love this," she said. "Tell me about it."

Surprised by the question, Iris didn't answer right away. She was used to people interpreting her paintings themselves, or asking where they were from. She didn't think she'd ever been asked to tell someone about it. Even more surprisingly, she found herself eager to answer it.

"Have I told you about the houses?" she began, realizing quickly she had not. Lucia reached for her tea and sat down, her face open and eager.

By the time she finished, they were each on their second cup, and

Iris was feeling quite pleased with herself. For the first time, she'd told the whole story—from the red farmhouse to Ruby's story, to the cow giving birth, and not once had she been embarrassed or unsure. On the contrary, a sense of pride was rising in her, particularly when Lucia kept repeating the word, "Amazing!" as she inspected every inch of the painting, her hand hovering just above the surface.

"It has such a beautiful energy, Iris. Have you ever thought about doing portraits?"

She hadn't thought about it at all, at least not since last summer. The echo of that spirit voice reverberated in her head, and she was momentarily breathless. Then, with a start, she realized she wasn't afraid. She was curious, and deeply so. "Do you think I could? How would I even begin?"

"I would think the same way you do these," Lucia answered. "Let spirit show you someone, and then you just draw what you see. Let the sitter tell you if they recognize it or not."

"Oh, okay. The houses just come to me on their own. You're saying I do this like doing a reading for someone? Gather evidence and give it to them?" It was beginning to make sense, and a comforting heat was spreading through her like the way the hot tea warmed her up.

"Exactly," Lucia said. "I'm not an artist, but that's the way I understand it works. You are an artist, so doing the portraits shouldn't be hard. You're also clairvoyant. So I think all you need is to try. See what spirit can do with you."

It sounded right. She thought of the conversation the other evening about magic and being excited. The feeling was back, stronger than ever. This *was* right. All of it.

A week later, she had her first sitter.

<h1 style="text-align:center">CHAPTER 45</h1>

Iris sat at her easel, putting the finishing touches on a new piece. The sound of the mail carrier outside drew her attention away from her work. His truck had a distinctive rattle she had come to recognize over the years. The door closed with a metallic clank, and she heard a rumble as the truck drove away.

Deliberately, she moved her attention to the outdoors, trying to envision what she was hearing. The pavement was wet, amplifying the sound of traffic on the road out front. It had snowed overnight, and she could hear the scrape of shovels on pavement as she imagined the snow being pushed into piles and scraped off of car windows.

Drawing her attention back inside the studio, she considered all the works in progress, the growing pile of commissions waiting to be delivered, and finally, the "Wall of Wonder." That was the name they had come up with for her display of what Ruby called her spirit houses.

On a small table in the corner was the sketchbook where she had been practicing spirit portraiture. She'd been nervous before the session Lucia had arranged last month, and so had sat and sketched from memory any of the spirits who had come through during circle. They were rough but had given her the confidence to try sitting with a real person for the first time.

The sitting had been with Lucia's sister, Marta. They'd been careful not to reveal who she was until the day of the sitting, so Iris wouldn't have any preconceived notions. They might have kept it secret until the end, but when Iris saw Marta's face, she so closely resembled her sister, they never would have been able to keep it a secret.

As she had settled in with her pencils and sketchbook, Marta had sat quietly, hands clasped in her lap, an expectant look on her face.

"I'm going to begin by drawing what I see, and I'll tell you about it as I go," Iris said. "Sound alright?"

Marta nodded encouragingly. "Lucia told me I should just answer your questions and see what spirit brings through. I've seen mediums work before, so I think I'll be okay."

Iris nodded, grateful she was the only novice here. Turning to her sketchbook, she allowed her mind to still, waiting for an image to appear. Her mind filled with yellow flowers, and she began to sketch them in, filling a large bit of the page with them. She reached for her pastels, adding color to the image as she went. Suddenly, in her mind, she saw a little girl—a very small one. She swallowed the sudden wave of sadness that filled her and did what she had long ago learned to do. She began to draw what she saw.

First, there were the pigtails, pink ribbons sitting on top of the brown-haired little head. She was dressed in overalls, with mud on her hands and green boots on her feet. Iris drew quickly, knowing Marta was waiting to see what she had done. She began to tell her what she was seeing.

"Spirit is showing me a little girl, who seems older than a toddler, maybe four or five years old." Marta put her hand to her mouth and nodded firmly, tears forming quickly in her eyes. Iris turned away, letting her eyes lose focus so she could see the image in her mind, but also so she didn't have to see the tears in the face in front of her.

"She's laughing, and now I'm hearing a song. Do you remember 'You Are My Sunshine'? Does it mean anything to you?" She could see it did but needed to hear it.

"That's my daughter. She died when she was four. I used to sing that song to her every night before bed." Marta was smiling through her tears, encouraging Iris to continue.

"She's dressed in overalls, and she's all muddy—like she's been out in the garden. I think there's something about the garden, too, because I keep seeing flowers. Tell me, do you have another child—a boy, maybe?" Marta shook her head.

Shivering slightly at the negative response, she refocused, asking the spirit to try again. Once again, she heard the word "son," but this time she saw a brightness in her mind as she heard the word.

"Oh, I'm sorry," she said. "I think I misunderstood. She was saying 'son,' but I think she meant the sun in the sky, because it's what she's showing me now." She began to add beams of sunlight behind the little girl, adding a palpable warmth to the image.

Marta grinned. "Yes! She's saying her name—Soleil—but it means sun, like in the sky. That's why I sang that song to her!"

Iris laughed, silently reminding herself it only needed to make sense to Marta, not to her. *Trust in spirit*, she said to herself. *Just give what you get, and they'll take care of the rest.* Grateful for the discipline of her training, she kept going.

"Your daughter is showing me a baby carriage now. She's holding a doll and singing to it—she's singing the same song, I think. And she wants me to tell you something." She took a deep breath, offering a silent prayer that she would be as accurate as possible in conveying it. "She says to tell you not to be afraid. What happened to her won't happen again. She wants you to know it's going to be okay. And she says she'll always be there."

Iris had been staring at the drawing as she spoke, her mind blank as she let the words flow freely. As if coming back from a daydream, she blinked, her focus returning to the room. Marta was fully crying, and for a moment, Iris wondered if she had said something wrong. "Are you okay?" she asked gently.

Marta nodded, wiping her face with a tissue. "Can I see the drawing now?" she asked. Iris turned the drawing toward Marta, watching her face to gauge her reaction. The response was instantaneous and beautiful.

"*¡Bendito!* That's Soleil. That's her face, and her hair, and her muddy little boots. Those are even the buttercups we planted all around the yard after she died. *¡Ay Dios!*" she cried, touching a finger softly to the edges of the image, her other hand cradling what Iris now saw was a pregnant belly. They sat there in silence until finally Marta reached across to grasp her hand, saying simply, "Thank you."

A gust of wind rattled the windows, unleashing a shower of snow from the eaves, drawing Iris's attention back to the studio. Her stomach growled, reminding her she hadn't eaten since breakfast. Using the opportunity presented by the mail delivery, she headed across the yard to the cottage. She grabbed the stack of mail from the box, tossing it on the table while she made a snack.

Just the brief walk through the yard had produced an actual chill this time, and she was grateful for the cozy chair, a sunny window, and the special tea and biscuits Jeremy had sent last month. She realized how much she missed him, and wondered when, or if, he'd be back.

She began to sort through the mail, setting aside the bills and tossing the ads in the recycling bin. Tucked in the back was a letter with a familiar British postmark. *Jeremy*, she thought, with a grin. Her scalp tingled, and a warmth rose up inside of her, feelings she was becoming increasingly familiar with. She might have once called it a coincidence she was thinking of him before she knew the letter was there, but not anymore. There was the tingling she was coming to recognize, and it happened far too often to be coincidence. She whispered a thank you to the universe.

She had last emailed Jeremy expressing some of her doubts amidst the mass of questions she always had, and she had been wondering when he'd respond. Her puzzlement at his sending a regular letter was minimized by her excitement at seeing what he had to say.

Dear Iris,

I received your email just yesterday and wanted to respond to you quickly but thoughtfully as well. Unfortunately, my computer stopped working in the interim, and it will be a week before I get it back. This is too much to type on my phone, so I thought the best course of action was to write you a good old-fashioned letter. If I get it in the post today, you should have it by next week. I hope you don't mind..

You have a lot of questions, which is natural, and which I will speak to. But my first priority is to speak to you of the doubts you are feeling. Be reassured that too is natural, but if left unchecked, it can be discouraging. So, I hope I can dispel them for you now and provide you with something to use in the future when other doubts will invariably arise.

Spiritual unfoldment happens slowly. It is very much like the opening up of a rose, one petal at a time. If you have ever watched a rose in the garden, you will know buds can seem to be opening quite steadily, day after day, and then a stretch of cold or rain can seem to halt its progress. After a time, the dreary weather passes, and the rose continues to open up until one day, it is in full bloom. It's opening up is finished.

This is where the metaphor falls short, my dear. You won't one day be like a rose, fully developed, without any more growth or unfoldment possible. For that is never the case with any of us. We are always opening up to new things—to learn, to experience, to grow from. I would like you to think of yourself as a rosebush.

All through the season of growth, new buds form, and others reach a peak and then fade. Your experiences of spirit and mediumship will be like that. I suspect you have already recognized the houses, which were once all you saw clairvoyantly, have given way to other images, like the sketches of my mother-in-law and the portrait of that child you did. Congratulations on taking another step forward. You provided real healing for her mother, I am sure.

Remember, just as the rosebush doesn't cease to grow when a bloom fades, neither will you. One will lead to the next, and so on. You will also—I need to forewarn you—experience times when it seems all has stopped, and your development has gone dry. Again, think of the rosebush, dormant in winter, but very much alive inside, working on the buds that will spring forth in the summer.

You are always growing, Iris. And you will always be learning. Let no one tell you this journey is otherwise. You never really complete your training, nor stop developing. As long as you live, you love. And as long as you love, you grow.

This is only the beginning, my dear friend. You have such a gift in both your vision and the ability to translate that vision into something others can see and understand. You have always had this gift, Iris. It is the ability to take what you see, or hear, or feel and turn it into something others can see. Your vision is so beautifully clear, and those you touch are the better for having met you.

You asked me why it is that other mediums knew of their gifts as a child. I can't answer that, but what I can tell you is you have been on this journey your whole life, whether you realized it or not. At some point, you turned a key, and a door opened up onto this world for you. I promise, life will never be the same. You have discovered the miracle of knowing life is eternal, and you now hold the keys that will unlock this secret for others. THAT is the reason we are mediums—to show others what exists beyond their sight. You have the ability to be the eyes and ears for those on this side of life, and the voice for those on the other.

It is a precious gift we have been given, Iris. I see the love you bring to it, and it is that love which will continue to lead you forward in this life. Trust in it. Trust in yourself too. Your own spirit is as wise and wonderful as the guides and helpers who exist in the world of spirit. They will be beside you all the way, working with you and your spirit to help you to know what paths to take.

I envy you in a way, Iris. We can only start this journey once. You will be discovering magic and wonder in ways you never imagined. Let it be joyful. Know it is full of love. And know your dearest friends, the ones gathered around you now, see the wonder that is you and love you for it. Believe in their love, believe in yourself, and know the vision you have will take you everywhere you wish to go.

With admiration and affection,
Jeremy

P.S. I've just received word from The Sanctuary that they would like to have me back again. I guess this old medium did some good there last year. I am greatly looking forward to seeing you again in person, sometime around the first of May. ~J.

CHAPTER 46

Iris wandered out to the backyard, admiring the freshly turned over beds and flats of annuals she had picked up the day before. She had planned a quiet, contemplative day at home, with nothing more challenging than planting a few flowers out back. But gardening allowed her mind time to wander, which was the last thing she needed right now.

She pulled the slip of paper out of her pocket again, then stuffed it back in without reading it. She wasn't meant to be thinking about it at all. But ever since Lucia had called to tell her what she had written down, all she had wanted to do was think. It was taking every ounce of her discipline not to.

Realizing she needed to do something to occupy her mind, she went back inside and searched for the most complicated baking recipe she could find. She'd promised Ruby a plate of brownies for her party but figured a fancy cake would be welcome instead. Between the pastry cream, the frosting, and the cake itself, she figured this would hold her focus for at least a couple of hours.

Ruby pored over her list and was happy to see so many things checked off. Tonight was a big night, and she couldn't be late. Her apartment was ready at least, the wine chilling, the hors d'oeuvres ready to go. Charlie and Andre had dropped them off earlier and had helped move the furniture around while she strung the fairy lights on the porch as she had wanted.

All that was left to do was to grab the flowers she had ordered earlier in the week, pick up Jeremy, and get to Lucia's in time to get what she needed downstairs before heading up to the studio.

Lucia looked up as they rushed through the door, the wind chimes tinkling in their wake. "Hi, Ruby! Hello, Jeremy!" she called, "I wasn't expecting to see you until tonight!"

Despite their hurry, they stopped to talk. Lucia would be nervous about hosting her first student demonstration, and they both knew it. "Are you ready for tonight?" Ruby asked.

Lucia straightened her necklace, clasping the crystal pendant reverently. "I'm as ready as I can be. The rest is in spirit's hands!" she said, looking skyward. "I just hope everyone's nerves don't get the better of them. How's Iris holding up?"

"Last I heard she was up to her eyeballs in some recipe she decided to try. She said it was the only way she could keep her mind off what you gave her." Ruby leaned closer, speaking in a stage whisper. "So, what exactly is it you gave her? She said she's not allowed to think about it. She wouldn't even tell *me!*"

Lucia chuckled, "It's not that she's not allowed to think about it. If that were the case, I would have made her wait until tonight. She's just not supposed to plan what she is going to say, so she is able to allow spirit to inspire her speech."

"Ah," Ruby nodded. "I understand . . . I think." She still couldn't quite make sense of all of it. "Iris is nervous, but okay, I think. And she's bringing the cake tonight, so if her speech bombs, at least we'll have chocolate to drown our sorrows in later!" She winked, then turned to Jeremy. "Here, help me find something just right."

Jeremy called over his shoulder, "It's Iris's birthday tomorrow. But don't say anything—we want to surprise her." Lucia touched a finger to her lips. "Your secret is safe with me." Then, with a wave toward a young woman who had been lingering behind the counter, added, "Kathy here will take care of you. I've got to head upstairs and get ready. See you tonight!"

ris looked around the small room and tried to gauge the level of nervousness the other students were feeling. Alex was sitting with his back straight, staring at the clock on the wall opposite. His plaid shirt was buttoned all the way up and his tie tight enough to choke him. She caught his eye and motioned for him to loosen the tie a bit. He did so, then seemed to relax as he breathed deeply for likely the first time in an hour.

Philip, on the other hand, was bouncing around like a little kid on the first day of school. He had rolled and unrolled his sleeves several times and was currently pacing as much as one could pace in the small room where they waited. He was going to be the first to demonstrate, and Alex second. Iris would be doing something different.

"What's an inspirational address?" Charlie had asked when she invited him to come.

"It means I'm going to get up there and speak without writing anything in advance. I'm not really supposed to even think about it. Lucia will give me the topic that morning, and I can meditate on it, but nothing else."

"So, you just speak off the top of your head?" he'd asked.

She'd explained if she relaxed enough, spirit would be able to inspire her words, offering a message meaningful enough for everyone present to hear it. She knew it could work, having seen others demonstrate it several times. But still she was nervous.

She fingered the key hanging around her neck, its old purple ribbon frayed and worn. Michael's spirit was nearby, and she silently thanked him for being there.

Her other hand reached into her pocket, feeling the warmth of the gemstone Ruby and Jeremy had given her when they arrived. The warmth spread through her chest as she recalled what Ruby had told her about it. "I picked this one," she had said, "because it lets the light shine through. And that's something I think reflects you so beautifully. You let the light shine through, Iris. Through your vision, I'm able to see how beautiful the world is and how full of light it is. Even in the darkest days, I can look at your artwork and see the light shining through the waves or clouds or the windows of a house. And when you smile, that light shines right through you. You are beautiful, my friend, and I am so, so lucky to know you."

"We've got a nice little audience here for all of you," Lucia announced, peeking her head in the doorway and knocking Iris out of her reverie. "Remember, these are your friends, and on the other side of the veil are your spirit friends. There is only love and support here tonight, so if you begin to get nervous, just remember that. Love is all around you."

Ruby and Jeremy had taken seats on the raised bench at the back, making themselves visible in case she needed some reassurance. Thanking them silently, she straightened her jacket and walked onto the platform. She stood behind the podium, gave a wink to her friends in the back, and spoke one word, the one at the top of her card, "Imagination." The word hung in the air for what felt like a very long time. Then, very deliberately, she let go of the podium, took a step to the side, and began to speak.

"Imagination is a strange thing. It can be magical, allowing a person to venture into new worlds, scenes from a story, or a life longed for but not realized. It can also be seen as wasteful, or unrealistic, because it takes a person's mind away from the here and now. And yet imagination persists, and even fierce critics of it can find pleasure in losing themselves in daydreams. Imagination leads to invention. It leads to hypotheses, which lead to theories and real discoveries. Imagination makes us human. It separates us from other animals. It is how we learn to exist in an ever-changing world.

"Imagination is how we do what we do when we sit here in circle, or when we get up on this platform and demonstrate for all of you. Imagination is essential to mediumship. Without it, the spirit world would have nothing to work with, and no evidence would come through.

"We have talked about imagination, and about how it can interfere with our work, too. It must be harnessed, and nurtured, and learned from. Because while it is essential, it can confuse or distract and must be understood and acknowledged in order to be the essential tool we need.

"I am an artist. I draw and paint, and imagination has always been central to my work. I have always thought of it as something I drew on, a world I entered by choice. As a child, I learned to suppress it in order to be accepted by those around me. This town changed that. This town—this place of art and creativity—changed me. You allowed me to be who I am and to create as I pleased, and I have loved every minute of being here with all of you.

"I could try to explain to you how my imagination works with spirit to create the visions I see of places and people beyond the world around me. I could try to tell you how it is done—how I turn it on and off with a thought, how I channel the energy I feel into the pencil and brush, and how that leads to creations I am only beginning to understand.

"But that is not what I am going to do, because I know I couldn't do it justice. I am going to talk to you about your imagination, and about how it is as essential to you as it is to those of us sitting up here. Your imagination is where your heart plays. Your heart knows what you want; it knows what you long for, deep inside, and, astonishingly, it knows how to find it. But it doesn't know it immediately. It knows it because it listens to you and learns from you and feels what you feel when you imagine.

"When you were young, you didn't know what you would be when you were grown, so you imagined. You saw yourself as the teacher or the athlete or the author. You tried each of those things on in your mind, and, eventually, the one that felt right for you is the one you listened to. I hope you were each lucky enough to have gotten it right the first time. Not all of us are, and some of us need to move through life a little slowly, or a little haphazardly, learning as we go, trying out different roles, until eventually our imagination catches hold of us, and we learn to live as we always intended to.

"I stifled my imagination for a long time when I was young. I was embarrassed by it and tried to live as unimaginatively as I could. But then I took a chance, and let it creep back into my life, a little bit at a time. And then, about a year ago, I let my imagination run free, and here I am. Imagination did that. Imagination led me here. Imagination helped me to see what I had always known I would see. It helped me to see myself, who I am, and who I want to be.

"Someone very special gave me this key I wear around my neck. We used to imagine it would unlock a treasure chest, or a secret room, or the door to the future. We tried to unlock everything we could find for a while, but then we gave up, and I tucked it away in a box. You'll notice I didn't get rid of it, though. I didn't give up on it completely. That key was important, and something inside of me knew it, and so I held onto it, and trusted, and here I am.

"Imagination is what makes us vibrant, and witty, and wise. It lifts us up and shows us the way. It helps us to find who we are and to be what we want to be. Remember that when you imagine—freely and fully and openly and honestly— you will find your heart, you will find your way, and you will be extraordinary. Thank you."

"You should be very proud of yourself tonight, Iris. You did a brilliant job."

Jeremy tipped his wine glass toward her in a casual toast to the evening. It was a balmy night, and they had stepped out onto Ruby's porch to get some fresh air. She was grateful for the break. It seemed as if she hadn't stopped talking for hours.

"Was it really okay? I didn't babble?" That was what had worried her the most, that her inspirational talk would devolve into a nonsensical blather of unrelated thoughts.

"It was lovely. I mean it. Just lovely. I realized about halfway through that you had left your little card on the podium. You did it all from your heart, Iris, with some spirit inspiration thrown in. And what comes from your heart will always be beautiful." He paused, looking down at his glass as he added, so softly she almost missed it, "As will you." Then he slipped back inside to join the party.

She lingered outside, allowing the magic of those three words to fill her with a sense all was once again new. She leaned against the porch railing, staring out into the twilight. The air was filled with the sound of cicadas and the smell of lilac. She breathed in deeply, savoring the moment of quiet and the lovely knowledge tonight had gone well.

She thought back to this time last year, when she had stood outside her studio, marveling at the same smells and sounds of early summer. *How things had changed*, she thought. The world was still the same as it always was, yet she was different. Inside, her friends were gathered, happily enjoying one another's company. A year ago, many of them were strangers, and now here they were, celebrating something she hadn't even known was possible that day.

"Penny for your thoughts."

Startled, she looked up to see Ruby standing in the doorway. "You were a million miles away. Everything okay?"

Iris grinned. "It is. It really is." She could feel the excitement still bubbling inside and repressed the urge to laugh. She took a slow sip of sangria, savoring the sweetness. "I was thinking about this time last year, before all of this started. Do you remember how we didn't even know what mediumship was?"

Ruby rolled her eyes. "Oh, I remember," she said, joining Iris at the railing. "The funny thing is, sometimes I can't remember what it was *like*. It's as if the way it was, the way I understood the world, was so completely different from the way I understand it now, that I can't reconcile the two. I can't imagine life ever again being the way it was before."

Iris nodded in agreement. "And I don't think we can ever go back. I know I can't unlearn what I know, and I can't even imagine not knowing—really knowing—that my parents, and Michael, are still here. It's astounding to me I ever could have wondered if it were true."

Ruby didn't answer right away, her eyes fixed on the lights in the distance. "I know I've said this before, Iris, but thank you. Thank you for being in my life, thank you for listening to your heart and painting my grandparents' house, and thank you for trusting me enough to include me in all of this."

"Ruby, if it weren't for you, I might not have even figured this out. It was you who started it all, and it was you who helped me to see I should continue." She stopped, recalling those dark days last fall. "I am the one who should be saying thank you."

"Well, if it weren't for the two of us, neither of you would have gotten anywhere!" Lucia called from the doorway. Jeremy stood behind her, his eyes reflecting the fairy lights and a huge grin on his face. Lucia motioned for them to come inside. "Everyone is wondering where you went!"

There were a few people gathered around the painting of the red house hanging on the wall in Ruby's living room. Iris had given it to her last summer and was so pleased it was now a loved piece of art rather than a painful reminder of the past. As she admired it, she noticed a photograph on the table below. It was a picture of Ruby's family standing in front of a set of barn doors. Ruby was in the middle of everything, looking happier than Iris had ever seen her. Looking more closely, she noticed something on the wall to the side of the doors. Ruby walked over just as she lifted the photo up to take a closer look.

"It's the plaque, Iris. It's the same one you drew in your painting. It was how I was sure it was Gram's house. What I didn't know was my grandparents had salvaged the plaque from the ruins of the fire. They had kept it packed away, but my dad found it and had it attached to his barn." Iris glanced from the photo to the painting, filled with the same sense of wonder she had felt when she first learned what it was.

"My dad just sent me that photo—we took it when I was visiting last fall."

"What's the significance of the plaque?" Iris asked.

"My great-grandfather fought for the Union Army. He was given a land grant after the war, which is how they ended up with the farm. The plaque was put up by the historical society at some point. It was one of the reasons my grandfather was so devastated by the fire. My dad says he thought he had let his family down by letting the house burn."

"Our histories are full of remembrances and regrets, aren't they?" Jeremy said. "I think the history lives on in the stories we tell and the memories we share with others. Your family's story most certainly lives on, and now with this photo to go with the painting, you have a great way to make sure your story is remembered."

"Do you think what we do, bringing evidence to people of their loved ones in spirit, is a way of keeping those stories alive?" Iris asked.

"I think that's just it," Jeremy replied. "For Ruby, it most certainly kept it alive, because it encouraged her to go back and ask those questions."

"Remember, it can do more than bring histories to life; it provides actual healing, too," Lucia added. "Some would say that's what mediumship actually is—a form of healing—a healing of hearts and minds, but a healing nonetheless."

Jeremy motioned toward Philip and Alex, now looking totally relaxed after a successful evening. "What those two did tonight was bring healing to the recipients of their evidence. You could see it brought them comfort, which can sometimes be such a profound gift that it changes someone's life. It is a sacred gift you have all been given, the ability to connect the world of spirit with our physical world. If you can remember that, your mediumship will always do what it was meant to do, which is to heal souls, on both sides of the veil."

Lucia seemed pleased. "Speaking of healing," she said, "I haven't told you. My sister Marta had her baby yesterday. Her name is Esperanza."

"Hope," Iris said. "Perfect."

"It is. She had such a hard time believing things could ever be better, but when you gave her that drawing and the message, everything changed. She's been a different person since, and I know she'll make sure little Esperanza understands her big sister is looking after her."

Iris peered over at Charlie, who had been sitting with Andre, quietly listening to the conversation. He smiled, pointed up at the sky, touched his hand to his heart, and finally pointed toward Iris. She put her own hand over her heart, held it there, and nodded in understanding. Michael would love what she was doing.

"Are you planning to do the arts fair this year?" Andre asked.

With a wink, Charlie added, "Or have you decided to become a professional medium?"

"Yes!" Iris answered with a grin.

Charlie gave her a tolerant look and asked, "Yes to which?"

She turned to Jeremy and Ruby, making sure they were okay with what she was going to reveal, then added, "I am doing something different this year." A flush of heat rose through her body, and sweat prickled at the back of her neck. She stopped and took a sip of wine, willing the excitement to settle down. As she set the glass back down, her hand trembled ever so slightly.

"I've asked for two tents this year. I'm going to display my houses, but this time it will be on purpose." She winked at Charlie, who blushed, and the nervousness she was feeling vanished.

"So how will it work? Will you have a helper for the other tent?" Lucia asked.

Ruby jumped in. "She is going to have a couple of helpers actually. I am going to help staff the main tent, where her traditional paintings will be on display, and Jeremy will be able to work in the other tent. Iris will be free to move between the two. On the off chance someone recognizes one of the scenes, she and Jeremy will be able to talk to the person and see if they would like to engage with Iris about it on a mediumistic basis."

"I don't know if anyone will be willing to sit with us," Jeremy interjected, "but I would like to be there to help out in case they do." He stopped and scanned the room, finally focusing on Iris and Ruby. "It is important for all of you to remember mediumship is now a part of your lives. You know it and won't be startled by it. The general public is still back where you were before this all began for you, so you need to always remember to tread lightly when the topic comes up. They won't always be able or ready to see what you see." His eyes were kind, conveying neither scolding nor judgment.

Ruby continued on, her face a bit flushed from wine and excitement. "Iris was a bit worried it would be like sending out a message in a bottle, hoping a specific person would pick it up. But we figured since it worked for me, then maybe it will work for others. We would be setting up an opportunity for spirit, hoping they would be able to lead someone to us."

Iris marveled at the joy on her best friend's face and the admiration on everyone else's. "I wasn't sure what to do with all of them, to be honest, and these two helped me figure out at least how to start. Tell them about the Wonder Project, Ruby. It was your vision, after all."

Ruby lifted her chin, clearly pleased to share this new venture. "So last fall I began to call Iris's house paintings her 'Wall of Wonder.' I couldn't help but think of someone like me, wondering about someone they had lost. And I wondered how their life might be changed if they saw these paintings. So that's where the 'wonder' part came from. The next part came to us this spring.

"We're going to put together a website of the paintings, and Iris is going to write what she knows about each of them. We are hoping it will help someone to recognize a painting as belonging to them."

"But the first step is the fair," Iris interjected. "It's something I already know, so it feels like it will be a good place to practice if someone actually does walk in and recognize something, and having Jeremy there takes some of the pressure off of me."

Lucia had by now heard the whole story and still marveled at how it had come about. "Wouldn't that be wild if someone walks in, just like Ruby did? Do you think it really could happen?"

"It already has." Everyone turned to look at Charlie as he rose from his chair and reached into his pocket for his phone.

"I was going to show you this later, but I think now might be the right time. I got an email today, sent through the contact link on the website for the fair. Here—there are a couple of photos you should see."

Iris took the phone from him and sat down on the couch as she scrolled through the photos. Her heart beat faster as she realized what it was before she even read the email. Placing the phone down on the coffee table, she cradled her head in her hands as if she could somehow contain the energy rushing from her gut up into her head.

"What is it, Iris?" Ruby asked, concern evident in her voice.

Iris closed her eyes, her heart pounding as her mind began searching for what this might mean. Then she grinned and began to read the email aloud.

Dear Mr. Hatch,

I am writing to you in the hope you might recall an artist who was at your fair last year. She had a lot of pictures of the ocean, if that rings a bell. She also had a painting of a small white house, which was very familiar to me. I couldn't place why at the time, so I took a photo of it to see if I would remember once I got home.

Well, life got busy, and I forgot all about it until last week, when I was going through some of my parents' things and stumbled upon the second photo I attached here. It's black and white and old, but it's of my dad standing in front of his childhood home when he was a young boy. He always had it on his desk, but I hadn't seen it in years.

You will see why I found the painting so familiar. It looks like the exact cottage my dad lived in as a child. He came to the States as a young man and was never able to afford to go back home to Scotland until long after their cottage was torn down to make way for the new motorway.

I was hoping you might be able to put me in touch with the artist. If it is still available, I would like to buy the painting. My parents are still quite well, despite being in their nineties. I am sure my dad would love to have this painting to hang in their apartment.

I am also hoping, perhaps without reason, that she has some connection to the cottage, perhaps through family herself. If you think she might be interested in speaking with me, I would love to be in touch with her.

Best regards,

Jonathon Stewart

As she took in the view of the room full of friends, Iris realized the immensity of what was possible. Jeremy beamed, reaching to take the phone so he could see the pictures. He set it down and smiled, first at Ruby, then at Iris. Then, pointing to the phone, he nodded at the two of them, saying simply, "And so it begins."

THE END

lease visit brendasheridanauthor.com for a list
of book club discussion questions and updates on
future projects.

ACKNOWLEDGMENTS

I would like to start by thanking everyone who has ever believed in me, even when I didn't believe in myself.

I am eternally grateful to my parents, Bob and Peggy Sheridan, whose unconditional love sustains me to this day. I am equally thankful for my siblings: Rebecca, Christopher, Jennifer, Luke, Bernadette and Justin, who have always made sure I know how much they love me, while keeping me grounded enough to appreciate the simplest things in life.

To all the wonderful mediums who have encouraged my unfoldment, particularly at the Arthur Findlay College in the UK, thank you. You made it all so easy . . . and beautiful.

I would also like to thank my spiritual companions who kept me grounded in faith, but open to the wonders of God's work in and through me, especially Fr. Bob, Fr. Peter, and Dixie.

I am grateful to the writing communities at The Lit Forum and The Creative Academy for Writers who encouraged and critiqued and challenged and gave me the confidence to finally move this book from my computer out into the world.

And a final thanks to the wonderful team at Paraclete Multimedia for their beautiful editing and design work. You turned my manuscript into a real book, and I am so grateful.